Moonlight Awakens
a sex-trafficking story

John Matthew Walker

Copyright © 2020 John Matthew Walker

All rights reserved

The characters and events portrayed in this book are fictitious. Any similarity to real persons, living or dead, is coincidental and not intended by the author.

No part of this book may be reproduced, or stored in a retrieval system, or transmitted in any form or by any means, electronic, mechanical, photocopying, recording, or otherwise, without express written permission of the publisher.

ISBN: 9781735597515

Cover design by: John Matthew Walker
Library of Congress Control Number: 2020915624
Published in Indianapolis, Indiana
Printed in the United States of America

DEDICATION

To the invisible, the forgotten, the shamed.
We see you. We remember you. We treasure you.

JOHN MATTHEW WALKER

CHAPTER 1
Emma

Sledgehammers battled in my head as the bed beneath me wobbled and moaned. Ear-splitting music rattled the paper-thin walls, and the pounding bass shook the ceiling. I felt as if I were waking up to CPR. I blinked at the shadowy figure bouncing on top of me. His sweat dripped onto my face.

My stomach lurched and pain shot through me as I relived my nightmare. I tried to roll onto my side, but I couldn't turn. His massive thighs crushed my hips. The bed stopped bouncing. The room stopped spinning, and the puzzled, angry john glared at me. His sweaty hands clutched my shoulders and smashed me against the mattress. His grip and his eyes said he was going to finish, no matter what.

I swallowed my tears and the salty foam in my mouth. *Just get it over with.* I lay still and hoped the drugs would help me forget. Although my mind surrendered, my stomach jolted. My body whirled sideways, and I heaved my insides on the bed, the wall, and the floor.

The loud smack of his fist quaked in my ear. My cheek burned. The nameless man grabbed his pants with one hand and clutched my throat with the other. His eyes cut through me. "You owe me money." He shoved my face into the mess and said, "I'm not paying for puke."

He said a lot more, words I've worked hard to forget.

The door slammed behind him, and the room went dark.

I was a long way from home but closer than ever to the nightmare that had driven me away.

* * *

I'd always felt unwanted. Raised by aging Puritans who seemed irritated by my existence and acted as though they wanted nothing to do with me unless I was causing trouble. When my older sister, Mandy, got out of prison, they wanted nothing to do with her, either. Said she was only coming home for a handout.

They had crammed her few possessions into plastic grocery bags and used cardboard boxes. They had tossed them at the front door as though they were hoping for a quick hello and good riddance. But I saw Mandy first. I'd waited for her on the porch. No idea why. When I was a kid, she was almost never around, and when she was, she was stoned or asleep. I'd never liked the way she looked at me—stared at me—or through me as if I didn't belong or she wished I'd never been born. I figured she was jealous, since she'd been the only child for sixteen years until I came along.

A cab slowed in front of our sun-scorched yard and dropped her off at the end of the driveway, and there she stood. I couldn't see her tears, but her shoulders shook, and she rubbed her face. "Hey, Mandy."

No running with arms wide open. She plodded toward the house with her head down, kicking at the gravel and wiping her cheeks. Our eyes met for a second. She looked spent. Her face, blank.

Mandy stared at her clothes spilled across the porch and the plastic bags that couldn't hold them. She shoved one of the cardboard boxes and sat on the porch. I guess Mom didn't think Mandy was worth a laundry basket or anything extra. I looked over my shoulder into the living room thinking I'd see my parents. Nothing. Entryway. Nothing. Apparently, there wouldn't even be a quick hello.

I sat beside her and half-expected her to pull out a cigarette or a joint, but she pulled out her phone.

The screen said "Yellow Cab" and she tapped it. "Looks like I don't belong here or anywhere, Em."

I offered a nervous laugh. "Not sure either of us do. I'm half-surprised they haven't tossed my stuff onto the porch already."

"You know what it is, don't you?" I'd never seen such sadness in her eyes.

"What what is?"

"I'm sorry I couldn't be everything I should've been for you."

Mandy folded her hands in her lap and stared into the distance. Nothing to see but miles of corn and the haze of an Indiana summer. Her eyes swelled until a tear trickled down her cheek. The trickle turned into a flood. Her lips quivered. Nose sniffled. "I'm sorry, Em. I didn't know what else to do. Mom and Dad cared more about hiding my shame than they cared about you or me."

I scooted closer and wrapped my arm around her and squeezed her shoulder. "It's not your fault." I cried too. My big sister was home from prison. No excitement. No banner. No party. Not even a smile, a hello, or a hug. And Mom and Dad were nowhere to be found.

She shook her head. "You don't understand."

"What's to understand? You're my sister."

The trickle turned into a flood, but despite the waterworks, she kept looking at me. She studied my features as if memorizing every detail. She gently held my face in her hands, locked her eyes on mine, and kissed my forehead. Her arms wrapped around me, and she held me against her chest.

I couldn't stop my own tears as I felt hers drip against the back of my neck. Our bodies shook as she held me.

"They never told you."

"Never told me what?" I slid from her arms as she wiped her tears.

MOONLIGHT AWAKENS – a sex-trafficking story

Finally, she drew a deep breath. "I was fifteen. Rusty was eighteen. I thought he cared about me." She shook her head and flicked her hand as though waving off the painful memories. "When he found out I was pregnant, he dumped me. You were born nine months later."

My stomach dropped onto the sidewalk. My sister was my mom, which meant Mom and Dad were my grandparents—my lying, uncaring grandparents.

* * *

The cab pulled up again. Same number. Same driver. What did he think? I helped Mandy load her things into the trunk. She wrapped me in a hug, and I didn't want her to let go. I didn't want her to go.

But I heard the familiar creak of the front door and saw a new wave of pain cross Mandy's face. She slunk into the cab and disappeared from my life.

I turned around and glared at the smug Pharisee standing in the doorway. Mandy was the scapegoat for his failures, and I was a constant reminder of shame. He and Mom—Grams, as she became to me—always seemed to resent me and did their best to ignore me.

After saying goodbye to Mandy, things only got worse. I'd tried to confront them about lying to me—about driving Mandy away—about being hateful and controlling. Big mistake. What little care they may have shown disappeared. The only smiles I saw from then on were the masks they wore in public.

By the time I hit middle school, Gramps and Grams were completely over round two of parenting, and I was over them.

Nothing I'd ever done pleased them—or even grabbed their attention. It was time to stop trying. Time to stop following their rules. If they couldn't love me, surely someone else could.

CHAPTER 2
Emma

Johnny Paul had seemed nice at first. He was like one of those dreams that make you want to stay in bed, fall asleep again, and keep dreaming. One day during sixth grade, I was called to the principal's office for talking during class. I missed the bus home. How could a school make a kid miss the bus? They let me use the phone to call home, but I wasn't about to let my grandparents know I'd gotten in trouble. As the principal watched, I punched some numbers then pretended to talk to Grams.

I told him she wanted me to walk next door to the church, and he bought it. As soon as I lost sight of the principal's window, I headed home. It was only a couple of miles.

That's when Johnny Paul first eyed me. I was eleven years old and still a tomboy. Short brown hair. Never gave a thought to wearing makeup. No boobs. No interest in boys. And no clue.

He was sixteen. His driver's license was still wet, and he was driving his daddy's car, a black Crown Victoria everyone recognized as the preacher's car. He slowed beside me as I walked.

His smile was soft and seemed genuine. I still see that little crinkle of a dimple when he first smiled at me. Smokey blue eyes. Brownish blond bangs and a clear complexion. He was the first boy I'd ever really noticed, and I felt so special climbing into that car.

Riding home with him became a habit.

I pretended to walk to the church for piano lessons. He would pick me up and take me home.

Over time, I stopped wearing jeans to school. I wanted to look nice for him. I'd snitch some of Gram's seldom-used makeup, maybe even a touch of perfume. My efforts did not go unnoticed.

When I turned thirteen, there was no more tomboy. I was all girl. Hair. Nails. And everything an eighteen-year-old boy could dream of.

But Johnny Paul did more than dream. One day after school, I snuck around the side of the church as always, ready to hop into his car. But it wasn't his daddy's car anymore. Johnny Paul had saved his money from detasseling corn and delivering pizza and bought himself a used pickup.

I climbed in. He smiled as he turned the key and revved the gas. He bit his tongue like Michael Jordan getting ready for a slam dunk as he shifted into gear. The truck bounced across the gravel parking lot and onto the main road. It wasn't the same gentle ride as his daddy's Crown Vic.

"I've got a surprise for you," he said.

My heart leapt, imaging flowers or a necklace. Maybe a peck on the cheek.

My excitement changed when we turned onto a side road. "Where are we going?"

"It's a surprise." My butterflies were throwing up in my stomach. His face didn't look right. Glazed stare. Beads of sweat on his forehead. Flushed cheeks. And it wasn't even hot outside.

After a few more turns, I lost track of where we were. Some unnumbered gravel road inside a giant maze of cornfields.

Eventually we went off-road altogether and parked on a farm lane out of sight and out of earshot of anyone.

My mouth was so dry, I couldn't speak. Palms dripping. I saw no surprises in his truck. Nothing in the back. Only Johnny Paul and me and miles of corn between us and anyone else.

"I'm scared."

Sweat drizzled down his splotchy cheeks, and he was panting as he slid closer. A nervous smile stretched across his face. "There's nothing to be afraid of."

The truck suddenly felt hotter, and I choked on the mix of corn dust, gravel, and exhaust. He pressed against me, his arms clumsily wrapping around me, his lips wobbling in front of mine. It wasn't how I'd imagined my first kiss. Warm. Wet. Extremely short. And awkward.

As awkward as it was, his lips against mine opened a whole new world. I felt wanted. For the first time in my life, I felt desirable.

Each day, I'd watch the clock and dream of school's end so I could hop in his truck and feel his kiss.

My English teacher even noticed. She smiled and winked when she welcomed me back to earth from one of my daydreams. I'd been lost on an island with Johnny Paul. He was my world, and I was his. Or so I'd thought.

But he graduated and disappeared for a couple of years. College girls were more mature and more fun, I guess, but I still thought of him, missed him, maybe even thought I loved him.

But I doubted he loved me. He must've loved the attention. My smile. My kiss. Surely, he'd loved my innocence and vulnerability. I'd always thought the only reason he hadn't taken it further was fear of his father.

I started riding the bus again when he left for college. What a nightmare. Even the younger kids called me Johnny's slut. The bus couldn't move fast enough.

But one October afternoon. Johnny Paul was home for fall break. He pulled up behind my school bus in his truck. I could feel his sweet lips already.

When the bus dropped me off at the end of the lane, he pulled up beside me and rolled down his window. My smile flattened when I saw his glossy eyes and smelled alcohol. It was just after four, and he was drunk.

He smiled and slurred. "Hop in."

"Hell no!" Two years of nothing, and he showed up wasted and expected me to hop back into his life. Being forgotten, overlooked, and scorned already filled enough of my life. I didn't need any more of that. I didn't need Johnny Paul. I didn't need anyone.

I walked toward home. He gunned it, pulled off the road in front of me, hopped out of his truck, and came toward me, half-staggering, half-running. My legs couldn't run as fast as my heart. He tackled me, dragged me into the cornfield, and had his way.

I was fifteen. He was twenty.

I guess going off to college made him feel more like his own man and less like the preacher's son. Alcohol suppressed his fear, and he ignored mine. Or maybe enjoyed it.

"Keep your mouth shut about this," he said with his finger in my face and his sweat dripping on my naked chest.

Those cutting words were unnecessary. Who would I tell? He was untouchable. I was white trash. My real mother couldn't have raised me if she'd wanted to, and Gramps and Grams only raised me because they wanted to avoid hell. And our little outhouse of a town wouldn't allow that kind of scandal.

I snuck into the tall corn to get dressed. Thank God he hadn't torn any of my clothes. How would I ever explain that?

When he'd put himself back together, he dropped me off a little closer to home but far enough away that Gramps and Grams wouldn't see his truck.

It was the first time he'd had his way with me, but it wouldn't be the last. He dropped out of college after that semester and started working at the co-op. He didn't pick me up after school like the old days. He'd wait down the lane, out of sight of the school bus. My almost daily ambush.

He'd get off from the co-op just before school let out. He'd wait for me all covered in corn dust, saw dust, horse feed—you name it. At least sometimes he'd smell like molasses instead of compost. I was just a stop on his way home. His afternoon treat for working so hard.

I learned to go along because I was scared. And because I didn't think I had a choice.

He started to pretend he liked me. Even brought me presents. When

I was sixteen, he gave me herpes. When the doctor told Gramps and Grams, I became the town whore in their minds. It didn't matter that the preacher's son had forced himself on me regularly. They'd never thought it strange when I threw up at school and didn't want to ride the bus home. Never thought it strange that I had no friends and never wanted to be around other people. Never wondered why I'd come home from school covered in corn dust or smelling like a barn. Never wondered why I didn't want to go to church or why I sat in the pew staring at my feet and white-knuckling the seat.

I no longer mattered to them. Mandy had scarred their reputation, I ruined it. I became sin in their eyes.

They no longer mattered to me.

When preacher-boy offered me to a couple of his old college buddies, it was more than I could take. I could have screamed, and our deaf little town wouldn't have heard. My last tiny trace of self-respect died in that cornfield. When they'd each had their turn, they laughed at mud-covered, naked me, then pissed on me and left. They each took a piece of clothing as a trophy.

I lay there in the mud and mashed corn stalks staring at the stars through the tassels. I should have been freezing to death, but I felt numb. I was nobody. And I felt nothing. Worthless. A discarded piece of trash. I couldn't move. Didn't want to move. I just wanted a combine to run over me and grind me up with the cornstalks. That'd be my one claim to fame. *Local Girl Killed by Combine.* I smirked imagining they wouldn't even post my name—to protect my upstanding family.

But I was still alive. As much as everyone hated me and I hated myself, I was still alive, and my skin was prickling with goosebumps. October nights in central Indiana are pretty darn cold when you're naked. I thought maybe I'd die there after all.

Then I saw a flicker of headlights through the corn and heard a familiar engine rumble. Johnny Paul to the rescue. Maybe he felt guilty. Maybe he was coming back to claim what was his. Maybe he didn't want to make the papers when they found me dead with his DNA in my rape kit. No matter. He was there, and I would have to go on living my miserable life.

"Get in." I couldn't see his face, only his silhouette. As I started toward the cab, his hand thrust onto my shoulder. "Nope. In the back. You're not leaving any of your mud and filth in my truck."

I'd sooner die than get in the back of his truck. I couldn't imagine my naked skin on that cold metal bed, let alone the shame of being tossed in the back like a sack of feed.

I turned and walked back toward the corn, but he grabbed my arm.

It stung like a you-know-what, and he pulled me into his arms, lifted me, and dumped me onto the truck bed. My hips and shoulders slammed the cold metal. The pain quaked through my whole body. I hadn't thought I had any feelings or tears left, but Johnny Paul found them. I ached and sobbed as I bounced toward town.

He stopped on the gravel lane that ran behind my house. It was hidden by the small stretch of corn that lined the road. He dropped the tailgate and swung his arm. "Get out." What a gentleman. His daddy would be real proud.

His truck-bed light was just enough for me to see his eyes. Even in the dark, he looked me up and down. I felt like a wadded up, discarded porn magazine.

But I also felt an unfamiliar resolve. I looked into his eyes and saw no soul, just an empty wannabe user who'd used me for the last time. I wasn't about to touch him or let him touch me, but in my mind, I slid up beside him and gave him one last kiss on the neck. I felt like a black widow. He'd had his way, and now he'd become my prey.

As I turned my back on him and walked into the corn, he scooted up behind me and swatted my butt. "Let me know when you want another ride." He chuckled.

I didn't look back. I didn't say a word or show any reaction, but I thought *you'll never get a ride from me again.*

Only another hundred yards, and I'd be home, but my calves and even my toes started to cramp. Shivers riddled my body, and my teeth chattered. I was bruised inside and out and could barely move. I crawled out of the corn and hobbled up to the back door, hoping no one was home.

But Gramps was standing at the kitchen window. He looked through me, unfazed, as I snatched a sheet from the clothesline and covered myself.

He turned his head and shouted, "The tramp's here. Fetch her some clothes."

The sheet and fresh hurt mixed with anger and warmed my tired body. I ran to the door, stumbling, almost blinded by my tears. I prayed Grams would open the door and at least try to smile, but as I got close, the door opened and she tossed out jeans, panties, and a T-shirt. "You'll not come into this house like that. Go to the shed and put your clothes on."

That was it for me. No sense in staying where I wasn't wanted. I waited until they were asleep. I knew where Gramps kept his cash. He thought it was safe—thought I didn't have a clue, but I knew every little secret he and Grams held so dear. I was forgotten, but never forgot anything. No one paid attention to me, but I paid attention to everything.

I nabbed Gramps's stash and Grams's too. I snatched their cell phones and cut the phone line. I grabbed as many clothes and snacks as I could cram into my backpack and snuck into the garage where Gramps kept his precious truck. Grams's car was in the driveway. I took the spark plugs out of his pickup, slipped out the side door and into Grams's rust bucket, a prehistoric Ford Falcon. I called it the Pterodactyl.

I plugged the keys into the ignition, gripped the steering wheel with my left hand, and, before I started the car, spoke a prayer. "God, I can't imagine you're here. Can't imagine you're listening, but just in case you are, you know I've got to get away. Please let there be a better life for me—anywhere else. I'll go anywhere. Please."

I started the car, and left Middletown, Indiana, forever.

CHAPTER 3
Emma

A thousand miles from home. No one knew where I was. No one cared. The summer breeze rushed through my hair. I had escaped in my stolen clunker.

I hated to admit it, but I hadn't been thinking when I'd left my grandparents' house. There'd been nothing to think about. I'd seen no future and wanted nothing to do with my past. I'd left Middletown and all of Indiana without shedding a tear. Just driving. Kentucky. Tennessee. Alabama. Florida. Maybe I'd drive into the ocean.

But I suddenly felt I was burning a trail from nowhere to nowhere. Then the tears began. No windshield wipers could clear my view. I drove through a downpour of fear mixed with a faint glimmer of hope. I scoured my thoughts for one good memory. As I thought of Gramps, I only saw hollow eyes that looked through me or past me. That phony Puritan was always thinking of another woman or another beer. I was only another anchor holding him down.

Grams was too frazzled to think of me. It was a wonder there was ever food on the table, not because we couldn't afford it, but because she was paralyzed by neglect. She only married Gramps because he'd planted his seed and hoped to run, but her dad's shotgun had changed his mind—or at least his plans.

Nope. I had not one positive memory for either of them.

But I had one good memory—one beach vacation away from Gramps and Grams. Aunt Gladys and Uncle Bud had invited me to go with them—just the three of us. They'd never had any kids of their own. Maybe I was a test run, or they must have known the family secret and felt sorry for me. We all had a great time until we got home. Gramps never told Aunt Gladys thanks and barely made eye contact. They never made the trip from Iowa again.

That vacation was the one and only time in my life worth remembering.

And I remember everything about it. The cheesy hotel smelled like lemon and moth balls. Early bird specials with every old person in Florida fawning over me. Walking the beach and holding hands with two people who really cared.

I remember wading along the shore, the waves sloshing against my feet. A huge wave—huge-to-me, anyway—slogged me in the chest and stung my eyes. Uncle Bud chuckled as he plucked me out the waves and held me close. Aunt Gladys dabbed my eyes with her towel, then Uncle Bud set me on his shoulders.

I stayed there until sunset. On his shoulders, the waves were no threat. They were enticing and peaceful. Unaffected by anyone. Always there. So calming.

That was what I needed. Calm.

How I missed Uncle Bud and Aunt Gladys. A car accident stole more than their lives. It stole mine as well. I needed them more than anything, but all I had were memories.

When I saw the Florida state line, I set my course toward Panama City.

I stopped at the first beach. People everywhere. Not exactly what I wanted, but it would have to do.

I wore my bikini under my jeans and T-shirt. I grabbed a water bottle and a towel I'd swiped from the previous night's trashy hotel, and I ran to the beach.

White sand. Umbrellas. Food stands. A mix of salty air and cigarette smoke. Not like the beach I remembered. But the ocean was the same—blue-green like a dazzling jewel. Hypnotizing.

I waded among people before I could wade in the water. I kicked the waves, smiling because the waves didn't care, and neither did I. Life had kicked me around long enough. Not anymore. I was going to toss and roll like a wave, unaffected, uncaring.

"Bring it!" I shouted like an idiot. I smiled, knowing people would be staring, but I didn't look. I kept kicking the waves as I walked along the shoreline.

My jeans were soaked to the knees. I draped the towel around my neck to keep it dry.

Finally, I reached a clearing in the hoard of sun-worshippers. A lonely stretch of sand with a smattering of dunes, an empty lot between hotels. I walked away from the tide, tossed my towel on the ground, and stripped off my jeans and T-shirt. My feet danced on the screaming-hot sand. Thank goodness for the towel.

I stretched it across the sand, plopped down, and stared at the waves, sipping my water. The sun slowly drifted closer to the horizon. I lost track of time. I lost track of myself as the rhythmic breeze and splashing captivated me. The ocean seemed so vast, and I seemed so small. Insignificant.

As the hours passed, the lonely stretch became like my own private beach. Parents and grandparents packed up their chairs, coolers, and kids and headed to beat the crowds at the restaurants dotting the coast.

Looking both ways, I saw no one anywhere close to me. I felt a twinge of guilt as I crushed the empty water bottle and heaved it into the surf. It bobbed up and down, empty and helpless against the tide. I should have picked it up and carried it to the trash can. Instead, I watched it as though I were watching myself. My life played out by a plastic bottle tossed into the ocean.

I wasn't a wave after all. I was the crushed water bottle, garbage in the sea of life.

I drew a deep breath and pulled my T-shirt over my head. I heard footsteps squishing through the sand and felt someone brush past. A shadowed arm stretched out and snatched my crumpled water bottle from the surf. The imposing silhouette of a man stood over me, and I almost jumped out of my suit.

The crushed plastic bounced in his hand, then he said in a chocolatey smooth voice, "I think you know better." I could hear the smile, and I pulled the towel out from under me and covered myself, ignoring the still-hot sand. I didn't care for the sudden feeling of sand in my bikini bottoms, but I had no time to worry over that. I was alone on a beach with a stranger.

I was blinded when he stepped out of the sun and stood beside me.

"What's a beautiful girl like you doing out here alone?"

I looked up past well-defined calves to solid abs, a broad chest, and a chiseled chin. The man was bronzed. He handed me my guilt in a crumpled mound of plastic. "It's not really my job to pick up trash on the beach."

I reached for the bottle, but he snatched it away and pulled his other hand from behind his back. His fingers clutched the necks of two beers, limes poking from each.

He sat on the sand beside me, apparently immune to the heat, and handed me a beer. He rested his forearms on his knees, the beer dangling between them, and stared at the waves. "It's a good place to be when you need to relax." He turned and smiled. His voice was like silk, but I wasn't so naïve as to share a drink with a total stranger, especially when I felt his eyes peering through my shirt and roaming up and down my body. I was a corpse, and he was the medical examiner doing his thorough inspection.

My unease faded as he squeezed his lime into the bottle then took a sip. He closed his eyes and breathed, almost meditating.

While his eyes remained closed, I slid my hand into the pocket of the limp jeans beside me. Shoot. I'd left my phone in the car. I had no one to call and no one to call me, but a 911 operator might be friendly voice right now.

Sure, the man beside me seemed calm and unthreatening. But he was ripped and could overpower me in a second if he wanted.

I glanced at him as he stared at the gentle surf. He seemed as unaffected by the world around him as the waves.

Not like me. I was the floating trash, tossed by the whims of the world.

I didn't dare touch that drink.

When he finished his, he stood. "You should enjoy that beer, and you should enjoy your life." He took a step back and waved. "I hope you find what you're looking for." With that, he walked away.

I waited until he was well out-of-sight before I squeezed the lime into my beer.

CHAPTER 4
Emma

Eyes closed, I fought the sledgehammer headache and the memory of the john who'd pounded me into that flimsy bed. I prayed it had only been a nightmare, but the bed moaned, and I lurched as someone sat beside me.

I looked up. Hollow eyes stared into mine. The girl looked about sixteen. Thin platinum blond hair and dark eyebrows. She smiled. "You okay?" Her girly voice sounded so out-of-place.

My pulse quickened as my future stared back at me.

She washed my face with a warm cloth. "I gave him his money. The boss doesn't need to know, but we have to get you cleaned up or there'll be hell to pay." Two other girls entered the room with a bowl and towels. The clean chemical smell was a welcome reprieve.

One girl wiped down the wall—nasty green concrete block with tiny windows close to the ceiling. Big enough for slivers of light to get through but nothing else.

No escape.

Another girl mopped the floor with her foot and a wet towel while the girl beside me wrapped up my sheets and scurried toward the door.

"Where am I?"

She turned around and shook her head. "There's no time to talk." Starved for sleep, she looked through me with bloodshot eyes. "He's going to find out you're awake. I'll change your sheets, then you'll need to lie down and pretend you're still asleep."

"I don't understand."

"Right now, it's about survival. We'll talk later."

Neither of the other girls said a word. They finished the clean-up as though it were a normal part of their day then slid out the door. The skinny blonde bounced back into the room and stretched clean sheets across the twin bed.

Her eyes widened as a door slammed and footsteps approached.

Shoving me onto the bed, she said, "Close your eyes and don't move."

* * *

"Selene."

My blood curdled at the man's slithering voice, the winsome voice of the man who'd handed me that one beer. I lay perfectly still and silent as the weight of his body settled beside me. I refused to react as he traced the length of my limp, naked body with his finger.

"I'm so glad you had that drink with me. You are indeed a treasure to add to my collection, and so aptly named. How's my little moon goddess?"

My name is not Selene. I prayed that my face showed nothing, but I could feel my eyelids quivering as I swallowed my tears.

He grasped my hand, lifted my shoulder, and rolled me onto my back. "I know you're awake. My client said you were quite *expressive* right before he asked for his money back and stormed out." His gentle grasp turned into a tight squeeze. "If he couldn't get his money's worth, then you will have to pay me yourself."

Holding me down with one hand, he unzipped his jeans with the other.

My stomach, though empty, was still screaming. I poured sweat, soaking the sheets. As he leaned against me, I blew hot vomit-breath in his face.

He raised his free hand, and I braced for another slap, but his face softened as he looked at my cheek. "He hit you. That bastard. Now he owes *me* money. No one messes with the face of one of my girls."

Then he dug his thumb and fingers into my side. Pressing just above my hip, he squeezed like a vice. The searing pain was too much. I dry-heaved and wet the bed.

He rolled me over and blistered my behind with his belt.

When he stopped, I could hear him panting, waiting silently for me to acknowledge him. I remembered the young girl's words. *Right now, it's about survival.*

The only thing I had to live for was the hope that someday, I would have something to live for. Mr. Ripped saw no value in me except to pedal my flesh, but that girl had come in here, brought others, to protect me. Maybe she'd even put herself at risk in order to do so. If a teenage whore could see value in herself and me, I could at least try to believe.

Sometimes, hope is a tiny thread, but that thread is strong, so I held on, and in that moment, I rolled onto my back and let him stare at me in all my glory. I had nothing to hide from him or anyone else. Life had taken everything from me except me. Even in that pit, I knew there was something worth living for. If I never found it, its pursuit would have to be worth it.

I had nothing else.

He smiled at my nakedness. "My Selene." He spread his arms and looked around the room as though he imagined an enchanting palace. "You'll be a light in this darkness. You will bring joy to many." He laughed. "And much money to me."

He started for the door. "The girls will help you freshen up so you'll be ready for our guests." He turned and looked at me once more. "If you need another beer to lower your inhibitions, that can be arranged."

He closed the door behind him.

I thought I'd felt alone before, but that was nothing. Nothing.

What I wouldn't give for one scornful look from Grams or one snide remark from Gramps. My hate for them was true love compared to this hell.

CHAPTER 5
Emma
A Few Weeks Later

Those first few days were a blur. I cried every night and tried to suppress the memories, or swallowed some drugs to numb my brain.

Pain quaked through my head as one of the other girls flipped on the light and parked herself beside me. Her girlish ponytail bounced with the bed. Everyone called her Bliss. I remembered that much, and the place surely needed some bliss.

I rolled onto my side and pulled a bucket from under the bed. I stared at the pile of used condoms and beer bottles in the bucket and wondered what I was doing.

"Hurry up and puke so we can play." She bobbed up and down, smiling and patting my knee. Her eyes said *get over yourself*, and she waved a deck of cards in my face.

I heaved into the pail as Bliss tapped her foot and held the deck of cards next to my face. I wiped my mouth and groaned. "Can I at least brush my teeth?"

She laughed and smacked my behind as I stood. "This is *our* time. Don't waste it." She waved me off.

It was a Monday morning. I soon realized Mondays were our "off days." I imagined the boss was passed out from a long weekend bender. The johns and occasional janes were all gone, back to their respectable lives.

Some of the girls were gone too. The ones who *chose* to work here could come and go. I couldn't understand that choice.

I trudged down the grim hallway and stumbled into the one bathroom. One sink. One shower. One toilet. On a Monday morning, there were six of us girls. On weekend nights, there would be as many as twelve with at least twelve tricks—twenty-four people and one toilet.

As I slumped onto the toilet, I remembered whining about Aunt Gladys's house only having one bathroom for all of us. What I would have given to use her toilet. The strangely squishy seat. The fluffy lid cover and crocheted Kleenex holder.

I missed her overpowering air freshener as I breathed a cloud of mold and urine. Staring at the floor, I wished I still had that bucket.

Hairspray haze covered the mirror. I could barely see myself. Thank God.

Streaks of mascara marked last night's tears. Eyes swollen and bloodshot. And crimson hair. When did I get blood-red hair?

"Are you coming?" Her platinum blond head popped through the door, and she waved the deck of cards.

I washed away yesterday's face and brushed my teeth. Neither act made me feel clean, and I didn't recognize the girl in the mirror.

Emma was lost. I was Selene, and Selene was no one.

* * *

"Do you have any kings?"

I turned my cards facedown and laid them on my lap. "How long have you been here?" I asked.

Bliss nibbled her lip like a nervous child. "Do you have any kings?"

"Go fish." As she drew a card, I asked again. "How long have you been here?"

Her face reddened, and she shook her head and kept shaking it as if to avoid thinking, to avoid answering. No one keeps track of time in hell. They just distract themselves with games and pretend the game is what's real.

She blew a puff of air through her bangs and tapped her fingers on the bed.

I said, "I'm sorry, do you have any tens?"

With a little girl voice, she said, "Go fish."

I drew a ten, added it to the three I already had, and spread them on the bed. "My name is Emma."

Stern eyes met mine. "Shh," she whispered. "Maybe someday, but here, your name is Selene." She glared at me as if I was supposed to know that. "No one uses their real names. No one shows their real feelings. That's how you hold on to that tiny piece of yourself you've got left."

"Okay, but what's your name?"

She rolled her eyes. "Like I told you, everyone calls me Bliss." She stood, tossed her cards on the bed, and said, "We're done, here."

"Bliss, I'm sorry. Selene is sorry."

A grin stretched across her face, and she picked up the cards and stacked them, then plucked the rubber band from her ponytail and bound the deck. Her hand reached for mine. "Come on."

She led me to the tiny break room. Broken down sofa with ratty, faded red cover. Refrigerator that hummed and vibrated. Small counter with chipped laminate from the seventies. Sink, coffee maker, microwave, and hot plate. A kid-sized table with two dinky chairs. And in the corner, an antique TV in a wooden chest like you'd see on an eighties TV show. A worn and abused portable DVD player on top.

"Want a cup of coffee?" Bliss poured a cup and handed it to me. "Thought you could use something stronger, but coffee will have to do. It's all we got."

"What you girls doin'?" A big girl voice boomed behind me.

"You must be Tawnya?" Smooth, dark chocolate. She stood with confidence that owned that doorway and every place she went. Her long black hair and manicured nails seemed so out of place.

"Mhmm. And you ain't nobody." She dusted past me and snatched my coffee without a "thanks" or even a glare. She whirled around and back toward the doorway, then she stopped, turned, looked me up and down, and disappeared down the hall.

Bliss poured me another cup. "You won't see her much. Tawnya is the evil queen. She doesn't work the Outhouse any more. That's what she calls this place."

"Kind of fits, don't you think?"

She bunched her lips, looked around the room, and nodded. "I prefer Hell's Outhouse."

We both laughed, and two more girls slid into the room. Candy and Alice. Candy was like a grown-up version of Bliss. Strawberry blonde. Weathered skin and tired eyes. But she could still make it all up and look screamin' hot—especially when the johns were wasted and the lights were low.

Alice. I couldn't understand having such a normal name in such an abnormal place.

I sipped my coffee and followed her as she walked toward the sofa. "Alice?"

"Yeah?"

"Why do they call you Alice?"

She gave me a wry smirk and an eyebrow tilt. "Bobby called me Dazzle. How ridiculous is that? But he dragged me down this rabbit hole, so I said, "You can call me Alice."

"Is that your real name?"

"Are you real stupid?"

"Ease off, Alice." Candy was the peacemaker. Go along to get along. She used to be the queen like Tawnya. She'd tried to escape, but Bobby's goons, Roberto and Mason, caught her. She'd shown me the scars on her back and behind her ear. Bobby was careful to protect his merchandise. She could still wear a sexy top and long hair. He'd preserved all her important parts.

Candy had no choice but to surrender. None of us had a choice.

"You done with your coffee? Let's get back to our game." Bliss held up the cards and motioned toward the door.

I hadn't played Go Fish since grade school. It was nice little escape, and Bliss didn't seem to mind that I was winning. She was lost in her little-girl world, hiding from our reality, and I was not about to spoil it.

Even if she could only escape in her mind, I would do everything I could to help her.

Looking into her eyes, I saw a lonely little girl who still held a tiny thread of hope, that tiny thread of the girl she once was.

If she could escape, I could too, but it wouldn't be enough to retreat into my mind. I set my thoughts toward playing the game, plotting my moves, and waiting until the stars were aligned and the time was right.

I'd escaped hell once before. I could surely do it again.

* * *

The door swung open and banged against the wall. Mr. Ripped stood in the doorway. Most of the girls called him Daddy, especially the ones who came and went as they pleased. Sick. They fought over him like jealous wives. They could have him, as far as I, or anyone with a brain, was concerned.

That Monday morning, he looked more like ripped-off than ripped. His hair was a mess. Scruff on his face. Eyes half-opened. Arm over his head. Scraggly arm pit hair saying "stay away—far away." And a cigarette dangled from his mouth. Every girls' dream-turned-nightmare.

"You're not allowed to smoke in here," Bliss shouted.

You go, girl.

He snickered as he crushed the cigarette against the door frame. His eyes fixed on me and roamed up and down. He smiled, but I knew there wasn't much to see, not on a Monday morning with no shower and no makeup.

"Selene." Arms wide open and all smiles. "It's good to see you awake. It looks like you and Bliss are having a good time." He looked at Bliss and nodded toward the door.

She gathered the cards and hurried past him to her room.

I cringed as he sat on my bed and slid his hand across my thigh. "Selene."

I barely noticed the stench of his breath over the stench of the old mattress.

He leaned closer, and I pulled away. His smile flattened along with his gaze.

Teeth clenched, grip tight, he squeezed my neck in one hand. The other dug into my thigh.

"My friends like what you do for them when you're trashed, but I would like to see what you can do when you're awake." He stared at my lips, winked, loosened his grip, and slid his hand up my thigh. He studied every inch of my face and every part of my body.

As his eyes locked on mine, I felt a sudden chill—not the kind a girl dreams of but one that ices her blood. Those deep dark wells screamed into my soul, and I heard the words just as if he'd spoken them aloud. *You will do whatever I want.*

He let go and smiled. "This isn't how I meant things to go. You're not like these other girls." He brushed my cheek and ran his fingers through my hair. "You're something special. You are spectacular, beautiful. You are like a jewel in my crown. I have big plans for you."

He kissed my lips. Very tender and gentle, but I tasted an ashtray and felt like one too—a trashy home for burned-out waste.

He reached into his pocket, pulled out his hand, opened his palm, and held up a pill. "You can take this if you need it, but you've had long enough to see how things work around here, and I don't know how long I'll let you test my patience."

His eyes shifted from me to the pill. He rolled it between his fingers. "It's hard to imagine how something so small can change the way you think, what you feel, even what you do."

The pill stopped between his thumb and index finger. His face crinkled as he crushed it and flicked the crumbs onto the floor.

He pulled at my T-shirt.

I closed my eyes and imagined I was running as fast as I could deep into a dark forest, but there was no place to hide. I felt branches scraping my arms, poking my side, and cutting me inside. The pain grew until I heard his whisper like a subtle growl in my ear.

"I know you're trying to hide from me, but there is nowhere to run. You're in my world now, and you need to embrace it." His arm slid around my back, and he squeezed me tightly. I felt more than heard his whisper. "You need to embrace me."

His full weight pressed against me. He loosened his grip but stayed atop me, trapping me. His sweat dripped onto my face. "I like your face. I like your body." He panted between words—between thrusts. "I like everything about you, and you can mean so much to me, so much to us and our business."

I closed my eyes as the bed shook. I felt out of control, worthless. The dark forest had turned into an Indiana cornfield, and I was lying in the mud. Naked. Used. Discarded. Forgotten. Emma buried herself deep inside, and I became Selene.

Our fused bodies steamed and pulsed. I'd dreamed of being with a guy like him, but my dream had become a nightmare.

His dripping body slid off me as his hands pressed against my hips. He pushed me aside and sat on the edge of the bed to catch his breath.

I stared at the blank wall and heard the bucket slide out from under the bed. The bed creaked and bumped the wall as he stood behind me. He ripped the sheet from my hands and tossed it. I was totally naked.

Exposed. Vulnerable. But it didn't matter. Not anymore.

I stared at the blank ceiling, imagining stars above cornstalks. I heard the thudding and spattering of his urine into the bucket and imagined the sound of a combine rumbling toward me, ready to chew me up and spit me out.

He chuckled as urine splashed onto my bed and across my back. It wasn't a first for me and probably wouldn't be a last. And it was only warmth I'd felt in that miserable hell hole.

After he finished, he kicked the bucket back under the bed. "You really need to clean this room. People are going to get the wrong idea about you."

I prayed he'd leave so I could clean myself, clean the room, cleanse my sheets, and wipe my mind of every taunting thought of the hell to come.

I was jealous of Bliss. I wanted to be like her, shut everything out, do my job, and somehow pretend to be a little girl.

But he was still there. His panting slowed. I could hear him wrestling with his jeans. I felt a hint of security at the sounds of his zipper closing and his belt buckling, but I heard no footsteps. I could feel him still standing over me, feel his eyes still glued to my body.

"I know it must be hard for you," he said. "But I have a good feeling about you, Selene. What you can accomplish without trying or when you're totally high—I can only imagine what you'll be able to do when you put your mind to it. But let me be very clear. I don't give a rat's ass how hard it is for you. Everyone's got it hard. You think I wound up here by choice? You think this was my dream?"

I shook my head like a good girl. I grabbed the urine-spattered pillow and covered myself as I rolled over to face him. Emma tried to tremble, but I shoved her back inside. I buried her tears and ignored the ache in my throat as she whispered from my soul. *Please let me die.*

"You've got it better than most, baby girl. You caught my eye. I've got an eye for beauty and talent, and you've got both." He raised his voice, and the bed moved as he propped his foot and leaned against it. "You have chance at a great run, a good life—money and classy guys, not the scum you find here."

Like you?

"Do as I say and to do it with passion. I don't care if you have to fake every single second. Give it everything you've got."

Emma didn't move—didn't breathe. She willed my heart to stop, but I knew her only chance to survive was for Selene to live—to thrive. Emma wanted to disappear, so she did.

I nodded without expression, but I must have been too slow and unconvincing.

He shoved the bed against the wall so hard that I lurched and banged my head.

He leaned close to my ear and whispered, "Do. You. Hear me?"

I nodded.

His hand rested on my shoulder. "Look at me."

I rolled over. He plucked my pillow shield and tossed it into the corner. He gently gripped my arms and lifted me to my feet. His eyes burned into me. I felt branded. Owned. I dared not gaze at my prison as the warden looked into my eyes. He owned me, as master owns a slave. A chill ran over me. I knew he would kill me, or worse, if I crossed him.

He narrowed his eyes. "You're finally starting to get it. Do what I say, when I say, and you'll get your high-class johns and your share of the cash before you know it. If you don't, I don't need you pretty or healthy to work here." He sniffed, smirked and looked at the squalor. "I don't even need you conscious."

He kissed my cheek, let go of my arms, and walked to the door. "Be a good girl and clean your room. Our guests will be arriving any time now."

I flopped onto the soiled bed. The urine smell grew stronger, and I felt the scum-covered walls closing in. The darkness and stench awakened painful memories. Johnny Paul's callous words. "Don't worry, guys. She won't tell anyone." Gramps's angry grip on my arm as he shoved me into his truck. The cold steel and the surgical lamp in my face.

I squeezed my eyes shut and shook my head, trying to bury the memories, but nothing could bury my reality, and I couldn't stomach the thought of being here for the rest of my life.

I stared at the cobwebs and smoke stains on the ceiling. A fly buzzed around and paused dangerously close to a spider web. Oblivious and unaware, it flew away unscathed.

That fly had more freedom than I did. It might even outlast me.

Light footsteps reminded me I was not alone. Had to be Bliss. Nobody else ever came to see me. Alice was in her own nightmarish wonderland. Candy wanted to pretend we were one big, everybody-get-along family. Tawnya, we never saw. She must've had her own thing going. But Bliss had become my one hint of light—my one friend.

She played the little girl beautifully, but sometimes and every working night, she turned into big girl Bliss. All business. Get to it. Do it. No nonsense. Even then, she could sell the guys and the ladies on the little girl act.

Big girl Bliss had laid out the rules of the game, and I clung to her advice. *Survive.*

For any hope of escape, I had to play the game. I had to ignore feeling small and alone. Insignificant. Forget that no one knew where I was. No one cared. If my grandparents were looking for me, it was likely only to get their crappy Ford back. I couldn't live in those thoughts.

My survival was all on me. How long could I hold on? Would I last long enough? Would there be enough of me left when I escaped? If I escaped?

And when I thought of all the other girls, escape seemed impossible. I wished we could all escape, but I couldn't picture a way to get everyone out. I had to find a way out, but I couldn't leave Bliss. I had to find a way out for her as well.

CHAPTER 6
Emma

Days turned to weeks as I went through the motions for "Daddy." That's what the "wives-in-law" called him. Like I was going to call him that, or consider the girls "in-laws." He was not my boyfriend. He was my pimp.

We were his slaves.

But I played the game and called him *my* Bobby. It was my way of pretending I owned him. Every time I said it, I could see the puzzled look in his eyes, and I knew he wanted me to call him Daddy. Even so, his wry smile tried to tell me I was special, different from the other girls.

I wasn't about to fall prey to his lies. He could say and do whatever he wanted. Wave a wad of cash in my face. Hook me up with the richest schmuck in town. It didn't matter. I would not believe for even one second that he saw me differently. We were all the same. His meal ticket. Nothing more.

But as I became more and more detached from myself, my resolve weakened. His charms never wavered. The lies stayed the same, but a lie repeated over and over can begin to feel like truth. And I felt the growing danger of falling into his altered reality even though I wanted no part of that world.

As much as I hated him, it became impossible to remain disconnected all the time. One Monday morning he visited me like he did most mornings. But it had been a big weekend. Huge football game. The Falcons played the Patriots. Bobby had hired a crew to clean the place. They scrubbed it top to bottom, trashed our old mattresses and ratty furniture—even put in some decent light fixtures. Nothing fancy but more than a Goodwill lamp or a dangling lightbulb.

Hell's Outhouse felt more like Hell's Hostel. Still hell but almost livable.

Bobby sat beside me. I felt his warmth as I lay there. His hand gently touched mine. No groping. No forcing himself on me. No screaming. He was the dreamy hunk I'd seen on that beach.

"You had a big couple of nights, Selene. I'm going to give you a break this morning unless you're wanting some of this." He stood and stretched out his hand like a game show host showing off the next prize. Then he sauntered out the door, ducked his head back into my room, gave me a flirty grin and a wink, then disappeared into fading footsteps.

I couldn't believe it. He had a different day for each of his girls. I was his Monday girl. I'd always dreaded it, but in some warped way, I felt cheated. I imagined him coming back with a fresh bouquet of roses and a bottle of wine.

I had a split-second fantasy and pictured him and me together and happy.

The thought smacked me upside the head. I was becoming one of his wives. I slammed my fist against the wall, and electric pain shot into my elbow. That I could even *have* such a thought terrified me. What if those thoughts kept coming? What if they grew? What if I started to believe them?

No way. Those thoughts had to die.

I was not going to become like the girls who called him "Daddy," dote on him, play off the "wives-in-law" to win his favor or avoid his fist. I saw the way they looked at him. The way they looked at me. Each believed he was her boyfriend, that he cared about her more than the cash she brought him—everyone except Bliss and me.

That fleeting frightening fantasy became my motivation. I'd buried Emma, but she was still alive, and survival was no longer enough. I wanted out. As unwanted as Emma had been, I realized *I* wanted her. I wanted to be Emma again. I would be Selene and play the game while I looked for a way out.

Day after day I became Selene, and Selene became whoever the johns wanted. She was gorgeous, sexy, and willing to go through the motions. And the motions were all they would ever get.

CHAPTER 7
Emma

As the months passed, I'd adapted to my disgusting routine while plotting and waiting for the right moment to escape. Sometimes, I'd even start to believe I was Selene. I'd not seen any rich johns or celebrities or any real cash. I was still working on scraps and working for scraps.

I gave Bobby whatever he wanted. I'd decided to fake my way into his trust, hoping he'd trust me like he trusted the girls who came and went as they pleased. If he trusted me, he might loosen his grip, lower his guard.

One Friday morning, he walked by the break room and tossed a DVD into my lap. No box. No label. Just Sharpie marker that read *Dance*.

"Tawnya's sick. Looks like tonight's your first chance to escape." He winked and added, "Watch it and learn. It's your gig for tonight."

He chuckled as he walked away.

I popped in the DVD and slumped onto the sofa. Sagging cushions and the smells of cheap perfume and ashtray swallowed me.

Bliss swung through the door as the DVD started. "I hear you get to go out dancing tonight."

I imagined club hopping or slow dancing with fraternity brothers, but the video showed Tawyna stripping. I might've expected pole dancing in a club, but she was in a living room surrounded by surly, pants-down men sitting in a circle around her. Tongues wagging. Eyes glazed. Groping her anytime she got close enough.

I couldn't watch. I turned it off.

Bliss looked at me with her frightened little-girl face, and I knew I had to turn off my emotions and turn on the DVD. She sat beside me and held my hand as we watched. Tawnya turned those men into boys and those boys into puppies. She owned them, knew what they wanted, knew every hot button, every move. She turned it all on and shut them down like toys on Christmas night—batteries drained and dying. They had nothing left, and she was still standing.

Even Selene wasn't ready for this gig. Tonight, I was going to have to be Tawnya. It was all about the mindset. It was all about finding the right moment to escape. I didn't want to become like Candy, a scarred has been or never was, but I had to take the risk. I could only be Selene or a pretend Tawnya for so long. I had to escape.

I spent most of the afternoon feeling sick. I don't think I ate anything all day.

When evening came, Bobby handed me a couple of pills. "You'll probably need these, since it's your first time out." He smiled as he eyed me up and down. I was dressed for the part.

He placed his hands on my shoulders as Roberto and Mason walked up behind him. In a different life, I might have seen myself with Roberto. He was muscular, smooth, and always gentle. I felt like he really liked me and wanted to love me. After I'd been then only a short while, he'd quit using any of the other girls. He'd stroke my hair afterward, and he'd whisper "My Selene" or "I love you" in his deep Columbian accent. I was glad he was going. He'd make me feel safe.

Bobby's tug on my shoulders drew my attention away from Roberto. Bobby's smile disappeared, and his eyes narrowed. "Don't let these guys be rough with you tonight. I know they might be a little upset that Tawyna's not coming. She's the girl they requested. So, too soften their hearts, I'm sending Bliss with you as a bonus."

Bliss? This was definitely it. I didn't want to imagine leaving her and didn't have to. She was going with me. Our chance to escape. I dared not say anything to her. Who knew what she might've said or which personality would've been listening? No. I'd have to plan the escape myself. The hardest part would be toggling between Emma and Tawnya. I had to make those men think I was totally into them and look for a way out at the same time.

Bobby led us out the back door to a sleek black van. It was backed up against our building—doors opened, blocking any escape on either side.

Although it was my first time outside since my abduction, there was no time to enjoy it—not even time for one deep breath. Mason nudged me toward the van. He wasn't like Roberto. He was wiry but strong, and he used all the girls except me. Once Roberto had claimed me, Mason steered clear, but his perpetual scowl let me know he hadn't forgot and still wanted his turn. Thank God for Roberto.

Mason didn't care which girl he used. It didn't matter. He liked it with anyone. And he liked it rough. Everyone hated him—feared him, except Roberto. I couldn't tell where he was from. He may have had an accent, but who would know? He never spoke. He'd nod. Squint. Wink. Sneer. He said everything he needed to say with his face. If that didn't work, he'd use his fist or the back of his hand.

I lifted one foot into the carpet-walled van and felt his nasty grip on my rear, shoving me the rest of the way. Roberto gently lifted Bliss into the van. She curled her lower lip between her teeth and winked. Roberto and Mason climbed in behind us and closed the doors. Behind the wheel, Bobby turned and pointed at Roberto and Mason. "No freebies. These ladies are working."

We sat on opposing futons, obviously placed to unfold into one large bed. As trashy as that sounds, the van was the nicest thing I'd seen since I'd been there, wherever *there* was. I'd assumed I was still in Panama City, since that's where Bobby found me, but that brief walk outside had felt cooler than I'd expected, and hearing guys talk about the Falcons and Patriots made me think Atlanta. I smelled no salt air, no fish odors. Only pine trees and exhaust.

Roberto sat across from me and kept his eyes on Mason. The tension was palpable. *Don't touch my girl.* His stare spoke louder than words.

I'll make her mine if I want. I couldn't read their minds, but I felt their shared hate and respect.

Bliss was in clueless-little-girl mode—all smiles and leaning against Roberto as though he were a giant teddy bear. I was stone cold—all business on the outside. On the inside, I was just glad I hadn't eaten anything all day. If I was lucky, between the drugs and the empty stomach, I'd pass out and never know what happened.

As we pulled onto the street, I strained to see through the windshield. Mason, the passenger's seat, Bobby, and the fluffy dice hanging from the mirror made it difficult to make out anything, but I wanted to know where I was and where we were going. I was a long way from Middletown. This street was narrow, lined with forgotten-looking homes, unkempt yards, barred windows, closed businesses. Before I could see more, a blind slowly lowered between Bobby and us. Mason glared at me as he pulled it down.

There were no other windows, just midnight blue carpeted walls, mirrored ceiling, unlit lights, a tiny disco ball, a mini-fridge, and a small shelf holding a stereo system. Roberto read my mind and said, "It's mostly Tawnya's van." He raised his eyebrows and smiled. "But it's yours tonight."

Mason groaned. An actual noise came out of his throat. No words, but it was something.

"How much farther?" I asked.

"You anxious to meet your new friends?" Bobby asked. I could hear the smile in his voice. "No matter how long it takes to get there, you'll have all the time you need. Do a good job—or should I say jobs—and I'll let you keep the tips. That goes for you too, Bliss. And take as long as you like. These guys are paying by the hour."

I had no idea how any of the money worked. Since I'd never worked outside, I'd never seen what the johns were paying. I didn't realize what I was splitting with Bobby were just the tips. I'm sure he liked it that way. Not only did he make more money, but he kept us feeling worthless. And none of it mattered since we had no place to spend it anyway except to buy stuff from Bobby. I hadn't been to a store since I'd run away from Gramps and Grams.

But it was money, and Bobby made it sound like we might get quite a chunk if we worked hard. What a twisted universe I must've fallen into. *Don't forget your real job is to find a way out.* Yeah, I had to find a way out, but in the meantime, I still had to survive.

Bobby patted my knee. "You listening? These guys are paying by the hour. That means make it take as long as you can, and remember these college boys can be crazy tippers if you get them drunk and give what they want."

I'd had enough of college boys, and they'd gotten more than they deserved from me. But tonight, I wasn't me. I wasn't Selene. I was pretending to be Tawnya—put-it-all-out-there, exhaust-those-little-school-boys Tawnya. Three personalities. One crying. One terrified. One cracking her knuckles and ready to crack some knuckleheads.

A split-second part of me grinned when I put it all together and realized these guys were paying a lot for their turn with Tawnya.

Deep inside, I could feel Emma shaking her head. *Don't measure your worth in money or what anyone else thinks.*

I liked Emma. Sometimes she showed a little spunk, but she'd have to save her spunk and stay hidden until I could figure a way out.

The van finally stopped and backed into a driveway. Bobby lifted the blind. I saw a quaint, older neighborhood. Cute fifties-style houses with picture-perfect yards. Everything seemed so normal, not at all like the slum or the frat house I'd expected.

My heart sank and pounded out of my chest when I caught a glimpse of an old pickup in one of the driveways. It looked just like Johnny Paul's. Heart pounding. Acid churning. Sweat beading. These men were going be just like him—church boys, husbands, businessmen, hypocrites and cheats, every one of them.

Thank God my stomach was empty. If I had eaten anything, it would've blown all over Mason, and my life would be over. The way he looked at me, I'd always felt like he'd get as much of a thrill from watching me die as from working me over.

When Bobby killed the engine, my heart skipped a beat, and I had to catch my breath.

"Might want to take one of those xannies," Roberto said. I think he actually felt sorry for me. He handed me a water bottle and a baggie with some extra pills. I popped one and stashed the rest.

The van doors opened. Bobby stood there, all smiles, dollar signs in his eyes. "It's show time, ladies."

Mason slid out first, then Bliss and me. Roberto followed and closed the door.

Bobby gave a sideways nod toward the house, motioning Bliss and me to go first. The three of them flanked us as we approached the door.

We didn't even have to ring the bell. A young man, early twenties, opened the door and stuck his head out. He was holding a beer and smiling like a puppy. "Great! You're here." His eyes popped when he looked at the two of us. "Your brought two of 'em. Bonus! But where's the one we saw in the ad."

"Sorry, bro. Tawnya's a special girl, all right, but she's sick, and you wouldn't want her that way. So, to make up for it, I've brought Selene. Bliss is a bonus at no extra charge."

"Sweet." His tongue was practically dripping.

"What's the occasion?" Bobby asked.

The young man chuckled and burped. He was already half drunk. "It's my buddy's bachelor party. He made me promise his fiancée there'd be no strip club." He sipped his beer. "So screw it. We brought the strippers here."

Bobby held out his hand. The young man gave him an envelope, and Bobby said, "Bottoms up. Tops down." They laughed together.

Bliss and I smiled on cue and tried not to throw up.

The young man stepped inside, stretched out his arm, and said, "Ladies first."

The cozy living room didn't match the thumping bass and the spinning lights. Guys sinking into the ancient sofas struggled to stand. How quaint. The gentlemen stand to welcome the ladies. They reeked of booze and cheap cologne.

Looking past them through the dining room, I spied the kitchen with its tacky countertops, metal cabinets, and that stainless-steel-looking trim around the edge of the counters. And straight through the kitchen was the back door. *Our escape.*

Mr. All Smiles said, "Can I take your coat?"

I reached deep inside for my inner Tawnya. She looked that school boy up and down. He had no idea what he was in for. Tawnya smirked and stepped past him. Selene hid inside, and Emma had disappeared.

Bliss bumped into me as the door closed behind us. I'd expected Roberto and Mason to follow us inside, but they stayed on the porch. I guessed they would just listen and respond if we screamed.

I heard the van start. Bobby was leaving. I guess he had other girls to attend to—other money to collect.

Another twenty-something approached me. His tongue wasn't wagging or even hanging out. His wide eyes struggled to focus on mine.

Nervous smile. Flushed face. Sweating. He extended his hand to shake mine. "My name's Michael."

Mr. All Smiles opened his mouth and revealed his true identity, Mr. Douchebag as he said, "Don't tell her your name. She's a ho."

Michael's eyes dropped, and his flushed face turned crimson. I couldn't tell if he was angry or embarrassed. I suspect both, since he turned around and disappeared into the kitchen.

Mr. Douchebag ushered us into the living room, where a mix of smiles and surprised faces greeted us. Two of the guys brought chairs from the dining room and shifted the sofas and chairs into a circle. Douchebag turned up the lights just a hint and cranked the dance music. The boys danced their way into the living room with beers in hand. One of them winked and turned the lights all the way up.

There we stood like two stunned school girls who'd just seen their first joint. I looked at Bliss and smiled. The drugs were working. Her scared little-girl face had morphed into Bliss, and she was ready to strut her stuff. Emma awakened inside me and hid behind a trembling Selene. I wasn't Tawnya, and pretending wasn't working.

Bliss tossed her hair, nibbled her lip and began a slow twirl. The way she rocked her booty while she spun dragged those boys into a coma. She owned every eye in that cramped room.

The thump thump thump of the bass shook her and the house, every inch of her body in motion. We were dressed as naughty meter maids. Tiny hats strapped on with tiny little strings. Tight blue tops with snaps instead of buttons. Short peekaboo skirts with no panties. And, of course, high-heeled stripper shoes, the kind every meter maid wears.

As Bliss worked into a sweaty dance trance, I popped another pill and unsnapped one, two, three buttons. I could feel the pulse of every hungry young man in that room. Their hearts pounded with the kick drum.

I leaned forward, bending from my waist. My hips swayed and bobbed with the music. I looked into the wide, wondering, wandering eyes of a baby. He was twenty-something going on eighteen, smooth cheeks that rarely needed shaving. I smirked at the sweat on his forehead. His hands trembled as he balanced his beer on his lap. His breathing quickened as though he'd never been this close to a girl.

I put my hands on either side of his chair, and his beer jostled in his lap. I captured his eyes as I started to taste the bitterness of my dissolving Xanax. I lowered my head into his lap and sucked a mouthful of beer. As I swallowed that bitter pill, the panting pup next to him unsnapped my blouse the rest of the way.

I wasn't sure there was going to be enough beer and Xanax to get me through the night.

Bliss tapped me on the shoulder and shouted over the music. "I see some naughty boys." She did a little spin with one hand on her hip and the other shaking her pointer at those "naughty boys."

"I'm giving each of you a parking ticket." Their mouths dropped as Bliss handed each of them a condom and said, "Next time be careful where you park." Every eye followed her—her eyes—her hair—her dreamy body.

She owned them. They sat in that circle like obedient puppies waiting for their treats. Eyes wide open. Tongues hanging out.

As we circled the room, one of the young men looked at me and swallowed hard. His hands were empty. His jeans still zipped. His belt snug. He looked at my eyes, not my chest. He had no color in his face. He rubbed his hands on his knees.

He was the groom, had to be. As we looked each other in the eyes, I felt like I was staring into a mirror. We were both desperate for a way out.

Bliss stepped between us and stood in front of him shaking her finger. "Looks like you're trying to double park." His hands didn't move when she offered him a condom. She unfastened her top, bent down, straddled him, and sat on his lap.

His eyes popped. His jaw quivered. He leaned back against the chair, shoved her shoulders, slid out from under her, and bolted toward the door.

As he ran, I saw myself running through a cornfield—laughter and footsteps chasing me. I'd felt the fear I saw in his eyes. Fear that must have exploded as his buddies tackled him. They rolled him onto his back, laughing as they stole his pants. They held him against the floor while Bliss went to work.

I didn't remember anything else. Thank God for those pills and the beer—lots of beer.

I woke up on the sofa, nothing left of my uniform—not even the little choker. Bliss tossed me my trench coat. "It's time to go," she shouted over the music—still blaring. The floor still bouncing with the bass.

The room was dark. Guys lay passed out, half-naked. The groom was nowhere to be seen. And I never saw Michael again after we'd almost shaken hands. I guess he didn't want to touch a ho.

Bliss started toward the door, but I grabbed her arm and nodded toward the kitchen. My head throbbed.

"We need to go." Her tone was half-protest, half-command.

"I need a drink of water."

The music faded a little as we entered the kitchen, enough that I could talk without shouting. Barely alert and certainly not sober, there was enough of Emma awake in me and screaming to get out. I grabbed Bliss by the arms. "Now's our chance."

"Chance for what?" She was all big girl. Stern eyes. Sharp tone. No nonsense. I still have no idea how she maintained that persona.

"Our chance to *escape*." Even I could hear the desperation in my voice.

"Girl, you are *nuts*." Bliss jerked her arm loose and shoved me away. "There *is* no escape. Go ahead. Try it. Make a run for it. I'll watch the doors."

The doors. My heart sank. "What do you mean?"

"What do I mean? What do *you* mean? When are you gonna wake up? You are no longer you. Kill that girl, whoever she is." Her hand shot up in my face before I could speak. "And don't say her name. You are and forever will be Selene."

I could hear the cry in her voice. Whoever she'd been was screaming to get out.

I looked out the kitchen window. Mason was covering the back door. He and Roberto weren't our bodyguards. They were guarding our bodies, because that's all we were to them and to all the men who'd used us. Bodies.

They stood guard so we wouldn't try to escape. How I wished I'd had more pills, a whole bottle of pills. How many times could my life feel like it was over but keep going?

We climbed back into the van and rode home. I never saw any tips. If there were any, I was too drunk to know it.

I buried Emma again.

CHAPTER 8
Michael

I knew Kyle had made a mistake when he'd chosen his fraternity brother to be his best man. Jordan was a real piece of work. The guy'd never grown up, and to him my best friend's bachelor party was a frat party gone crazy.

I'd never seen so much alcohol—two kegs, Jim Beam, and Captain Morgan. There weren't enough guys there to handle that much alcohol. They'd all be drunk before they got to the second keg, especially considering I don't care for alcohol.

At least Jordie had followed through with his promise to not go to a strip club. Even so, I felt like giant sequoia in the mud. *I don't belong here.* That was what I'd told myself. Don't get me wrong. I'm no better than anyone else, and I love Kyle more than I love my own brother. But my stomach was practicing Boy Scout knots. I wanted out of there, but I couldn't leave Kyle stranded. He sat in the corner of the cramped living room, sipping his beer alone. I could tell he felt almost as awkward as I did, but what was he going to do? It was his party.

I wanted to talk to Kyle, but the music was so loud, it was impossible. He sipped his beer and lay his head back as though he was staring through the ceiling. He set his beer on the end table and folded his hands on top of his head. He had to be thinking about Samantha.

Everyone called Kyle's fiancée Sam. She was drop-dead gorgeous. Wavy blond hair, tiny dimples. And her smile could melt a glacier. How could he not think about her? She was perfect, and the next day, she would be forever his.

I left him alone to dream about Sam and I stepped outside to get some air. I didn't expect to choke on the smell of weed. I think Jordie had invited as many guys from their old frat as he could. Thank God only a few of them were able to make it. Kyle had four groomsmen, but there were about ten guys crammed into that tiny house. It looked like it was built in the fifties or earlier. Mostly brick. Stone chimney. Stone archway over the front porch. Driveway barely big enough for one car. Old fixtures, solid wood door frames. And hardwood floors that buzzed with the thumping bass. Jordie had rented it for the weekend, and he seemed fully prepared to trash it.

Too much noise and alcohol inside. Purple haze outside. It didn't feel like much of a choice. I stepped off the porch. My truck was sitting there, begging me to drive it home. The sun was working its way down. It would be dark in another thirty minutes. I figured Kyle was going to be too drunk to remember when I left the party, so I stepped toward my truck.

But a black van backed into the driveway and blocked my exit. Great. More guys, as if the party wasn't ridiculous enough. I turned around and headed to the back door. I needed to at least talk to Kyle before I left, then maybe I'd figure out a way around that van.

I found him in the kitchen by himself. Head down. Leaning over the sink.

"Great party," I said.

He smirked. I'd seen that face a thousand times. "Yeah, right." He didn't even have to say the words. "I didn't expect them to smoke pot, and I'm scared to think what else Jordie's got planned." His face tightened with regret, and I sensed he wanted to get out of there too.

But he shook his head and heaved a sigh. "Have another beer, Michael."

I half-smiled. He knew I hate beer. He winked and re-filled his red plastic cup.

That's one way to leave the party. Or at least forget you were there.

He heaved another sigh and headed back to the tiny living room. Jordie was holding the front door open, but it wasn't more frat brothers. It was two girls in gray trench coats and matching fedoras. Weird. Two thugs stood behind them. The shorter one reminded me of Manny Pacquiao, the Filipino boxer, but I imagined this guy would rather rip my head off than knock me out. The other guy was huge, bulging muscles, Hispanic. I pictured him protecting some drug lord's little princess.

My desperate desire to leave exploded into a fear that I hadn't left soon enough. I broke into a sweat when I saw those platform heels and smooth, oiled legs, and I imagined the girls wore nothing under those trench coats.

But my nerd instincts ran deeper than reason. As the guys seemed to press around me, I stepped toward one of the girls, stretched out my sweat-drenched hand, and said, "My name's Michael."

Jordie laughed and opened his mouth, but I couldn't tell what he said. The girl's eyes told me she didn't want to be there. But those eyes, her face... Smooth, sturdy cheeks. Thick but neatly trimmed eyebrows. Stunning lashes. Golden brown hair that refused to hide under her tiny hat. And lips that begged for a kiss. It felt surreal—like I was staring at two people at once. A bombshell who could explode every hormone receptor in my body and a little girl who was screaming to get out.

I wanted to throw up. I didn't even look at Kyle. I couldn't. I had to get out there. Though I managed to make myself walk at a normal pace, inside I was sprinting. I couldn't get out of there fast enough. I ducked into the kitchen and bent down with my hands on my knees, panting like

Kyle and I used to do after running "killers" in basketball practice. I wanted to cry. I wanted to scream. I wanted to throw up, grab Kyle, and get the hell out of there.

But I convinced myself the alcohol would somehow protect him. Even if something happened, surely he'd never remember it. I stepped toward the back door and heard a collective "whoa." Middle school curiosity got the best of me, and I turned to take a peek. Everything inside me felt warm and tingly, the certainty that I was doing something exhilarating and wrong at the same time.

The trench coats fell to the floor, and the hats went flying. Little blue stripper outfits were my cue to leave.

As I stepped around the corner of the house, I saw a third guy opening the driver's door of the black van. A real ladies' man. Dark complexion. Contagious smile. Smooth, bulging muscles and dark hair with tight curls. "You leavin'?" he asked. "I brought my two best girls. They'll show you a real good time."

"Past my curfew," I said, and he laughed as he climbed into his van.

I wanted to rip that smile off his face.

Get your van out of my way, pretty boy.

* * *

I couldn't sleep. My thoughts ran a thousand miles an hour through a thousand what-ifs. Then I imagined Jordie blabbing about the party through his champagne bubbles and Sam sobbing and running out of the reception. We weren't in Vegas. We were in Westview, a suburb of Atlanta. And what happens in Westview, well pretty much everybody knows about it. How was he going to hide a sleek black van with two goons and girls dressed like flashers?

Poor Kyle. Poor Sam. Poor whoever those girls were.

I sat on the edge of my bed. Three AM. I had a sinking feeling—a feeling I couldn't shake—a feeling that something was terribly wrong. *Kyle.*

I checked my find-your-friend app. Kyle was still at that house.

That couldn't be good. Why would he still be there. You can only drink so much alcohol. Girls can only dance and spin so long. They only have so many clothes to take off. *Oh God, no. What if they were more than strippers?* I wanted to kill Jordie. *I've got to check on Kyle.*

I threw on a pair of jeans and snuck out the door. I'd decided to live with Mom and Dad until I paid off my student loans and until I met the right girl. They didn't seem to mind. I think Mom actually liked having me at home. I had to be quiet so I wouldn't wake them. After all, Dad had to officiate Kyle and Sam's wedding in less than twelve hours.

Twelve hours. Dang it. What are you thinking, Kyle?

He wasn't thinking. He was probably passed out on the sofa in that old house. Either way, it was way past time to get him out of there—for his sake and for Sam's.

The house was dark. My jaw dropped, and my heart sank as I saw that black van sitting in the driveway. I hopped out and ran to the front door. The front porch light flicked on as I ran up the steps just in time to catch that girl's eyes. Hollow. Sad. And glazed from drugs and alcohol. I caught a hint of smile, a smile that disappeared as soon as pretty boy said, "Nice work, ladies."

I stepped around the wiry goon, careful not to touch him, look at him, or even inhale the same air. When I stepped into the house, Jordie's stupid disco ball was still spinning. I flipped on the entryway light. No movement. Not even a groan.

Jordie lay on the floor in front of me next to a wadded-up condom. His pants were around his ankles, his legs almost blocking the door. The girls and their goons would've had to step over him to get out. I seized my chance to give him a swift kick in the gut.

What a.... I had no words, no decent words for how I felt.

He didn't move. Didn't even groan. I kicked him again, then turned to look for Kyle.

I cried. No way in the world I could've held my tears. My best friend, the night before he was to marry the girl of every guy's dreams, lay completely naked on the hardwood floor of a strange house. Empty Solo cups all over the floor. Used condoms. Dried you-know-what smeared into the wood. And there he lay surrounded by Polaroids of him and those two girls. The one girl barely looked fifteen. The other one I'd take home to Mom if she were a decent girl. No chance for that. And their lipstick was *all over* my friend.

I couldn't let him wake up to this mess. I walked toward the kitchen and felt my way down the cramped hallway. I tiptoed and didn't turn on any more lights until I found the bathroom. I closed the door and shut it as quietly as you can shut a sixty-year-old door, then I turned on the lights and looked for a towel and washcloths. Found both and a bowl.

Perfect.

I ran some water until it was warm. Stared at myself in the mirror as I filled the basin. "You left your best friend." I wanted to smash that face in the mirror. I'd like to think Kyle had saved himself for Sam. I was pretty sure they'd been frisky together, but I wasn't going to count that. The used condoms gave me a fleeting sense of relief, but the lipstick told me they hadn't made him use a condom for everything. I imagined poor Sam finding out she caught an STD from her husband on their honeymoon.

Stop it. Stop it. Stop it. What's done is done. Let's bury it and move forward.

Water spilled over the bowl into the sink. I dumped enough out that I wouldn't spill, then carried it back to the living room, leaving the bathroom light on so I wouldn't trip going down the hall. I felt like I was in a video game where you shoot the bad guys and their bodies just lay there for the rest of the game. Loser frat boys were scattered over the floor, the chairs, the sofas. Some of them were starting to moan a little, so I had to work fast.

I tossed the towel and wash cloth over the arm carrying the bowl and grabbed the kitchen trash can with my free hand.

First, I picked up the polaroids and tossed them into the trash—all except one. I used that one to scrape the dozen or so used condoms off the floor and add them to the soon-to-be-buried-and-forgotten polaroids. I snatched every cell phone.

I grabbed each snoozer-loser's index finger to activate their phones. I searched and deleted incriminating photos of Kyle. I desperately wanted to take pictures of each of them with their own phones and send them in a text message to "Mom," but I didn't. I didn't want anything to come back and haunt Kyle and Sam.

But I used my phone to snap incriminating pics of every one of them then buried the pics in a hidden folder. I went to the kitchen, searched the drawers, and found a pen and a small notepad. I scratched a love note for Jordie.

I've taken pictures of you and your buddies and copied your moms' and your girlfriends' contact information. One word of this party gets back to Sam, and I'll not only send those pictures, I'll track you down and chop off your little friend.

I took the wash cloth and the warm water and washed Kyle. I rolled him onto his side—even had to wipe a smudge of lipstick off his rear. Those girls had been thorough. I scoured the living room and the hallway until I found every piece of his clothes. I hoped it was his underwear. I couldn't really be sure.

As I got him dressed, he started to moan. I whispered. "You're not waking up here, buddy." I lifted him onto the sofa, leaned into his chest, reached under his arms, and wrapped mine around him. I pulled him close, stood him up best I could, and hoisted him onto my shoulder.

I'd never tried to open my pickup door with a friend heaved over my shoulder. It wasn't easy, but I did it, then I gently laid him on the seat and closed the door.

Jordie. I stared at the house, briefly fantasizing about lighting the whole thing on fire. Burn those jerks and this whole night and forget about it. They say "what's done is done," but the truth is, some things can't be undone, and they change you forever.

I prayed Kyle didn't get some creepy crawlies, a virus, or worse. I prayed the same for Sam. But I also can't help but pray for those girls—especially the one that shook my hand. I can't imagine she wanted to be there, to do the things she did. Those haunting eyes made me think she was slowly dying inside. Every night giving a piece of herself away until eventually there was none of her—the real her—left.

I whispered toward the starry sky. "God, I don't even know her name." *If I did, it wouldn't be her real name.* "Please help that girl—and her friend." I couldn't bring myself to pray for pretty boy and his goons. I didn't want to mess with those guys, but something in my gut told me I'd see them again.

I glanced at Kyle stretched out on the seat in my truck. Still dead to the world.

I looked back at the house. *No more bachelor parties for me. No way!* I never wanted to see any of those guys ever again. Unfortunately, I'd have to see at least three of them tomorrow—later today—at the wedding.

I wanted to get Kyle out of there and tucked into bed before he had a chance to wake up and remember anything, but I had one thing left to do. I ran back into the house. Juiced on adrenaline and lack of sleep, I flicked on every light, turned the stereo back on, and cranked it up. I took the love note for Jordie out of my pocket and stuffed in his. He was starting to wake up. I grabbed the bag of evidence/trash and headed toward the door. One last look around the room. Moans and groans. One guy stood and threw up over the air vent. Another one whizzed into the closet. "Great party, guys."

I stepped over Jordie one last time as I opened the door, banging it hard against his back. He opened his eyes for a second, squinted, and rubbed his head. As he closed his eyes again, I gave him one last kick. The throbbing in my toe satisfied me. I slammed the door and bolted toward my truck.

CHAPTER 9
Emma

All the showers in the world couldn't make me feel clean, but that warm water still felt good, and it helped me wake up and helped me forget. I liked to pretend my shower was some kind of baptism—my chance to start over or at least pretend. Drying off, I looked in the mirror. *You're still in there, girl. Don't you ever leave me.*

We hadn't escaped, but we'd still somehow find a way. I'd just have to wait for the right time and place. In the meantime, *survive*. Play the game.

I walked past Bliss's room. Sound asleep. I couldn't help but love that girl. She'd saved me last night. I'd froze. That guy Michael got to me. Shook me up, because he seemed real. Not like the other guys. He wasn't exactly a knight, but I guess we didn't look like distressed damsels either. That startled look in his eyes and the way he disappeared like an embarrassed little boy made me feel more exposed than when those twerps unsnapped what was left of my outfit.

I couldn't forget his eyes. Maybe the only set of innocent eyes I'd ever seen. *Bury that thought, girl. Bury him. Play the game. Survive. And when the time is right, escape.*

As I walked back to my room, I realized it was almost ten o'clock on Saturday morning. Bobby had let us sleep in. We must've done well.

As I stepped into my room, Bobby lay on my bed. Fully clothed, arms folded behind his head, face beaming, he said "I'm giving you the night off." He sat up. Hopped of the bed. Waltzed toward me. Stuff a stack of cash in my hand. Kissed my neck and slid by me and down the hall.

Money and the night off? Those ex-frat boys must have given him a serious wad or he cleaned their wallets while they lay passed out. Either way, I'd take the cash and the night off.

I slid into Bliss's room. She rubbed her eyes and gave me a why-did-you-turn-on-the-light look.

"I can't believe he's giving us tonight off."

Her eyebrows tilted into an instant frown. "What are you talking about? He never said anything about a night off." Her eyes widened. "At least not to me."

I saw a personality I hadn't met yet. This was tough girl, a take-you-out-behind-the-school-and-kick-your-ass girl, and I had no idea how to handle her. Hands up, I backed up. "I'm sure he just hadn't told you yet. I'll… let's go talk to him together."

Her face softened and Bliss was back. I didn't want to tangle with whoever that other girl was. Thank God if there is a God.

I hoped there was a God, because, I sure as hell need him. Actually, I'm not too sure about hell. Kind of hope there isn't one of those—at least not for me—but for Mason and Bobby, yes, there needed to be a hell for them. I looked through the ceiling. *God, if you're there, yup, I sure as hell need you.* I chuckled. Somewhere inside, I felt like there was a God and he knew I needed him. Hopefully, he cared that I needed him. Hopefully, he at least noticed.

I walked down our little prison hallway toward Bobby's door. There stood Mason, arms folded, chewing on a toothpick. His eyes never saw clothes. He was stripping me down in his mind even though he already knew what was there.

"I need to clear something up with Bobby."

"Mmm." He actually made a noise. Wow. Then he gave a little chin lift, head nod, and stepped aside.

As I reached for the doorknob, Mason slid between me and the door. Greasy smile. Warm ashtray breath in my face. I think he somehow thought that smile might win him another freebie. I stared, emotionless until he opened the door, and I slid past, Bliss behind me.

"Selene." Bobby stood up. As much as I hated his guts, there was no denying he looked good in jeans and a bleached-white wife beater. Muscles twitching, wide smile. If I didn't know what kind of scum he was, I might let him give me a beer and have his way.

"I need to talk to you."

"Anything, precious. You were great last night. Those boys gave us an extra five hundred bucks." He handed me an envelope. "I was going to keep half of the tips, but you deserve it all." He nodded to Bliss. "Yours and sweetheart's. You guys split it however you like."

Bliss grabbed it. "Half?"

I nodded, staring at the cash. Bewildered. I looked at Bobby. *What am I supposed to do with money? I'm trapped here. I can't go anywhere. I've nothing to spend it on. And I don't even have a safe place to keep it.*

"It's money," Bobby said. "You don't know what to do with money? I listened to that guy on the radio. He said there's only three things you can do with money. You can spend it. You can save it. Or you can give it away." He held his arms out as if to say, *your choice.*

"How can I spend it if I never go anywhere?"

He smiled, and I felt another *gotcha* coming. Bobby never smiled unless there was something in it for him. I was too dumb to figure it out, but this smile was all about trust, manipulative trust.

"I've got a surprise for my Selene." Arms wide open like he was expecting a hug.

I shrugged, looked at him as flatly as I could, let one shoulder drop, and cocked my hip. All I needed to do was smack my gum, and I'd have just done that stereotypical hooker thing you see in the movies when they're not impressed. But I never chew gum.

He put his arm around me. "I'm taking you out tonight. Just you and me. We're going someplace special, and I'm taking you shopping beforehand so you can pick some new clothes." He stepped back, nibbled his lips as if he were thinking, pointed at my chest, and said, "Tell you what. I'll even pay for the clothes and let you keep your money."

I couldn't hold the flat face, and his eyes told me he knew it. As his smile grew, so did mine. *Damn it. Why can't I just hate this guy.* He'd ruined my already ruined life, but he was contagious—like a disease I couldn't get rid of.

The *tap tap tap* of Bliss's foot reminded me why we were there. "Sounds nice, *my* Bobby, but I don't want to go without Bliss." Scared to death I was overstepping, I softened my tone, did my little open-mouth tongue slide, and said, "Don't you think she deserves a night off too." I raised my eyebrows. "We could be a threesome." I knew the sleazy perv would go for that.

He eyed Bliss up and down. She was in full-on giddy-little-girl mode. I didn't think I'd ever know who she really was or if the real girl was even still in there.

"Sure." He pointed at Bliss. "But you got plenty of clothes. Just pick out something classy and don't go showing off your goods at this place." He looked at us both. "And no stripper heels, just regular. Okay?"

Bliss and I looked at each as if we were sisters who'd each gotten a pony for our birthday. No sleazy men tonight. No *up-standing* citizens. No middle-aged frat boys. No work. Only shopping. New clothes. A night off. And dinner at a classy restaurant.

I honestly couldn't remember the last time anyone had taken me shopping and let me pick out clothes. Grams dumped hand-me-downs on me. The rare times I got anything new, she'd buy me a dress fit for a nun. If I tried to pick an outfit, she'd mutter, "Makes you look like a slut."

Despite being the worst of jerks, Bobby was doing something no one else had ever done for me, and—I couldn't believe I let myself feel this way—I felt loved. I felt special, and I wanted to make him happy—because he'd made me happy. Just once.

I was happy, and that was a feeling I'd not had since Johnny Paul gave me that first ride home from school.

* * *

I tried on so many dresses, I felt dizzy from twirling, giving Bobby his own little show. He smiled at each one, and I felt like Mel Gibson's daughter in "What Women Want," trying on dresses before the prom.

I stopped twirling. Emma had tried to sneak out—tried to be that young girl, Daddy's princess. But Bobby was everybody else's daddy. He wasn't my daddy. And I wasn't his Selene. I was Emma, and I had to hang on to that girl—even if I had to keep her hidden. I couldn't become one of "the wives."

I turned my back to Bobby kept my head down, eyes closed, and swallowed my pesky tears. I knew I was standing in front of one of those three-fold mirrors, but I couldn't look at myself. I wouldn't recognize who I saw anyway.

If it were Bliss and me picking out a dress, I would have loved it and loved every moment. Or if it were *Mandy and me*. I fought tears at the thought of her and what life could have been. What it should have been. *Prom dress. Wedding dress. Any dress.*

I shook my head and swallowed my tears. *No time for Emma.* I had to be Selene.

Eyes still closed. I heard Bobby's footsteps behind me and felt his breath on my neck. I flinched at his hands on my shoulders. He lifted my chin and whispered. "Don't be shy. Open your eyes."

I felt the corners of my mouth rise as I gazed at Selene. Dazzling. Standing tall. Poised. Head up in a form-fitting floor-length gown. Cliff-diving V neck. Open back. Shimmering black. Covered with dainty threaded beads that danced with every move.

But the dress was only lavish packaging, and I was the package.

"You may not feel it, Selene, but you are my princess." Bobby touched my shoulders once more. A cool tickle bounced on my skin as he draped a string of pearls around my neck. He gently turned me around and gave me a soft kiss.

He stepped back. Huge smile. Arms wide open. Eyes running up and down my body. "The only thing missing is the glass slippers."

* * *

There was no shady black van. Bobby's friend let him borrow his limo and his driver. The interior still felt cheesy—very expensive cheese—but nonetheless cheese. Velvet walls. Rhinestones on the minibar. Some kind of fancy rope lighting running around the edge of the ceiling. The backseat folded down into a bed. Snazzy shaded window between the driver and us.

Bliss giggled. I could see why Bobby hadn't wanted her to come. When she wasn't working, she acted like a child. And the little school girl could get downright annoying. She leaned forward and plucked open a tiny drawer in the minibar. Condoms. Of course.

Bobby shook his head. "It's your night off."

We had driven several blocks before I realized the windows weren't overly tinted and weren't covered. I'd been looking at homes and businesses going by, but hadn't really paid attention to what it meant. A new warmth rushed through me. This ride, the new dress, the money, and the night off were telling me I'd pleased him. I'd done a good job. And I must've earned some tiny measure of his trust.

But he would never earn mine.

I winked at Bliss. Playing the game was working. I was surviving, and if I played it right, surviving might become thriving. What kind of life would I have been able to make for myself anyway if Bobby hadn't taken me? I'd certainly never imagined myself cruising in a limousine.

Selene, you can do this.

We passed block after block. Luxury homes. Big churches. High rises in the distance. We turned onto Martin Luther King, Jr. Drive. We certainly weren't in Panama City. The new warmth disappeared into an icy chill. Where was I? We passed Booker T. Washington High School. We could have been in any city in the US.

But when we passed Clark Atlanta University and saw signs for Morris Brown University, it reminded me I was no longer in Florida and no longer in control. The same man I met on the beach, the same slime who drugged me and dragged me to Atlanta, that slime was in complete control. And his cocky grin agreed.

Emma was trying to sneak out again. Tears trickled down my throat as Selene slid her fingers across my neck and around my necklace. *Get over yourself. There is no more Emma.*

Emma had nothing. No one who loved her. No one to rescue her. No place to go. I buried her once more and swallowed the last of my tears.

I opened my purse and stared at my emergency stash of Xanax. Deep down, Emma wanted to pop one, but Selene was in control. *You don't need one. You are Selene.*

I closed my purse.

Finally, the car slowed and pulled onto a winding drive. Stone walls and trees lined the way. My skin tingled when I saw a police car. A bulky cop stood beside a squad car. I thought for a second, he could be my way out. Tell him everything. Watch him cuff Bobby and haul him away, but fleeting hopes fizzled when he nodded and waved at our driver.

At the top of the hill, we stopped, and our driver opened my door.

What the heck? This is how a girl's supposed to live.

Bliss clapped and bounced in the seat beside me. I grabbed her hands and said, "Let's be a big girl now." Her eyes narrowed, and fear shot through me because that look was take-you-out-behind-the-school-and-kick-your-ass girl. And even though that glance only lasted a split second, I'd hoped to never see tough-girl Bliss again. That girl was scary.

Her stare softened, and she frowned her little-girl frown.

I kissed her hands and whispered. "It's okay, just don't clap, and don't jump up and down." She smiled and nibbled her lip as she climbed out of the limo. I looked at her. She looked at me. We were dressed like a million bucks a piece. Two wannabe princesses.

Her hair twisted into a stylish topknot with a few well-planned dangling strands. Subtle earrings and makeup. Bliss looked as though a professional cosmetologist had spent an hour on her face. She was perfect. This night off was going to be great.

Her little-girl grin transformed into a wide-eyed, mouth-opened, head-tilted stare. I turned around to see three stories of rough-cut stone and glass. Dark windows stretched from the ground to the top of the building with the name SinS in huge letters at the top.

Not what I had expected or hope for. Why should I have hopes anyway?

Apparently, Bobby's idea of a stylish restaurant was an upscale strip club.

As I stared at the club, Bobby's hand touched my shoulder and slid around my back. Emma hid deep inside while Selene fake smiled as though looking into a bright future. Bobby pulled me close. His strong arm felt good.

His lips sent a tingle up my neck. "Come on, let's go."

As we approached the door, he whirled in front of me, beamed, and gave me a quick look up and down. Then he took my hands in his. His glossed-over eyes looked into mine. He drew a shoulder-lifting deep breath and exhaled as though he were a debut actor taking his first step into the big time. He kissed my cheek. "Don't say anything. Just stay close to me."

Just stay close to me. I felt a chill at those words—scary words. Why would I need to stay close to him?

He squeezed my hands, both of them in his left hand and led me toward the building. "Bliss, be a good girl and stay behind Tawn…Selene, and keep your mouth shut."

He almost called me Tawnya. Illusion over. I was simply another one of his girls. Nobody special. Nobody at all.

Nobody or not, I couldn't let it get to me. Why should his opinion matter? I was Selene, and I had the night off. And Selene was going to relax and enjoy it. I'd always hated that phrase, but that unfortunate phrase had become my survival plan. I plucked my left hand from Bobby's grip and reached for Bliss. I squeezed her hand, and we shared a smile as we neared the oversized doors.

Atlas and Roberto's doppelgänger stood guard. Arms folded. Suits intentionally a little small. Rolexes. Huge rings. And diamond studs in each ear. They both sniffed and nodded as we approached.

A saucy blonde wrapped in floor-length sequins and diamonds waltzed through the open door with outstretched arms. "Welcome to SinS." Her smile probably melted what was left of Bobby's soul, but I saw daggers when she looked at me. The way she looked at Bliss... I about died. She sparkled like a real-life Barbie, clapped her hands, did a little hop, and giggled. I couldn't tell if they were connecting or if she was mocking my friend.

Bobby bumped against my shoulder as he opened his arms and said, "Donny." His voice made it sound like he'd just seen a long-lost friend.

Donny. How appropriate. He stood in the doorway behind real-life Barbie, flanked by beefy goons. He had the saggy jowls, salt-and-pepper hair, thick eyebrows, and pinstripes. He was Donny alright. *The Don.*

He folded his arms and didn't take another step. "Robert! What a surprise." He raised his eyebrows and offered a tight-lipped grin. "Thought you'd *never* come back." His gravelly words sounded like a veiled threat—like *you'd better have a good reason to show up on my turf.* The Don tossed me a passing glance then peered over my shoulder, curling his lip as though looking for someone in particular. "Where's Tawnya? She was supposed to be here at three, and she's not with you."

Bobby dropped his head. "She's sick." He lifted his chin. "Not sure she's gonna make it."

Not sure she's gonna make it? Instant acid churned in my gut and climbed up my throat. *He killed her, and he's hiding it.* What else could I think? Why else would he be so cryptic about Tawnya? No one had seen her or heard from her.

The Don glanced at my heaving chest. As I held my breath, trying to avoid a panic attack, he glared at Bobby and said, "This is gonna cost me, and if it costs me, you know it's gonna cost you."

I closed my eyes, drew a slow deep breath, opened my eyes wide and faked a smile. No use.

The Don wrinkled his nose and looked *through* me.

Looking past me, he pointed at Bliss. "What's little miss Nutcase doin' here? I told you to never bring her again."

"Donny, I'm sorry. I thought you were kidding. It won't happen again. I promise."

The Don's crinkled brow and clenched jaw didn't look like a face that would ever kid. He stepped past me and nodded to his boys. "It won't happen *now*! Get her out of here."

Fire shot through me—through Selene like nobody's business. *It doesn't matter what Bliss may have done, nothing is going to spoil Selene's night off.*

I stepped in front of the Don in full-on Selene mode. One finger tugging on the V in my dress, my other hand slid up his chest, and I used my smoky, Ginger Grant voice. "Please let her stay. I'll make sure she behaves."

His eyes softened. He threw up his hands then patted my shoulder and gave me a wink. Spinning toward the door, he glared at Bobby, pointed at Bliss, then pressed his finger into Bobby's chest. "She does anything to screw up my night, and it's on you."

It was the first time I'd seen Bobby sweat. "My Bobby." I rubbed his shoulders and kissed his cheek, then whispered in his ear, "Don't let that big, mean man scare you." I laughed inside as sweat beaded and drizzled down his cheek. His nervous smile couldn't fool anyone.

He nodded toward Bliss's hands.

I grabbed her hand again. Then Bobby led us inside to a massive room drowning in high tech sound and lights. He shouted over the dance mix. "Let's get some drinks." As we walked toward the bar, the floor pulsed with the bass.

I glanced over my shoulder at a sea of men amid large round tables with pristine, white tablecloths. Plush centerpieces. Ice sculptures. Decadent desserts. And a broad assortment of young women filled the room. The girls were clinging to the men, climbing on them, dancing for them.

Some kind of night off. I couldn't grab a drink fast enough.

With all the noise and commotion, it seemed odd that nothing was happening on stage—yet. I leaned against the bar, lifted a hand and tried to catch the attention of the twenty-something bartender, but she was working it for the men with the glazed eyes and the open wallets.

I wriggled between her admirers and looked into her eyes. She raised her eyebrows and did a little chest bounce. I gave her a thanks-but-no-thanks smile for the bounce and said, "Closest rum you can reach. Neat. Fast. And a double."

I wondered why she was working a bar like this one. Smart haircut. No tattoos—at least none I could see. No piercings. Nothing wrong with any of those things, but she didn't have any of them, and she didn't really fit the scene—at least not to me.

She played the part with her expressions and movements. Her figure wasn't enough to own that stage or even take a whirl, but she had more than enough for the guys nosing up to the bar. And she had the bar as a shield between her and them. And I had no such shield.

The rum spun out of her fingers as she glanced at me and nodded toward Bobby. "It's on him."

I nodded, lifted the glass, and downed it. The buzz went straight to my head. Selene could get through anything now.

One of the girls bumped into me and giggled. I wanted to smack some sense into her, but I could see the drugs in her stupefied stare. She tapped Bobby's shoulder, gave a little twist and bounce, then took us to a booth next to the stage.

As the lights dimmed, our bubbly chauffer shuffled toward our table carrying a large pink box. "Cake," Bliss blurted. I sensed a little bounce coming on. I grabbed her hand and smiled. "Wait 'til we blow out the candles." As annoying as she was, I couldn't help but mirror her girlish smile.

I looked into Bliss's glossy eyes, but she had the googly stare of a six-year-old waiting for the Easter Bunny. I held her hand and gave her a wink. We'd been through a lot in our short time together. There would be nothing Selene and Bliss couldn't handle.

Until Bobby pushed the box towards me. I could barely look at. I could feel Bliss coming apart beside me. Lip quivering. Eyes twitching. Hands wringing. Then I heard her sigh and waited for the explosion.

I focused on Bobby. "It's for both of us, right?" Eyebrows up. *Please say I'm right.* He frowned. I'm sure he was way past sorry he'd brought Bliss. I looked at her again with the most girly smile I could fake. "We'll share it." I looked at Bobby again. "I'm sure Bobby has a gift for you too."

He puckered, shook his head. "I got you covered, Bliss. I forgot and left your present at my place. We'll get it after."

Big liar. But he'd saved the night. Who knows what she would have done. She'd obviously already ticked off the Godfather's daddy before.

"Open it. Open it."

I wasn't quick enough to stop the clapping and bouncing, but it was a present. I grabbed the box and pulled it closer. As I tucked my finger inside to break the tape, Bobby said, "Wait a second, show's about to start."

The lights came down even more. Stage lights lit. The low hum of strings vibrated the stage. "They have an orchestra?"

"Nah. It's all digital. Just wait for it."

The music slowly built like the start of an epic movie. I expected a Broadway musical or something, but the curtains slowly parted, and the spotlight hit an empty spot on the floor.

I jumped at the dish-rattling sound of a fist pounding our table. A fiery-faced Donny leaned across the table, got in Bobby's face, and grabbed his fancy shirt. "I sent that limo to pick up Tawnya. This was supposed to be her feature. And you come in here with Nutcase and Amateur Hour. Now where is my girl? We had a deal."

Bobby opened his mouth, but the Don shoved him, released his grip, and slammed the table again. "Deal's off." He pointed at the three of us. "Finish your drinks and get the hell out of my club." He waved his finger in Bobby's face. "I don't want to see you in here ever again. In fact, I don't ever want to see you again anywhere. Ever. Period."

He nodded to Roberto's twin and Atlas.

My night off was about to end if I didn't do something. The stage lights brightened and the house lights dimmed as his two goons pressed toward our table. I heard the clunk of stripper heels on the stage behind me, then the music kicked up.

I had zero desire to watch another dancer, but I wasn't ready to go back to my prison. Yeah, the Don was beyond angry, but what could he do to me that hadn't already been done? Kill me? Please. I wasn't living anyway, but I was learning to survive. I also feared Bobby would take his frustrations out on Bliss and me. Or worse, he might let Mason do it for him.

Not tonight. I went full-on Selene. Hopped out my seat and slid in front of the Don, ignoring his icy stare. "Donny?" I puckered in a little pout as I adjusted his tie. "I don't know what Bobby did, but I'd like to help you work something out."

Bobby stepped closer and shouted over the music. "Donny, this is the girl I was telling you about."

Donny looked me up and down like a meat inspector. The twitch of his lips indicated a "maybe."

The crowd heaved a collective "Whoa," and I turned my head in time to catch the dancer's rhinestone-covered boulder holders with my face. Bobby laughed as I peeled off the bra and hurled it at him.

I could see why the Don was aggravated. This girl could work it, but she wasn't Tawyna.

As she danced and twirled, she did something Emma would never do. She picked a tongue-wagger, and met his eyes. His face flushed. Sweat speckled his cheeks and brow, while her gaze held his eyes, and she worked her magic.

I jumped when she winked at him and smiled. He must be one of her regulars.

The music picked up and so did she. A chrome pole rose up from the floor. The bass thumping. Lights flashing and spinning. She grabbed that pole and owned it. She was toned, fine, smooth, and oozing sexy all over the place. As one song mixed into the next, two girls joined, then two more. Eventually there were seven girls working those dulled minds into oblivion. Smiles were gone. Plain dumb stares covered the audience. They were drunk on everything she and her posse were giving.

Bobby tapped my shoulder and handed me the box. "Open it."

As soon as I opened the box, I remembered what he'd said when I was trying on dresses. "The only thing missing is the glass slippers." And that's what I held in my hand. Clear stiletto platform heels just like Tawnya wore in her videos. I laughed and cried. Emma was way past dying inside. Selene had buried her and taken over.

I held those glass shoes in my hands, and I held my pain inside. Hopefully dancing would mean less touching and more looking. At least that's what I'd hoped.

My Bobby smiled that same little deceiver's smile he'd flashed when he'd handed me that first beer. "These aren't seventeen-hundred-dollar custom heels, but you'll work your way up to those."

I smiled back. I was surviving. Maybe that's what he was doing too. As dumb as it sounds, I couldn't help the thought.

The Don nudged me aside and stepped face to face with Bobby. "Not in my club. Not with you holding the strings." Then he looked at me as if I were merchandise, a bargaining chip, a slave at auction. "I tell you what. Give her some practice. Protect her assets." He wagged his finger at my chest. "Turn these Ds into double Ds, and I *might* make you an offer. Until then, I don't want to see you, and if I do—if I see you before she's ready…." He leaned in and whispered. Bobby's face went pale.

Without another word, without another sip, we left the club.

Bobby led us toward the limo, but the driver stood firm. Jaw set. Arms folded. He shook his head.

I'd never seen Bobby so dejected. Head down. Slouched shoulders. I could feel Emma grinning—almost laughing inside. *Daddy* had become a pouty little boy—a vulnerable, pouty little boy. The Don was a weak spot. Maybe he could be a way out.

Bobby plucked his phone from his pocket as we walked past the limo. "Roberto. I need you."

Fifteen minutes seemed like forever. We had strolled past the stone walls and the trees that lined the long driveway to the street. Bobby rubbed his face and his hair as he paced. Even Bliss looked nervous. She was half little-girl Bliss and half don't-mess-with-me Bliss. When she was in-between, standing next to her felt dangerous. I held her hand and swung her arm like a school girl. "What do you want to do when we get back home?" God knows it wasn't home, but it sounded better than—just about anything else I could think to call it.

Living with Bliss's ever-changing personalities felt like living with the Incredible Hulk. The Incredible Hulk with PMS and carrying a time bomb with a broken timer. I was the bomb squad and the tranquilizer. But when she smiled, I knew the little girl was back. And we were all calm again—for the moment.

Bobby elbowed me. "With you around, I don't even need to give her a Xanax."

Finally, Roberto and the sleazy black van arrived. We hopped in the back. Roberto hopped out so Bobby could drive, but Bobby waved him off and climbed in the back with us. He sank onto the futon and flopped his hands over his face.

When Roberto shut the doors behind us, Bobby glared at me. "Take off the dress."

"What? Now."

"Now." He tensed his jaw, nodded, and raised his voice. "Now. Take it off."

I couldn't stop the tears, and I couldn't stay full-on Selene. Selene didn't cry. Emma was back, and she was sobbing. Bliss wrapped her arms around me. "Don't cry." She pressed her lips into my ear and whispered. "Emma doesn't survive by crying."

Big girl worlds followed with her little girl bounce clap and childish grin. I honestly couldn't tell how much of Bliss was faking it versus just plain nuts.

But her hug felt genuine. I laughed through my tears as she tugged on my dress while I lifted my arms, all the while bouncing up and down in the back of van. I don't think Roberto intentional hit the curb on every other turn.

"Be careful." Bobby raised his voice. When I saw his eyes, I realized he wasn't talking to Roberto. He was talking to me. He yelled something in Spanish, but I caught the word Macy's. "We're taking it back." He reached around under the futon, pulled out a skanky top and a leather skirt, and handed them to me. Handed them. He didn't toss them. My crazed pulse slowed, and I took a deep breath. He wasn't mad at me. He was just mad.

"It's not your fault. You're can't be Cinderella yet, but it's not your fault. I'll let you keep the shoes. You're gonna need those, but the dress—I'll buy you a better, more beautiful dress later."

CHAPTER 10
Michael

Sam stood at the end of the aisle, sunlight bursting through the doors behind her. Even her silhouette was stunning. Perfect hair. Perfect subtle curves. As she stepped into the sanctuary, my heart fluttered, and I wasn't even the groom. Every eye in the room was on her. She was wrapped in a thousand soft white, flower petals. Her father beamed as he walked beside her.

The music built. Everyone smiled. Cameras flashed. Mothers cried.

I glanced at Kyle, thankful he was beaming, thankful I'd snatched him from that place before he could wake up and realize what had happened. Jordie stood beside him. His eyes red, hair tousled, hands folded. He winked and offered a smirk that said he'd do it all over again. As much as I wanted to smack him in the head with the candelabra, I had to forget about him—for now.

Sam's golden hair rested like a crown on her head, dotted with tiny pink flowers and baby's breath. Kyle said she'd had some fancy French stylist braid it, weave it, wrap it—whatever they do. A few intentionally loose strands caressed her cheeks and danced beside her crystal drop earrings as she walked toward Kyle.

When their eyes met, her smile grew even wider. Her smile could end a war. I just hoped the war would never start. My stomach rolled at the thought of tears in Sam's bright blue eyes. She didn't deserve what had happened last night. I'd like to think Kyle didn't deserve it either. Didn't want it. Hopefully never dreamed it could happen. But he'd made his choice when he asked Jordie to be his best man. My gut told me he knew what could happen, and it probably wasn't the first time.

I looked at him. Her eyes and her smile had erased any memory of last night—any memory the alcohol and who knows what else had left.

Thank God.

That would be the end of it—surely.

* * *

The sun kissed the few thread-like clouds over the horizon. Strands of lights stretched along the walkways through gardens to the breezeway. The Inn at The Wild Pony was the perfect venue. Open-air dance floor with a string quartet. Huge buffet under an expansive gazebo. Lighted fountains and ice sculptures. And an overflowing bar.

But the most perfect thing about the reception was watching Sam. The way she looked at Kyle. The way he held her. The way they danced. I melted with joy and jealousy as I watched them.

Kyle's face glowed beneath the lights as he held her close and looked into her eyes. Part of me wanted to throttle him. I prayed Sam would never find out what he'd done or that I'd left him at that house. I did more than pray, I sent *friendly* reminder texts to each of the groomsmen to keep last night to themselves. And I stayed close enough to Jordie to intercept anything stupid he might do or say.

He'd had more than his share of alcohol. I was surprised he could still stand, let alone walk. He stumbled across the dance floor toward the bar and bumped into the cellist. I slid beside him, smiled at the cellist, and pulled Jordie back onto the dance floor. He shrugged and shook me off then staggered toward the bar. As he leaned over the bar and held up his glass, I squeezed his shoulder, waved off the bartender, and grabbed Jordie's arm. "You're making a scene."

"Relax. It's a party."

I squeezed harder, grabbed his arm, and nodded for the bartender to take his glass before Jordie could toss it at me.

He slurred, "What're you're think you're doin'?"

"You've had enough, and you've done enough. Maybe one of your buddies should drive you home."

I'm sure I couldn't understand what he said next.

I walked him away from the bar and the dance floor, helped him slide onto a bench in the garden, then I brought him a cup of coffee. I hoped that would be it from Jordie, but he was back on the dance floor in a matter of minutes. He snuck another glass of champagne from the bar. The bartender glanced at me and shrugged as Jordie tucked a folded bill into the tip jar.

Jordie walked past the band, grabbed the mic, and lifted his glass and cleared his throat. "Everyone have a full glass of the bubbly? Kyle and Samantha deserve your full attention, and you deserve another round." He grabbed a spoon and clanked the side of his glass.

Sam blushed as Kyle closed his eyes, cradled her face, and gently pressed his lips to hers.

"Ain't they cute?" The guests clapped, but Jordie spoke over them. "I love you guys. Sam, you're the perfect bride. Gorgeous. Smart— doesn't take much to be smarter than Kyle, but you're smart either way. Kyle needs someone like you. You certainly have his attention."

My neck tensed and tingled as he spoke. I made my way behind the bar and the band and hoped no one noticed. My jaw ached from clenching my teeth as I walked toward Jordie. How I wanted to sprint and tackle him. *Dear God, make him shut up.*

He took a sip and shook his head. "Kyle, I love you like a brother. I can't *stand* my brothers, but I seriously love you, and I love the way you love to have a good time. Hopefully that doesn't stop just because you've tied the knot."

Faster, Michael. A few more steps and I could slide in behind him and grab the mic.

"Even if your marriage kills our fun, at least we had last night. One last hoorah. And don't worry, you wild-and-crazy guy, I won't tell anyone about all the parking tickets."

I snatched the mic from Jordie's hand. "To Kyle and Sam."

"To Kyle and Sam."

Glasses clinked around the room, and they kissed again. I breathed a hallelujah and looked at Kyle, who nodded. I leered at Jordie. He downed the rest of his Champagne and walked away. *Please, don't ever come back.* I never wanted to see him again.

I swallowed my frustrations with Jordie and with Kyle as I watched Sam's eyes. She deserved the perfect wedding and the perfect husband. I wouldn't be the one to pop that bubble.

"Kyle, I don't know what to say." There were so many things I could say, but I buried the ugly truth and lied as best I could. "I've never felt this happy for anyone. Although, I've got to say, I'm also a little jealous. I've never seen a more beautiful bride than Samantha."

I looked into her innocent, unknowing eyes. "Sam, you deserve more than any man I know can give you, but I don't know anyone who could come closer than Kyle. He loves you. He would do anything for you." Kyle looked at me. I could feel pain and fear in his eyes. Feelings I wanted to help him bury. "No matter what, he will always be there for you. He's been my best friend since we were kids. I know what kind of friend he is. And now, he's your best friend, your husband, and your one-and-only."

When she blushed again, I melted.

I glared at Kyle. *I'll do whatever it takes to bury what happened last night.*

CHAPTER 11
Emma

I felt like Cinderella trading her gown for rags. I still had the glass slippers, but I couldn't imagine any young prince swooping into my life to save me. And anyway, I had them both.

I stared at the stripper heels. *If the shoe fits....*

The ride home was quiet. Even Bliss sat in silence. No clapping. No bouncing. She closed her eyes and leaned against the carpeted wall until the van stopped.

As Bobby climbed out, I said, "Thanks for giving us the night off."

He tilted his head and rubbed his face. Even in the dark van, I could feel his eyes searing through me. "The night didn't go exactly as I'd planned. That's why we had to leave early." He clinched his fist as Roberto opened the side door behind him. "So, your night's not going exactly as planned either."

He pointed at my shoes and gave me a pouty smile as we climbed out of the van. We weren't home. We were in Sleazeville. A concrete-block dump nestled between factories and covered in exhaust and concrete dust.

"Since things didn't go like they were supposed to, I need you girls to make a few bucks to make up for it." He pointed at the two-tone rust-and-paint door. "Classy joint. Not like The SinS, but strictly hands-off. Looky-looky. No touchy-touchy." He held up both hands, squeezed at the air, and chuckled.

I felt sick. The place was as high class as the finest junkyard in the world. And I was about to wade through the garbage naked. No, I was being tossed into the garbage naked.

I was the garbage.

I'd forced myself to watch the videos. I'd learned from the best—Tawnya. What had happened to her? Probably waded in too deep and got buried with the other trash.

I'd seen her work it, but I'd never danced for anyone. Once, when I was about thirteen, I pretended to be a dancer like I'd seen in a movie. I was alone in my bedroom, and I imagined the glamour of being surrounded by handsome young rich men ogling me.

The rusted door scraped open, and a stocky Latino with tattoos like Mason's let us in. I left Emma daydreaming in the junkyard while Selene stepped into the club—the beat-yourself-over-the-head, wish-you-were-dead club.

More thumping bass. Flashing lights. Cloud of cigarette smoke with a hint of weed. The perfect place to find your prince charming. Bobby led us into a backstage bathroom to change. Scum-coated walls and the stench of aged urine.

I looked at Bobby and hoped beyond hope he would change his mind and take us home. His bronzed face looked somehow pale and defeated. He grabbed my hand. I opened my palm on cue, and he gave me a forget-everything-and-dance pill. I popped it and took a sip of his water bottle. I slipped on the heels. I could feel him watching me like he had the day we met.

I glared at him and held out my palm again. *This hell hole deserves more than one pill.* I didn't even have to say it. He knew. I grabbed the pill and washed it down, then I rubbed oil all over my skin. I pretended it was some kind of magic barrier—a force field to protect me from evil. There wasn't enough oil in the world. Too much, and I'd be slipping off the stage into even oilier who-knows-where-they've-been arms.

I slipped into the rest of my uniform—custom thong with a front pouch for tips. Selene was ready.

I stood off stage and watched other girls doing their thing. They'd obviously been self-taught, or they didn't have enough drugs on board to get loose. Selene was going to embarrass those women.

As I stepped toward the open stage, Bobby's arm slipped around my waist. He pulled me back against his chest. "I'm sorry about tonight. You may feel like rags tonight, but you will be my Cinderella someday."

I smiled. I couldn't help it. Every tiny sliver of reason left inside me told me to run fast and far as soon as I could get the chance. But reason was no longer screaming, just whispering, and the music was too loud. His hand around my waist was too soft. And his voice in my ear was too smooth. I'd left earth. For that one second, I was on planet Bobby.

The bass bumped up a notch as I stepped into the spotlight. Thank God for the spotlight. I could hear the whoops and cat-calls, but I couldn't see anyone. The beam, the fog from the smoke, and the haze from Bobby's pills were the perfect shield for my eyes.

I spun and planted a firm step with my back to the crowd. The floor vibrated up through my shoes into my legs. I let Selene take me to another place—any place but here. The lights spinning around me, I danced in another galaxy. I imagined pudgy green alien school boys clapping their fat three-fingered hands behind me. Everyone on my imaginary planet was sterile and impotent. I giggled as the Xanax and my daydream took hold. The schoolmaster was a giant blob of a woman alien. She had sterilized the school boys herself, zapping off their undesired members with a light saber.

The daydream died when I swung around the pole and felt a calloused greasy hand grab my rear. I squirmed, racing back to my daydream, still dancing as other rough hands touched anything and everything they could reach. The only thing that softened their touch was the crunch and crinkle of money.

* * *

I lay in my bed staring through the ceiling. I'd never remembered the part of Cinderella's story where the handsome prince abducted his princess before the ball and took her to a trashy tavern, but at least Bobby had saved me from those grabbing fingers. He even let me keep all my tips. Maybe someday, he'd take me to a store and let me spend it. Or maybe he just let me think it was mine.

Deep down, I knew he was a master manipulator. He controlled me. He controlled *my* money. He controlled everything. I couldn't imagine an easy way out or even a difficult way out. Bliss was right. Survive and wait for the right moment.

What if the right moment came? I had nowhere to go. No one to care for me. And no one I cared anything about.

Not true. I cared about Bliss.

As crazy as she was, Bliss was my closest thing to a friend, and I couldn't leave her.

This was it. This was my life. Emma and Selene sharing one body, and Selene sharing that body with anyone willing to pay. Selene would get by while Emma would daydream about her handsome prince.

MOONLIGHT AWAKENS – a sex-trafficking story

CHAPTER 12
Michael

I loved Sunday mornings. For me, Sunday represented a fresh start.

I lay in my bed, the room still dark. My alarm hadn't gone off yet. I grabbed my phone—six-fifteen. Why was I awake?

I opened Instagram and scrolled through everyone's pics from the wedding and the reception. Smiles. Little girls beaming and dreaming. Bridesmaids attending their princess. Kyle and Sam together, so obviously in love in every picture.

I scrolled down, and my heart skipped a beat. I sat up and stared. It was picture of me in that house—that blasted house that still haunted my memory. I thought I'd deleted all those pictures from their phones. They must've been posting them as they took them, or one of them left before I came back. My face felt hot and my stomach rolled as I feared what other pictures I might find.

There were a few of guys holding up their red plastic cups, but no more incriminating pics. I breathed a sigh and scrolled back to that photo.

Jordie was all smiles, wide-eyed, beer-in-hand, as he stood behind two girls in fedoras and trench coats. And there I stood, flushed cheeks, sweat beads, trying to shake hands with the stripper.

She was unquestionably beautiful, but her eyes looked so hollow. Suddenly, I was back inside that living room, hands trembling, heart thumping, and unable to process anything as I looked into her hazel eyes. "My name's Michael." What was I thinking?

But I could never forget her stunning eyes, her smooth cheeks, her eyebrows. Striking lashes. Golden brown hair. And how I wanted to kiss her lips. As I'd held out my hand, I'd felt frozen in time.

Now, as I looked at the photo on Instagram, that moment would be frozen in time for all to see, including Sam.

I pictured Sam's face sinking like the stripper's had when Jordie called her a whore. Innocence gone. Never to be found. I wanted to run again but not for myself. This time, I wanted to run for Sam and Kyle. I checked to see who'd posted it. *Alphafido?* It had to be one of Jordie's buddies. Who else would pick such a ridiculous name? He must've left before I came back to clean up.

I pressed the home button. "Call Jordan Scumbucket."

"Calling Jordan Scumbucket." It sounded so ridiculous when Siri said it. I laughed through gritted teeth as I waited for Jordie to answer.

When he answered, I said, "You'd better call Alphafido and tell him to clean up his Instagram now."

"Huh?" He sounded hungover again. I don't think the frat party ever ended for this guy.

"Jordan!" I shouted into phone hoping his head might split. "One of your 'brothers' posted a picture of those strippers at the bachelor party. Tell him to remove it now. Then check with your other buddies and make sure none of the rest of them are as stupid."

"Why are you getting so bent out of shape?"

I wished I could reach through the phone and choke him. "What do think is going to happen when Sam sees that picture—when Sam's *mom* sees that picture? What do you think's going to happen to you when Kyle sees that picture? I'm pretty sure Kyle didn't want those girls at his bachelor party. And I'm certain he doesn't want Sam or anyone else to ever know they were there."

"Give me a break."

"Which arm? I'm not kidding. You call Fido and have him take down the post before Sam sees it. And you'd better pray she hasn't seen it already."

"Those girls are still wearing clothes. I don't see the problem."

"If the picture doesn't come down, you're going to see—you're going to *feel*—a bigger problem."

"Are you threatening me?"

"I'm promising you. If your wild party breaks Sam's heart, I'll break more than your arm. Take it down."

"Okay. Okay. I'll call Alfie."

"Alfie?"

"Alfonce. Guys called him Alfonzo, Fido, whatever. I'll call him."

I sent Jordie the picture I'd taken of him exposed, totally wasted and collapsed in a recliner. I sent it along with the contact information for his mom and his girlfriend and a friendly reminder. "Don't forget."

I doubted Sam had seen it yet. She loved her Instagram, but it was Sunday morning and she had to be halfway over the Pacific on her way to Hawaii.

My stomach lurched at the knock on my door.

"Michael," Mom said, "are you awake?"

"Getting ready for church."

* * *

I'd never felt so guilty during church. I sang the songs and tried to bury my shame, bury Friday night. I should've been remembering my best friend's wedding, his beautiful bride, the kiss that sealed the deal. But all I could think of was that girl's face. I didn't even know her name—not even her fake name.

By the look in her eyes, I was sure she hadn't wanted to be there any more than I had—maybe even less. Her gaze had been hollow.

I couldn't imagine why she'd want to do that kind of work? She was beautiful. She could have any man she wanted. Find some rich guy and live an easy life. What had led her to a life of sleeping with strangers for money? Why wouldn't someone as beautiful as she seek a man who'd appreciate her for more than her looks—for more than what she could do to tease his fantasies?

That split second when I'd looked into her eyes, I'd seen a desire to run. I'd felt it. Why didn't she, then? Why do it if she hated it so badly?

That trench coat covered more than her body. It covered her shame, her guilt, and the nakedness of her empty soul.

I felt much the same as I sat in that pew. The songs were over. One of the elders had prayed, and Dad was halfway through his message when he said "sex." I hadn't been listening—didn't even know what he was talking about. But that word perked my ears.

"You've heard me talk about our ministry partners in India, Cambodia, and Thailand," Dad said. "We think of them as frontline soldiers in the war to end sex trafficking, but we have sex trafficking right here in Atlanta. In fact, Atlanta is a hub not only for air traffic but for sex traffic."

I felt like Dad looked right at me—right through me. "It's not what you think. You think of young girls in foreign lands kidnapped and brought to the states. I'm telling you it might be your neighbor's daughter. It might be happening in your neighbor's basement. It might be your daughter, your son. It might be happening in your basement. And it might even involve some of you."

I could feel the squirming in the pews. He was touching some hot buttons.

"Don't be naïve. Don't pretend to be innocent. We've all seen how the sex industry has permeated our world, our culture, our television and internet, our homes, and even our churches. But I'm not scolding. I'm not pointing my finger. I want all of us to open our eyes, our minds, our hearts. I want us to open our arms to help those trapped in sex trafficking.

"You may have seen one of these girls and not even known it."

His words burned into my mind along with image of that girl. That hollow I-don't-want-to-be-here look in her eyes. I couldn't help but think she had better things she could do with her life. Why would she choose to be a stripper, a hooker? Maybe it wasn't her choice. Maybe she didn't feel like she had a choice. Maybe she was just finding her way like everyone else.

Maybe you could help her.

The thought came out of nowhere and scared the bejeebers out of me. Here I was, the guy who ran away from two girls in trench coats. My heart pounded. The pulse in my ears drowned Dad's words as I thought of those girls who'd stood ready to flash more than their guns.

I wanted to bolt. My skin grew hot. My scalp tingled. I was sure everyone around me was watching me sweat. Dad kept talking, but I was back in that house watching those girls—imagining what they were about to do. When I ran that night, I'd flung open the door and almost tripped over the angriest-looking soul I'd ever seen. Short but muscle-packed. Scruffy face. Dark, stubble-covered scalp. Dark, deep-set eyes. Tattooed shoulders bulging from his wife beater.

He chewed on a toothpick and looked at me as if I wasn't worth the punch he wanted to drive through my face.

You may have seen one of these girls and not even known it.

I could still see Mr. Macho with his deep-set eyes boring through me, and I imagined him no longer as a body guard. He was a handler, a watchdog.

A sex-trafficker.

Maybe you could help her. I felt those words more than heard them. They reverberated through my cowardly soul. I was still living off Mom and Dad. I could barely help myself. How could I possibly help this girl?

How can you not?

My skin crawled, and my stomach rolled. I'd run from that house, but I'd never be able to outrun my thoughts or that voice in my head. The floor rumbled as the organ's notes rang. People stood for the invitation.

I had never been one to slip out during the invitation, but I did. I bypassed the foyer and sneaked down the seldom-used back stairs to the basement and the tiny one-seater bathroom. I shut the door and locked it, then turned on the fan to let people think I'd be in there a while.

You can't hide forever. "Yeah. Well, I can't exactly run away either." I shook my head as I sat on the closed lid whispering to my conscience and listening to the organ piped through the speaker above my head. I guess the church elders thought everyone, even those hiding in the basement bathroom, should hear the message.

As the music faded, Dad started his closing remarks. I sighed and dropped my face into my hands. "Please let it be done."

I knew Dad's flaws, his quirks. I had no misconceptions about him being perfect, but I knew his heart. I knew how deeply he felt his words and the immense faith that carried him more than he carried it. He was the reason I was still a believer though most of my friends had given up on church. And he had that preacher-deep, commanding yet compassionate voice.

"It's a big deal," Dad said. "Sex trafficking. More than what one person can fix. More than one church, one community, even more than one whole country can stop completely. But that's not what God is asking you today. Nod your head with me. Agree with me that you can't fix the problem. You can't stop sex trafficking. Now stop. Fold your hands. Close your eyes and open your heart. I want you to imagine one girl. One face. One heart. One forgotten child of God who needs to be remembered. You can't change the world, but maybe you can change the world for her. Make that your prayer."

I could imagine him bowing his head and raising his arms, hands toward heaven. "God, let this be our prayer. We cannot change the world, not without your mighty hand, not without your tender heart. Give us the will, the compassion, and the means to change the world for one girl at a time. Let us be your hands and feet—your heart where we stand, where we sit, wherever we are. Change the world through us. One heart. One person. One life at a time."

The speaker crackled as someone shut it off. I lied to anyone outside the door with my flush and handwashing. I felt so utterly empty.

Friday night had started with so many smiles. Seeing old friends. Lots of hugs and high fives. The wedding rehearsal had gone as smoothly and awkwardly as any I'd ever seen. The rehearsal dinner had been fabulous. If only that had been the end of my night—the end of Kyle's night. But that Friday night felt like the night that would never end.

I'd listened to Dad's plea. Great message. Great gift for saying the right words to soften hearts and call people to action. But I would probably never see that girl again, and I certainly didn't want to show my face in the places where I might find her. I could see the headlines. Prostitution Ring Busted. Pastor's Son Arrested.

I imagined my face on the front page and on everyone's Facebook and Twitter. No thanks.

I brought her to you before...

Stop right there. I held up my hand as though I could stop the voice in my head. It stopped, but I knew what it would say. *I brought her to you before, I can do it again.*

CHAPTER 13
Emma

It had been two weeks since we went to SinS. Nothing had changed. And still no Tawnya. The doorknob twisted and Candy kicked open my door. "She ain't coming back. You know that right?"

"Who ain't coming back?" *How did she know I was thinking about Tawnya?*

"You know who I'm talking about, and I suspect you understand what happened and what it means."

I stared at the ceiling and hoped she would go away.

"Ignore me if you want, but Bobby ain't gonna ignore you. He done set the stage for you to be the next Tawnya."

"And what does that mean?"

Alice stuck her head around the door. "It means you're next to go down the rabbit hole." She laughed her sick little girl hiccough laugh and trotted down the hall. Candy shoved me onto my side as she stood, then she smacked my rear and headed out the door.

Until Candy and Alice invaded my room it had been a quiet Sunday morning—the kind Grams would have destroyed by yelling me out of bed and kicking my butt into the bathroom to get ready for church.

I lay on my bed and stared at the dust bunnies on the ceiling while I imagined my grandparents, their smug faces, crossed arms, closed minds, and cold hearts sitting frozen in those ancient pews. They hardened a little more each week as they punched the attendance cards in their minds and racked up goody-goodness points for heaven.

If Jesus was real, if heaven was real, I couldn't imagine God wanting them or anyone like them contaminating his perfect world. If Satan was real, if hell was real, I had no trouble imagining my grandparents burning forever. Crispy, crunchy, blackened corpses. I could fall right on top of them when I died and crush what was left of them. Then I'd burn with them. My only heaven would be watching them suffer eternally.

The door at the end of the hall slammed. I tensed and braced for Bobby or Mason to come crashing through my door, but girlish clomping eased my fear and continued past my door and down the hall.

A dust bunny broke loose from the ceiling and drifted down. I pictured myself—a dirty little part of this dirty world—barely clinging before falling free.

That could be my escape. Selene was doing such a good job. She didn't need all those pills anymore. She was strong. She could handle anything and anyone—certainly any man. While Selene worked it,

Emma could collect the pills and stash them until the time was right—until she had enough for both of them to let go.

Death might be the only way I could control my life—my life which meant nothing to anyone. I had no life. Death wouldn't change anything.

You could run away again. Where would I go? I had no place and no one. I was a whore, human waste that no one wanted. Even the dirty hands that groped me—the men who have their way—didn't want me, they just wanted the fantasy, the rush, the feeling of power I gave them. And they resented me. Even the ones that acted like they liked me hated me because I wasn't theirs. I belonged to everyone but myself, and I belonged to no one.

I gathered my resolve and bounded out of bed toward the shower, wasting no time on clothes. I'd given up on the long-but-never-long-enough showers because nothing could wash away the filth. It had become a part of me. It wasn't that I'd accepted it. It was more that I'd rejected myself. No one else wanted me. Why should I want myself? I had become just another dust bunny, a nothing clinging to nothing. I would drift away unnoticed, forgotten, swept under the bed or blown out the door. It didn't matter. I didn't matter.

I was still in the shower when I felt a cool rush of air whirl around my wet body. "Shut the door."

No response.

"Bliss?"

I heard footsteps and the door closed. I finished my shower and pulled the curtain. I would've jumped, but Selene had buried those reflexes, so I didn't react at all when I saw Bobby standing there. He was that guy on the beach again. Cut-offs. No shirt. Huge smile. He was flipping a driver's license between his fingers—my driver's license. I knew he'd taken it as way to control me, but why was he waving it in my face?

His smile grew as he looked at me. He handed me a towel and watched me dry myself.

"What do you want?" I stared at his boyish eyes as they followed my towel. You'd think he'd get tired of it—being surrounded by it all the time. Any girl he wanted. All the time. His eyes were as wide as a middle-school boy's stealing a peek.

Emma blushed a little, but Selene stepped out of the shower and dropped the towel at his feet. "You gonna answer my question?"

His face crinkled like a silent giggle. He curled his fingers around my license, burying it in his hand. "You don't even know what day it is, do you?"

My birthday.

I couldn't believe it. Here I was at one of the lowest points of my life, and someone remembered and thought of me. One teacher, Mrs. Bobelia in third grade, had remembered my birthday. There was no mom to bring cupcakes. No special party. No friends. It was a day my grandparents wanted to forget—a day Mandy never added to her memory. She was probably wasted when I was born.

"It's a special day for you, Selene...Emma." He whispered my name—my real name. I didn't know what it meant that he'd used my actual name. I hadn't heard that name since Bliss had told me to bury it. I couldn't help it, but Selene was fading, and Emma started to cry.

As the tears streamed, Bobby held my license up to my face between two fingers. "Don't cry, baby girl. No one should cry on their birthday. Besides, I have a present for you." He tucked my license into the front of his cut-offs. "But you'll have to open the package to get it."

He closed the tiny gap between us—his skin against mine. Even though I felt owned, his hands were gentle on my skin. His lips felt soft and sincere on my neck. His manipulative magic was working. I was about to melt into his arms.

But he stopped and backed away. Hands on my shoulders, he looked into my eyes. None of the men ever looked into my eyes. If they caught my eyes, they always, always looked away. Mostly their eyes fondled me, undressed me, dreamed about what my body could do for them, was doing to them, and would do again and again as long as Bobby got his money.

But Bobby looked into my eyes. It felt like intimacy, though I had nothing to compare it to. I'd never known intimacy. Even if it was only my fantasy, even if it was only for a moment, I'd take it. It was more than anyone else had ever given me. I loved him. I hated him. He was smooth. He was harsh. He made me feel free when he looked into me. He made me feel like a slave when he looked *at* me. I *was* a slave—his slave.

My smiling master stepped back, held out the towel, and lifted his chin. I raised my arms like an obedient slave, and he wrapped the towel around me and tucked it in.

"Come with me." He took my hand, led me past my room and into his office.

Not here. Surely not here.

He let go of my hand. I looked at the solid steel back door with its tiny peep hole. The shades were drawn, and the blinds pulled, but along the edge, I caught a glimpse of the back lot. His car was right there. His keys lay on his desk. I imagined Mason standing behind us, watching the door from the hallway. Roberto must have been outside. Maybe he would look the other way if I ran. Maybe not.

I inched toward the desk, eyeing those keys as Bobby pulled the filing cabinet away from the bookshelf. I couldn't help wondering what he was doing. I kept my eyes on him as I leaned against the desk and slid my hand toward his keys. I heard a latch open, and I froze, expecting Mason to be standing behind me, but the door was closed.

Bobby stepped toward me and grabbed my hand. As he led me toward the bookshelf, he slowly swung it away from the wall revealing a hidden room.

"What's this?"

We stepped into a cozy bedroom. Surprisingly refined with ornate red-and-gold wallpaper. A decorative ceiling with no mirrors, and a stately dresser that looked like an antique. There was a matching vanity beside it. Bobby opened one side of the dresser, revealing a mini-fridge. He pulled out two beers and handed me one.

I took a swig.

I pretended it all meant something—that Bobby actually cared about more than the money I could bring him. That this room could somehow be my escape.

The room had three other doors. One stood open to reveal a private bath complete with old-fashioned tub with fancy feet, a huge shower with more shower heads than I would know how to use, and a separate room for the toilet. Another door opened to a walk-in closet. Nothing big by most standards, but to me, it was huge with racks stocked with dresses, blouses, and various costumes, and with shelves stacked high with boxes and linens. The final door had a peep hole. He didn't open it. I guessed it opened to the parking lot out back.

I did a twirl in the middle of the room. "What *is* this?"

He did that thing he does like a showman—arms stretched wide, broad smile, head tilted, chin lifted. "It's my boudoir."

"Boudoir? Isn't that what you call a woman's private bedroom?" I lowered my chin, hand on my hip, but it was hard to look disgusted, unimpressed, or threatening when you were standing alone with a man in his "boudoir" while wearing nothing but a towel.

He rested his hands on my shoulders, gently caressing them. "It's your boudoir now—if you want it."

My heart leapt as if it would jump out of my chest. My head pounded with my pulse. It felt like some kind of evil magic, and all magic comes with a price. Forget about strings attached. This room felt like it had ropes attached—one big noose, to be precise. And I was going to hang myself with any answer I gave.

This had to have been Tawnya's room. That would explain why we had seldom seen her. The fact that Bobby was making it mine suggested Tawnya was gone forever. He hadn't mentioned since the Don asked about her. What happened to her? What had Bobby done to her? What was he going to do to me?

Survive and wait until the time is right. It was time for Selene to wake up and take over. I needed her to let Bobby think everything was great.

I leaned into him, loosening my towel and dropping it to the floor. "My boudoir?" I used my darkest, silkiest voice as I whispered in his ear. Selene was selling it big-time. I could feel the heat from his skin as Selene worked her own magic. I pulled him close with my left hand, stroking his back with my fingers. I lay my right palm against his six-pack and walked my fingers into his shorts.

He grabbed my wrist. "What are you doing?"

I smiled at the angst in his voice as I wound my fingers around his gems. He had me locked away in a hidden room with no foreseeable way out, but his voice cracked with fear as his nuggets tried to retreat from my hands.

Mason was, no doubt, guarding the inside door. Roberto or someone else was surely outside. I had nowhere to go and no way out, but I felt as if I somehow had his life in my hands.

As his grip tightened on my wrist, I closed my hand. "This doesn't have to be hard."

He chuckled.

I let go and felt for my license, pulled it out, and tossed it onto the bed.

I had answered him without saying a word. As he softened in my arms, I knew he had believed the lie that I was his and had no plans to run.

Selene laid him across the bed and had her way. She was the embodiment of all the power Emma had lost and never had. She was Emma's anti-hero. The savior who might destroy her or save her.

And she worked Bobby until he collapsed like an over-cooked spaghetti noodle. He was done and undone. Passed out. Selene had cast her spell, and the manipulative prince had become a sleeping beauty—for the moment.

She slipped into the shower. When she stepped out, he was sitting on the edge of the bed. Cut-offs back on. He held her license in his hands as if he were holding a golden ticket. She grabbed a plush robe that hung on the bathroom door, wrapped it around herself, and sat beside him.

He almost blushed. "That felt more like my birthday present than yours." He smiled a shy smile. He'd been owned, and Selene knew it.

He handed me my license. "Here's your real present."

I held it. Emma was trembling, but Selene wouldn't let her hands show it. "What does this mean?"

He rubbed his hair and stared at the floor. "I'm sorry. You deserve better than what I've done to you. I know you have to hate me for it."

I didn't say a word. His silence led me to believe he wanted me to somehow absolve his guilt. I tightened my lips. Emma was in full-on hate mode. Selene was letting him squirm.

He looked into my eyes. "I hope you don't hate me forever. I took advantage of you." He shook his head and raised his guilty hands. "I don't want to insult you by telling you what you already know. So, I'm giving you your license to say you are your own woman, and you can do what you want."

It was a lie. It was plain to see this had been Tawnya's room, and no one believed his story that she got sick or ran away or moved to Florida or whatever his next story would be. Everyone suspected he'd killed her. It was the only reasonable explanation. No one escapes from Bobby or his goons.

"How do you expect me to believe that?" Selene wouldn't back down, but inside, Emma braced for a slap or a punch, or maybe he'd lug her back down the hall and throw her in her cell.

Without a word, he stood up and walked toward the closed door. He leaned over the end table beside the door, opened the drawer, and pulled out a key. It dangled from a gold chain with a fluffy pink poof on the end. He tossed it to me with one hand and opened the door with the other. "See, this door has been unlocked the whole time."

I caught the key.

He waved me toward the door. I clutched my robe as though suddenly shy and stepped through the door into a dimly lit hall with a door at the end.

"This is the back of the bar next door." He flipped the light switch, and I saw the stenciled sign on the door—Denny's Bar-n-Grill. Bobby walked with me toward the door, stopped about halfway, and pointed to a little nook on the left with a lighted exit sign over the door. Selene wasn't ready to hope, but Emma wanted to believe.

Both of us were crying.

"It's real." He pointed toward where we'd come from. "The room is yours. Your license is yours. And the choice is yours."

I wasn't ready to test the truth. I didn't trust him enough to run. My gut told me he would tackle me, or he'd let me run outside and right into Mason, or he'd let me run so he could hunt me down later. Free or not, I still felt like a slave—if not a slave to Bobby, a slave to fear.

He smiled at my tears. I don't know if he felt sorry for me, if he felt some regret or some kind of fantasy love, or if he realized he truly owned me. It didn't matter. I still belonged to him. Besides, who else would have me?

CHAPTER 14
Michael

I poured a cup of Kona. Hawaiian coffee seemed appropriate as I imagined Kyle and Sam walking the beach in Kauai, holding hands, swinging their arms and kicking sand. But the bachelor party hung in my mind like a brewing volcano.

As much as I'd wanted to erase that awful night and erase my guilt for leaving Kyle, I couldn't erase that girl—didn't want to erase her. Her eyes captured me.

And I couldn't escape the feeling that I'd see her again. I hoped I'd see her again.

* * *

On Saturday, two weeks later, I met Kyle and Sam at baggage claim. Tanned and glowing but exhausted. "You guys look great."

Sam rolled her eyes. "What've you been drinking?"

Even after fourteen hours on a plane, she could turn heads. Faded makeup or no makeup, hair flowing or wadded in a scrunchie, she was like a hit song, unplugged and still amazing.

Kyle nudged me as I looked a little too long at the bounce beneath her boho dress. Soft white with faint yellow flowers.

I elbowed Kyle. "You had a great time, I'm sure."

"Hawaii is so beautiful. We never wanted to leave."

I took one of the suitcases from Kyle. As I grabbed Sam's carry-on, she winced and trotted toward the bathroom. "Is she okay?"

Kyle gave a sideways nod. "She thinks she's got a UTI. It was a long flight. Let me tell you, when you've got to pee every twenty or thirty minutes, there can never be enough bathrooms, and fourteen hours feels like three days."

"At least you're still smiling."

"Are you kidding? I have to. I can't let Sam think her urine thing ruined any part of our trip."

Sam trotted out of the bathroom and the brushed her hair off her face then patted the sweat on her forehead. "Thank God for that breeze. Nothing like July in Atlanta."

None of us had any desire to stay in the heat. Kyle grabbed her suitcase and piggybacked it on his. "Let's get going."

As we walked toward the parking garage, I couldn't help but notice a young Indian girl in a faded school uniform. I would guess she was around ten or twelve years old. She stared at the sidewalk as she walked with a fifty-something man in a dull gray suit and scuffed wingtips.

It seemed odd that he led her by the elbow. Not what I would expect from a grandparent or a guardian. Odd felt even odder when they headed toward a silver minivan with deeply tinted windows. Not exactly a soccer mom's van. I tried to watch without staring.

As they neared the van, the door slid open from the inside, and a stubble-faced man with a shaved head stepped out. Dark eyes. Thick eyebrows. He scanned the area, then shook hands with the man holding the girl.

Then the stubble-faced tough guy grabbed the girl's arm and pulled her toward the van. The girl winced and turned her head. Her eyes caught mine. I'd never seen such desperation. The hair on my arms and the back of my neck bristled. A prickly chill surged through my whole body, and my stomach dropped as though I were in a falling elevator.

As Mr. Tough Guy hoisted her by the arm, I caught a glimpse of two other girls sitting in the van. Ratty shoes. Scrawny brown legs and ankles. Their hands resting on their knees. A hand from deeper inside the van covered the interior light. The two men shoved the girl into the van then examined the area once more as they closed the door.

I kept walking, looked away, and pulled out my phone. I started my phone's video and held the phone to my ear, pretending to make a call. I waved off a look from Kyle and pointed to the phone like I was listening to someone else. I quit watching the van and let my phone do the work. As we walked beyond it, I turned to my right looking up and down the road as though checking traffic. I wanted to make sure I captured the tag number.

My heart was pounding. I hadn't looked back, but I could feel the rough-looking guy staring at me. I imagined him coming after me.

I glanced at my phone. Stopped the recording and quickly sent the video to my email. I heard quick footsteps approaching, and Kyle's eyes grew wide. The video'd been sent. I deleted it and called Mom.

As I held the phone to my ear again, I felt a tap on my shoulder and heard a heavy Chicago accent. "What do you think you're doing?"

"Mom, let me call you back." I turned and held my phone at a safe distance so he could plainly see I was on a call but couldn't see that it had only been for a few seconds.

He shook his head, stepped closer, and tightened his fist. "Video. Let me see the video."

I tapped the Photos icon and held my phone closer.

Kyle stepped toward him. "Hey, man. We just got off a long flight, and we're tired. Our friend was just calling his mom to tell her we're home."

Mr. Chicago frowned and ripped the phone from my hand. His eyebrows joined together, as his face crinkled into an I-wanna-punch-your-face look."

He touched the last video. I breathed a sigh as he watched the clip of Sam and Kyle walking toward me from baggage claim.

He frowned. The older man walked up behind him and shrugged apologetically. "Never mind my friend. He gets paranoid when he sees a phone. Thinks his wife has hired an investigator to follow him."

I laughed. "I'm no investigator. I get caught even when I'm not doing anything."

Sam walked on ahead. Kyle and I laughed it off and followed her.

The two men climbed into the van, and it sped away.

Kyle turned to me, eyebrows lifted. "What was that about? That guy looked pretty rough."

"I think those guys are trafficking young girls."

I couldn't stop seeing that young girl's eyes. Dark. Hollow. Terrified. And Pleading. The video was a start, but I had to do more—felt desperate to do more.

As the van disappeared I called 911 and hurried toward my faithful Ford. That crimson Explorer had gotten me through college and grad school. Doubt she'd have enough left to make it through a high-speed chase.

The hopeless feeling grew with each passing second. I imagined that van flying down I-75. A girl no one knew—no one would ever know—disappearing and gone forever. Kyle's footsteps slapped the sidewalk behind me. I glanced over my shoulder and caught a glimpse of Sam. She stopped for a second, bent over, and held her stomach. I wanted to help her, but I couldn't stop thinking of that young girl. Hollow eyes filled with sorrow. Empty. Lonely. Emotions screaming. No mother to hold her. No father to provide for her. No friends. No joys. Only tears.

I feared those men would use and abuse her and ultimately discard her.

"Nine-one-one. What's your emergency?" *Finally.*

I described everything I'd witnessed—the girl, the men, the two girls sitting in the van, everything I could remember, but it didn't feel like enough. I thought I'd feel better after the call, but I felt hopeless.

I must have been staring into space. Sam stepped in front of me. Her supple hands touched my face. "Are you okay?"

I nodded and blinked to hide my tears. "There's got to be more we can do. They're getting away, and I want to stop them."

Kyle grabbed my arm. "Stopping them is a job for the police or the FBI or someone, not you. Not me."

We loaded the suitcases into my Explorer, I climbed in, stuck my wallet in the glove box like always. As I closed it, Kyle asked, "Why do you do that?"

"I don't like sitting on it."

"It's a bad habit. One day you'll forget and leave it, or, if your car gets broken into, they might steal it."

I shrugged and set my phone in its cradle. "We've got bigger things to worry about."

Kyle pointed at my phone. "What about the video. Maybe you captured something that could help."

I opened the email I'd sent to myself and reviewed the video. The van had a Florida tag. I screenshot the tag number and texted it to 911 along with good images of the girl and each of the two men, but I had only seen the feet of the other girls and had no video of them.

As we left the airport, there was no point in speeding. That van was long-gone, but it didn't matter. In my mind, every silver van was *that* van. I gritted my teeth and squeezed the steering wheel. The soul-crushing guilt felt the same as when I'd woken up after Kyle's bachelor party.

I glanced in the rearview mirror, expecting to catch the lovebirds smooching, but Kyle was staring out the window with Sam leaning against him—her eyes closed, grimacing in pain.

The Explorer thumped over the rumble strip and onto the shoulder. I jerked the wheel and swerved back onto the interstate. Kyle's body slammed against the door, and Sam moaned.

The moaning didn't stop but grew louder.

I glanced in the mirror once more. Tears and worry covered their faces. Kyle looked at me, and I'd never seen such fear in his eyes.

I tapped my phone and said, "Take me to the nearest emergency room."

CHAPTER 15
Emma

I sat on my bed—my new, luxurious bed in my new boudoir—my new cell. My mouth open, I sniffed my tears and wiped my eyes. I felt Bobby watching me—owning me with his eyes. The key in my hand. The door right in front of me. My escape.

But I was in his trap. He knew it, and I knew it. Still wrapped in a towel, I faced the exit—but felt no way out. I did my best to pretend they were happy tears.

Bobby slid close, cupped his hands around mine. I melted at his warm, gentle touch. Strange to feel such a twisted love—even an obligation to the slime wad who'd drugged me and stolen my life. He scooted closer and tilted his head down. His eyes met mine.

His eyes showed no tension. No drifting or glancing away. No lip biting. I couldn't read it in his face, but I could feel the lie coming like a pitcher winding his fastball. He was good—smoother than Satan himself. He released my hands, glanced at the key, then the door. "It's up to you."

I stood, clutched the key with my right hand, held my towel with my left, and slowly walked toward the door. I lifted the key, let the gold chain and the pink poof fall so he could see it.

Bobby stood and walked toward me. I could hear the soft patting of his bare feet on the plush carpet. His fingers caressed my shoulders and he turned me around. His hypnotic eyes trained on mine. "There's a lot of money to be made if you choose to stay."

I remembered Grams talking about the devil parading as an angel of light. I'd thought that sounded crazy, but there I stood in front of my angelic devil.

His eyebrow crinkled, and a hint of tension drew fine lines across his forehead as he watched my tears. His hands dropped to his side. A frown erased his smile, and I braced myself for a slap.

But he held still. No back hand. No fist. He opened his mouth, but before he could say a word, I said, "What happened to Tawnya?"

He gazed at the wall as though searching for his answer.

"Is she dead?"

He shook his head. "I don't think so."

A chill crawled up my back. His eyes looked through me as if he were staring into my soul, daring me to run, to find out what happened to Tawyna. Though he didn't speak, I heard him loud and clear. *You don't want to find out what happened to Tawyna.*

He glanced at the key then the open drawer on the end table. "I think you know what your best choice is—your *safest* choice."

Emma hid deep inside while Selene, trying not to pass out, lay the key in the drawer and closed it.

Bobby's mouth curled into a devious smile. He locked the door. "Can't be too careful. This is a rough neighborhood."

I trembled as he strode toward me. He leaned into me and offered his cheek. I wanted to bite it, scream in his ear and burst out the door, but imagined Tawnya trying the same thing.

I gave him a quick peck on the cheek. He patted my shoulder as though I were being a good girl, then he strutted past me toward his office door.

All I could think about was that key and the ridiculous pink poof. I wanted to grab it and run, but it was no use.

Bobby's office door creaked as he pushed it open. "You remember Donny? He's got a friend who's a modelling agent. He spotted you at Donny's the other night. He called and wants to offer us…you… a gig."

Emma threw up inside while Selene smiled. *A modelling gig.* Pictures and no sex sounded great. "How much?" I felt a sudden twinge of fear as those try-to-sound-tough words spilled out.

Bobby rubbed his hands and smiled. "Girl, you don't even know." He looked like he'd just won a high-stakes poker game. I was still the girl with nothing more to lose but her life.

* * *

I'd just finished my hair, makeup, and nails when Bobby opened the door and leaned into my room. He looked me up and down. "Someone's really gonna miss out tonight, but you, Selene, get the night off. For real this time. No tricks. No nothing." He smacked the door frame. "Just a night off."

I couldn't hold my don't-care stare. My cheeks rose and the corners of my mouth followed.

He winked.

Was it for real this time? No club? No junkyard? No greasy hands?

"Can Bliss have the night off too?" Bobby was a master manipulator, but Selene wasn't so bad herself. He wants a little extra from me—make me act like I care and do a little extra *for* me.

He smirked and nodded. Not sure what he was thinking, but he could think what he wants. I just want to hang out with my friend. And in my tucked-in-the-drawer dreams I wanted to find a way and a time for Bliss and me to escape.

"Sure, you two can do whatever, and I'll have Roberto get you a pizza or something."

Toss the dogs enough scraps, and they keep coming back. But one day this dog is gonna bite.

In the meantime, I grabbed Roberto and asked him to pick up a couple of movies. I made the mistake of letting Bliss pick. Thank God Roberto knew better than to get Bliss's choices.

"They were all out of *My Little Pony*, and I couldn't find *The Neverending Story*, so I got these." I smiled at the choices—*Avengers* and *Pride and Prejudice*. "Thought you might like at least one of them."

I hugged him and winked. "I owe you," I whispered. That got me a smile.

You and me, Roberto, in a different life.

Deep breath. Night off. No alcohol. No drugs. No sex. Just two girls watching movies. Roberto even made us some popcorn and brought us Cokes. No pizza. Didn't really expect it.

Bliss and I fluffed up the pillows and lay on my new huge bed. Bliss didn't look particularly jealous. I'd thought she might, but she didn't look around the room, mouth opened, gazing at everything. She'd been in here before. Maybe she'd watched movies with Tawnya or worked with her in this room.

A sudden icky feeling rushed through me as I imagined everything that had taken place in this room—on this bed. *Night off. Don't think about it.*

But there was one thing I couldn't stop thinking about. The key. As Bliss started the movie, I slid over to the end table, pulled open the drawer and grabbed the key. I started to unlock the door, but Bliss interrupted.

"Don't do it."

"Don't do what?"

No little-girl look. Bliss was Miss Serious. "Candy tried that, and you've seen her scars. I expect Tawnya tried it too, and that's why you'll never see her again."

As I dropped the key and slammed the drawer, there were no tears. I felt numb.

Miss Serious flipped back into little-girl mode and patted the bed beside her. "Forget about it for now, and come watch the movie." As I slid onto the bed. Bliss looked at me with those glossy let's-play-go-fish eyes. "We have to play the game to survive, remember."

I nodded and she said, "But forget the game tonight, and watch the movie."

As I watched the movie and nibbled on popcorn, I wondered if this was what normal people did on a night off. Who knew? Who was normal anyway?

Twenty minutes into the movie, Bliss crawled off the bed and headed toward the bathroom. I paused the movie and followed, concerned. Her face was a strange mix of pale and flushed. She hunched over and gripped her belly, and sweat beaded on her forehead. "I don't feel so good."

I caught her as she collapsed. "You're burning up."

Eyes closed, she moaned.

Her weight pulled me down. I guarded her head as we fell to the floor.

"Roberto!" I'd never screamed so loudly before. I'd had no decent friends in my life. I'd been used, abused, wanted for selfish reasons or not wanted at all—until I met Bliss. She only wanted a friend. And so did I.

As I held her in my arms, tears streamed down my cheeks. I imagined her dying right there. My only friend. The only person in the world who saw Emma *and* Selene and loved us both. She loved me as I was, and my heart told me she would love me no matter what.

Bliss was the perfect name for her. She held no judgment. Only love.

Footsteps behind me. Thank God. Thank somebody.

I lifted my head. "Roberto…" Except it was Mason.

"Wha' she doin'? She sick?"

It was the first time I'd seen softness in his tattooed face. No scowl. No frown. Not undressing me with his eyes. He knelt over Bliss, slid his arms under her, and picked her up. He looked like a lightweight MMA fighter holding a damsel in distress.

He nodded toward the back door. "Open."

I threw it open, rushed to the outside door, and opened it as well. With his tongue sticking from the corner of his mouth, Mason carried her outside. "Keys." He tilted his head toward his front pocket.

I plucked the lanyard from his pocket. Keys and his knife dangled from the large ring at the end. I unlocked and opened the van.

Conveniently, there was already a mattress on the floor. He shoved a few stray beer cans aside and lay Bliss on the mattress. "You sit with her."

His scowl was back. He grabbed the keys and hopped into the driver's seat.

* * *

I hadn't imagined so many bumps and sharp turns. And I didn't know Mason cared enough to drive that fast. Even though we were flying, the trip seemed to take forever, and Bliss wasn't opening her eyes. Her face was covered with sweat, but her hands felt cold. I lost my balance as we flew around a curve, and I bumped into her. My hand slid across her belly. She moaned and opened her eyes.

"Bliss! It's me."

She stared but didn't speak, her eyes distant and hollow.

I patted her cheek. "Stay with me, girl." I shouted at Mason. "Drive faster!"

* * *

The drive took no time at all compared to the waiting once we got to the ER.

Mason laid her across three chairs. Not exactly comfortable. but Bliss lay still, hands on her belly, eyes closed, occasionally groaning.

I expected an ER to be crazy busy and full of people, but from what I could see, it was full of people with more coming in, but hardly anyone coming out. The waiting area was packed. People crammed together on chairs. Staring at their phones. Reading. Sleeping. Babies crying. Homeless guy on the floor.

Two people sat behind a desk. And an occasional nurse would call out a name. Otherwise, nothing around us changed. No staff rushing to help. No concerned person asking, "Is she okay?"

I felt the stares—imagined if they weren't staring at their phones or messing with a fussy kid, they were watching us. Two whores and a thug. I could feel their contempt and their apathy. I was used to feeling exposed, judged, or ignored. But I'd expected this place to be different. I thought the ER might be the one place where people would see us without scorn.

I was wrong. Even the wandering eyes didn't care. When I sat and looked around, guilty people avoided my gaze. A mother pretended to console her sleeping child. A boyfriend suddenly took interest in his girl, who suddenly had to stare at her phone. Others just looked away.

But one young couple across the room kept looking at Bliss. A gorgeous young blonde with her handsome husband beside her. Disgust did not look good on her pretty face. Young Mrs. Perfect obviously thought she was better than us and didn't think we belonged in the same place.

Mr. Perfect didn't strike me as perfect either. He blushed like a turnip when I looked at him. I could almost hear him gulp from across the room. *Probably some john or a wannabe.* I straightened and did a little twist in my seat. As much as I hated the life, I hated the johns more. And I knew how to torture them.

Even in jeans and a T shirt, I could make him squirm. No stripper heels. No short skirt. No abundance of skin, but my shirt was tight, and I pulled it tighter as I sat up straight. The eyeliner, a smattering of glitter, and the studded fingernails told him who I was.

Every time he looked my way, I met his eyes. His gaze kept

traveling to Bliss. He looked as if he wanted to throw up or run away.

He was just another judgmental jerk. I turned to Bliss. Her eyes were still closed, and her limp hands lay across her middle. She wasn't even groaning anymore.

Mason paced—faster and faster. He chewed on a toothpick—twirling it like a tiny baton. Drove me nuts. "Will. You. Stop?"

He glared at me then stormed the desk. "We been here too long. My sister is dying."

The clerk, nurse, whatever stared at him with his tattooed brown skin, brown eyes, black hair, and short, wiry build. Then she looked at blond-haired, blue-eyed Bliss. "The nurse will be with your *sister* as soon as possible."

Bliss moaned as if on cue. She opened her eyes, wide with fear, then hurled all over the floor.

The janitor seemed to be the only one in the hospital with a sense of urgency. Go ahead and let the whore die, but we couldn't have any puke here.

A stout, don't-mess-with-me nurse strolled into the waiting-and-waiting-and-waiting area. She said, "Savannah Graves?"

Mason pointed at Bliss. "Right here."

Savannah? I felt a tingling warmth at the sound of a real name for my friend, and I couldn't help but smile. Bliss had buried that girl so deep, she'd never told me her name. I couldn't know for sure if it even *was* her name. It was likely an alias, since Bliss was probably only sixteen years old. I imagined Bobby had bought the identity of an older girl who'd died in another state.

"You coming?" The nurse's wide-eyed glare reminded me of Grams, and I tensed like a child waiting for a beating.

"She can't stand," I said, "I'm afraid she'll pass out again."

The nurse stuck her head through the door behind her. "Hey, Jimmy, bring me a wheelchair." She tapped her foot and checked her watch.

As much as I wanted to slap everyone in that ER, I wanted Bliss to get better. So, I swallowed my anger. As soon as that wheelchair poked between the double doors, I grabbed it and wheeled it around the check-in station to Bliss.

After Mason plopped Bliss into the chair, I pushed her toward the nurse.

"This way." She motioned us through the doors into the maze of monitors, lights, and alarms. A long hallway stretched beyond those magic doors. Rooms on both sides of the hall. Massive nurse's station about halfway down the hall. People moving. Working. Getting it done.

I marveled at the strange mix of clarity and confusion. The ER smelled so clean—sterile. But the filth of Atlanta's near south side and inner city filled the hallways and the rooms. Nothing felt clean.

I never felt clean—not since that first time in the cornfield with Johnny Paul.

The nurse looked at me as she pushed the wheelchair. "You gonna stay with her?"

"Sure," I said.

But Mason stepped around me and nudged me backward with his shoulder. "No. I stay with her."

The nurse scowled with a quick up-and-down look at his tattoos and his bleached wife beater. "Name?"

"Mason."

"Relationship?"

"Brother."

The nurse rolled her eyes as she turned the wheelchair toward a vacant room. She looked at me. "Only one visitor at a time. We're just too busy to deal with everyone tonight." She pointed me back toward the waiting area.

I kissed Bliss on her hot, sweaty forehead, gave Mason a you'd-better-take-good-care-of-her look, and trudged back down the hall toward purgatory.

I sat and flopped my face into my hands. Powerless. Not a single thing I could do but wait and hope.

Ha! Hope in what? I had nothing to rely on. No family. No other friends. No connections. No money. No god. No one but Bliss.

And she seemed to be getting worse.

I couldn't stop the tears. I ignored the silent eyes around me, the stone-cold hearts, the empty excuses. I had Bliss. What did they have? Money. Stodgy friends. Family who judged everyone the same way they did. Husbands and boyfriends who bought girls like Bliss, like me.

Did they get anything from us? Was it worth the cash for the momentary ecstasy? Why did they do it? Was it the thrill of doing something wrong? I couldn't get my head around it. It made no sense. And it left me empty? Did they ever feel empty like I did? Were they using me to try to fill some hole inside?

Why, God? I felt myself crying out to the one I wasn't sure I even believed. Was he the God who made my mom to be the useless sack of trash she turned out to be? Did he make those hideous people who lied to me for years about being my parents? Those same people who dragged me to church and dragged my shame in front of every person they knew and even those they would never know? Was he a god at all? Or just a flying spaghetti monster, a magic orb in the sky, a fairytale?

Real or a fairytale, either way, I didn't feel like a princess.

Soft, uncertain footsteps neared. The row of chairs where I'd planted myself moved as someone sat beside me. It had to be a man based on the way the chair moved, the heavy footsteps, the clunk into the seat.

He handed me a box of tissues.

"You look like you could use one of these."

"Thank you."

The young man had brown-green eyes and thick clean-cut black hair. T-shirt and jeans. Some churchy looking thing on his shirt—a cross and some words.

He looked familiar.

Then it clicked. *He's the guy from that bachelor party.* Heart racing. Palms sweating. Stomach whirling. I was all Emma, but Selene wanted to pour herself out on this hapless young man.

For once, Emma stood her ground. He'd given the tissues to *her*, not Selene. He wasn't buying anything or using anyone. He was reaching out.

I plucked a tissue from the box and dabbed my eyes.

"Are you okay?" His voice was gentle, deep, and felt sincere.

I feigned a confident nod and reached out. I forced myself to look him in the eyes. When I felt his grip, I shook his hand. "I know you."

His eyes grew wide as his mouth opened. He leaned back and released his hand.

He wanted to bolt. I could feel it. I imagined the little boy in his soul running for his life, wishing he'd never brought that tissue.

"Please don't go. Not yet."

His face softened, but he still looked scared to death.

"My name is Emma."

"Have we met?"

I shook my head. "No one knows me." I studied his eyes. I remembered them from that first night out—that awful night with those drunken still-wishing-they-were-frat-boys losers. What a way to celebrate getting married.

In the ER, his eyes were different. He was different. The blush was still there. The want-to-but-scared-to-death-to look was still there. But he hadn't stayed that night. I don't know if it was shame, fear, devotion. It didn't matter. He hadn't stayed. He hadn't used or abused me or Bliss.

"Your name is Michael?"

Eyes wider-than-ever, his face flushed, and sweat beads popped on his forehead and upper lip. He remembered.

I grabbed another tissue and looked down. I could feel him sliding away, hiding his eyes, hiding himself from me forever. I didn't blame him. I would hide too. I would run as far away as I could and never look back. I would pray to God to burn my memories to the ground and give me a new life.

But I looked up, and he was still there. His eyes were closed too, and a lone tear dribbled down his cheek. Forgetting myself, forgetting who and what I was, I touched a tissue to his lonely tear.

He grabbed my hand, not in the rough way I'd grown accustomed to, but gently. The way I'd hope a real boyfriend might grab my hand. He held my hand to his cheek and looked into my eyes.

I started to feel a little creeped out. Maybe he was a different kind of weirdo than I'd met before. But tears swelled and rolled onto his face.

He squeezed my hand tighter, held it to his lips, and gently the kissed the back of my hand. "Emma is your real name, isn't it?"

I smiled. I couldn't help myself. For a split second, I forgot about Bliss, the ER, Bobby, the life, everything. I nodded.

"That's a beautiful name." He sniffed his tears and tried to stifle his sobs. His shoulders shook. He still held my hand.

A deep voice behind him said, "You okay?" His friend was Mr. Perfect, the guy who'd stared at me earlier.

He waved his friend away. "Give me a minute."

Still holding my hand, he bowed his head, and my heart raced and fluttered. I knew it wasn't a proposal, but I grabbed onto that tiny hint of what a normal girl must feel like before a man pops the question.

"I'm sorry."

Here he was, the one guy in my life who'd never done anything to me except introduce himself and try to shake my hand, apologizing to me. "For what?"

"I shouldn't haven't let Kyle's frat buddy plan the party, and I never should have left him there."

I pulled my hands free, and my stomach churned. He'd seemed innocent and sincere. But my gut told me he didn't care about me. He was worried about himself.

He folded his hands as if he were going to plead with me. Or maybe pray.

I could smell a con. I didn't want to think all men were the same—looking out for themselves, but there we went again—this time a guilty conscious with a savior complex. *I'm gonna make myself look good and feel good by saving this poor sinner from her sinful life of sinning. Then I'm gonna sweep her off her feet—and into my bed.*

When I withdrew my hands and leaned back, I fully expected him to leave. But he didn't. He was just as clueless as he'd seemed that night when he'd tried to shake my hand.

Maybe he thought he was being nice. Maybe he thought he really cared about someone other than himself. Maybe he wasn't just staring at my chest and plotting a polite way into my bed. But maybe he was just like every guy I'd ever met.

I wanted to yell—to smack him—find a baseball bat and beat him senseless. I imagined clenching my teeth, squeezing that bat, and pounding a homerun into his face. He would slump to the floor and I'd keep pounding. Blood spattering, people screaming and scattering. I would be killing Johnny Paul, Bobby, Mason, and every pathetic john who'd ever stolen a piece of me.

Michael's eyes widened as he looked over my shoulder.

Then I felt Mason's stinging grip on my elbow and his spitting whisper in my ear. "You can't turn tricks here. You'll get busted."

I rolled my eyes, jerked my elbow free, and glared through his hollow eyes into his vacant skull. "How's Bliss?"

He gave me a sideways nod and pointed at the door.

I felt every eye follow me as I popped up and scurried toward Bliss. The hallway was abuzz with alarms beeping, patients on carts waiting for rooms, nurses and techs bustling about. I ducked into Bliss's room. She lay on a hospital bed. Eyes closed. Face calm. IV dripping. Monitor beeping with her heart.

I gripped the bedrail and stood beside her. She opened her eyes partway.

"You okay?"

She smiled and closed her eyes.

If Bliss were in better shape, I'd grab her and run. Even so, as soon as I'd try, Mason would be there to stop us.

But he wasn't there. It was just Bliss and me. I watched the drip drip of her IV like a clock ticking by the hours. It seemed strange that Mason hadn't come back. He's so controlling and not one to leave us unattended. Surely he hadn't left us alone. No way he trusted me to stay put, but why hadn't he checked on us? As much as I hated him, I felt uneasy not knowing where he was. Something was wrong. He was always up in my business when Bobby wasn't around.

Bliss hadn't moved. Not a noise except for breathing. I hated to leave her, but she'd be fine for a minute. I needed to get a drink.

I opened the door and peeked into the hall. The stodgy nurse was talking to a police officer. She caught my eye then motioned to the officer with a chin lift. He glared at me, and I backed into the room and closed the door.

My phone vibrated in my pocket. A text from Bobby. *Mason arrested. Get out of there.*

What? I couldn't leave Bliss. Bobby wasn't looking out for me or her. He was afraid I would squeal. *Screw you, Bobby.* I wasn't about to leave Bliss. They'd have to drag me away.

The door swung open. The nurse and the police officer looked at me, then a doctor stepped in front of them and walked toward me. Stiff jaw. Stiff brown hair. And starched white coat. No extended hand. No smile. I would've read his name badge but it was flipped around.

"How do you know Miss Graves?"

"She's a friend."

The nurse and the officer followed him into the shrinking room. Three sets of eyes glared at me—looked through me. I felt like the three of them were ready to pounce, throw me in jail, and wait for the judge to sentence me to more hell than I'd already seen.

The officer took a step but I ignored him and spoke to the doctor. "Is she going to be okay?"

Dr. Stiffcoat motioned for the cop to back off. "She should be fine, but she has some serious issues and some big decisions. We need to contact her family for consent to treat."

"She can give consent."

"Can she?" The officer stepped closer. "Miss Graves looks a lot healthier than I'd imagined."

"What do you mean?"

"We ran a background check on Savannah Graves. She would be about twenty-two, but she died when she was seventeen. So, who's your friend? And what's going on?"

Bliss, what have you done? Bobby, what did you do? "I have no idea."

The cop closed the gap between us. I backed away, stumbled on the chair and fell against the wall. It didn't stop him. He came even closer, and I slid to the floor, and curled into a ball as he raised his voice.

"Who's your friend? And who are you?" I closed my eyes and squeezed to hold back the tears. I felt naked and alone. The tile floor felt cold. I was fifteen years old again, shivering and alone in an Indiana cornfield, wishing a combine harvester would run me over.

"You'd better start talking, or you'll be coming with me."

Eyes closed. I shook my head. "I don't know her name."

"You don't know your friend's name?"

I cried like a lost child. I couldn't help it.

"How about your name?"

I looked up. His jaw was set and eyes burned into me. It hadn't taken long in the life to realize I couldn't trust cops, and it was obvious this one didn't trust me.

"Name?"

"My name is Selene."

He offered a massive eye roll and a firm squeeze on my elbow. Different day. Different man. Same pain. Same ache and emptiness in my chest. But it wasn't Bobby or some random john. The officer pulled me to my feet and led me toward the door.

I glanced over my shoulder. Bliss was still asleep. I suddenly felt like I might never see her again as the door swung closed behind me.

CHAPTER 16
Michael

The ER is a great equalizer. No one is special. Sam waited like everyone else.

The only one who got special attention was an older man with chest pain. One of the nurses calmed his wife and walked with her while the other gently lowered him into a wheelchair then sped through the doors.

A woman beside me cradled her infant son. She caught me looking and said, "Fever." He looked healthy to me, but I'm not a mom, and moms know their kids.

"He's cute." Dimples. Curly hair. Little overalls. One shoe on. One off.

She jostled him in her arms.

An older couple sat together across the room. They didn't seem to notice the drunk sprawled across the seats beside them.

A family stood in the corner—most of them crying. Nail biting. Pacing. Worry on every face.

I don't think I could ever get used to the noise, the bustle, or even the smell. We weren't in the best part of town or the best ER. It didn't even get two full stars, but it was the closest, and Sam was in a lot of pain.

After twenty minutes, I wasn't sure closest meant fastest. Sam clutched her abdomen and leaned into Kyle. I was ready to grab one of the nurses myself.

But then I saw her—the girl from the bachelor party. Same dark hair. Dazzling eyes. Perfect features. My palms moistened. My mouth dried. My face warmed.

"You okay?" Kyle asked.

I nodded.

"You look like you've seen a ghost."

A ghost indeed. One I feared was about to haunt Kyle and Sam. Right beside that girl was the other one from the party and that creepy dude who'd guarded the back door.

Strange and twisted as it may seem, I could hardly take my eyes off her—except when she looked at me. I felt so exposed when her eyes met mine—as though she could see through me—read my thoughts, my desires, my guilty fears.

I made myself focus on my friends.

When the nurse finally called for Sam, I looked at that girl again. She was by herself. Creepy Dude must have gone back with the other girl. I felt that nagging compulsion like those haunting thoughts I'd had when Dad was preaching. I needed to talk to her—wanted to talk to her. I was a nervous ten-year-old boy wanting to talk to a girl but too scared to open my mouth.

I imagined Jordan walking in and laughing at me like he had that night. Maybe I was naïve, but maybe it didn't matter. Maybe she was just a whore like he'd said. Maybe she wasn't worth anything—a throwaway—white trash—whatever.

But maybe she was like everyone else—broken and hurting—needing someone to talk to.

She cried into her hands. She wasn't dancing or selling anything.

I grabbed a box of tissues from the reception desk and walked toward her. Everyone was watching, though I'm sure no one cared.

I held the tissues in front of her. She grabbed a tissue and held it to her face. Crying turned to sobbing. Her body shook. She smacked her hand against her knee then grabbed another tissue—and another.

I forgot I was standing in the middle of a crowded waiting area. I stood dumbfounded, mesmerized by the crying beauty before me. Somehow, I couldn't look at her as Jordan had seen her. I saw a terrified young girl hiding inside a fragile fortress.

After several minutes, her sobbing slowed to a trickle, and she stopped shaking.

When she wiped her last tear, she glanced at me, and I reached for her hand. She held mine like a lifeline.

My skin tingled. Thoughts whirled. I was back in that house where she'd stood bedazzled and cloaked in her trench coat and meter-maid hat. My face screamed with heat. I was ready to run away, hide, crawl in a hole and die.

I pulled away, but she squeezed my hand, her eyes pleaded with me to wait. My sweat-drenched palm slipped free, and I sat beside her and looked into her eyes. Fresh tears puddled and dribbled down her cheeks.

"My name is Emma."

Emma didn't sound like a stage name. It had to be her real name. She was no longer a temptation shrouded in a trench coat. She was a real person with her own dreams, her own feelings. More than just a dancer, a stripper, a prostitute—more than a product of bad choices.

I could hear Jordan saying they do it because they like it, and they're getting paid for it.

I may have been naïve that night, but I remembered her eyes and her I-don't-want-to-be-here look.

My stomach wrenched. If she wanted out of that life, I wanted to help her.

But I had no idea how to help or where to start. I couldn't tell you what I said to her. I wanted to say I was sorry without making her feel like I was pitying her.

My feeble attempts to right my wrong seemed to confuse her. She pulled away. I didn't know if she was going to run or slap my face.

Then I saw Creepy Dude again. He grabbed her arm. The tiny Chuck Norris inside me wanted fly out and go all force-of-one on him. Instead, I went missing-in-action.

He mumbled in her ear and pointed her toward the ER. She darted toward the doors without looking back.

I doubted I'd ever see her again.

I felt a hand on my shoulder and jumped.

It was Kyle. "What's going on?"

"Why aren't you with Sam?"

"The doctor needed to do a *female exam* and Sam gave that *get-out-of-here* look."

I paused to shove my heart back into my chest. But it thumped even harder as Creepy Dude slowly strode toward me—rocking his shoulders and chewing the heck out of a toothpick. Despite being at least four inches taller, I felt incredibly small. He leaned into me—bumped his chest against mine, and thumped two stiff fingers into my collar bone.

I held his eye contact.

He stared through me. "What you lookin' at?" I could feel him slicing me to pieces in his mind.

Kyle stepped between us. "Never mind my friend. He's waiting to see a doctor like everyone else."

Creepy Dude bounced on his heels and pointed at my face. He spit his words through gritted teeth. "He's going to *need* a doctor if he don't mind his own business."

Kyle urged me away. As he eased me toward a seat, Creepy Dude paced and snarled. I was sure he was going to charge and smash my face.

But he looked past me, sat beside an older woman and her husband, and stared at the floor. I didn't expect him to shy away so easily.

Then I could see why he did. A police officer walked across the waiting area toward him. The officer slowed, scanned the room, then nodded toward another officer then another. How had I not noticed them?

As the officer approached, I scooted further away from Creepy Dude, down the row of seats while three other officers moved in from all directions. Two wore plain clothes with their badges on their belts. The three slowly approached Creepy Dude. Then the officer in front of him stepped toward the older couple and motioned for her to move aside.

When the couple had moved, the officer stepped closer to Creepy

Dude. "Mason Morales?"

Morales tried to jump and run, but the officers behind him grabbed his shoulders and slammed him into the seat while the officer in front aimed a Taser at his chest.

Morales glanced at the red dot, frowned, and held his wrists out to be handcuffed. As the officers led him toward the door, he glared at me, curled his lip, and snarled.

I hoped that would be the last time I'd see him, but my gut wasn't so sure.

The ER returned to business as usual. No worried faces. Almost no reaction at all as though the staff and those waiting expected someone to get arrested. But for me, it was a first. I'd never seen anyone placed in handcuffs and hauled away by police.

I watched the officers yank him out of the ER into the night, and shove him into a police car.

Two of the officers came back inside and scanned the waiting area. One of them looked right at me. Instant racing heart and dry mouth. I imagined their handcuffs digging into my wrists. I'd done nothing wrong, but they must have seen me talking with Emma, and they started walking toward me.

I wanted to disappear, but there was no way out—nowhere to run. As they drew closer, my pulse throbbed in my ears and pounded in my chest. I held my breath and closed my eyes, but their footsteps passed by, and they kept walking deeper into the ER.

Minutes felt like hours as I tapped my foot and chewed my nails.

Then the doors burst open and the two officers came out with Emma—head down in handcuffs. Tears streamed down her cheeks and dribbled onto the floor. An officer held her arm. She couldn't wipe her tears, and she couldn't stop them. She looked over her shoulder toward the doors behind her, obviously worried about her friend.

The officer tugged her arm. As she turned toward the exit, her eyes caught mine, and I melted. What a mysterious, beautiful puzzle with so many missing pieces.

Her eyes bore through me and she nodded toward the hallway. Did she want me to check on her friend? I pointed at myself then the hallway, and she nodded then looked away as the officer nudged her out the door.

CHAPTER 17
Emma

Handcuffs and a handgun left me no choice but to leave Bliss—and Michael. As the cops dragged me through the ER, I felt like a naked whore paraded toward the stockade. Every person looked at me, through me. Judged me. Everyone except Michael.

He seemed like a decent guy—if there were any decent guys. I imagined him saving himself for his someday wife and had a fleeting fantasy that I could be a wife—a faithful wife—and that a man could be a faithful husband.

Impossible thought.

The officer's grip kept me in reality and pushed me along. I strained to look toward Bliss, nodded at Michael, and hoped—maybe even tossed a weak prayer that he could be her guardian angel. For a second, his eyes held mine, then pain shot through my neck as the cop jerked my head and shoved me outside.

I glanced over my shoulder once more and saw Michael walking through the double doors. *He's going to check on Bliss.*

* * *

I felt like that young girl bouncing in the back of Johnny Paul's pickup, but they were going to toss me into a cell instead of a cornfield. No difference. I was trash whether they tossed me aside, buried me, or recycled me to be used again and again.

I didn't matter anymore.

But Bliss did. I'd never met anyone so naïve and helpless, so brave and fearless, so optimistic and vulnerable, so selfless and loving. Bliss mattered, so, for the moment, my life mattered too, if only for her.

CHAPTER 18
Michael

I tasted salt and felt my stomach trying to jump into my throat. The doors into the ER grew closer and darker. Fear loomed over me. *I can't do this. Not like this.*

Lying always struck me with terror. I was the kid who was always good because any time I wasn't, I'd get caught. As I stood in front of the double doors, the person at the check-in desk gave me one of those what-are-you-doing, raised-eyebrow looks. I paced for a few seconds to act like I was nervously waiting, then the thought hit me to go to the main entrance and talk to the person at the information desk. No one there had seen me. Maybe I could pull off the lie.

I thought of a news clip about a missing girl who looked enough like Bliss that I could fake my way through a story. I remembered the story because we shared the same last name.

Walking around this two-star hospital at night was a bit creepy. Line of people smoking near the ER entrance, even one in a wheelchair with an IV pole. I swore I heard a gunshot a few blocks away. I stayed on the sidewalk and kept my eyes open and ears alert.

As I walked through the main entrance, an elderly woman smiled over the top of her granny specs. She sat behind the information desk with her blue curls and blue smock with a volunteer badge. "Can I help you?"

"I'm looking for my sister."

"What's her name?"

"It's complicated." I prayed she couldn't see the sweat beading on my face. "Her name is Hanna, Hanna Williams."

She lifted her glasses and leaned into the monitor. "I don't see a Hanna Williams? Would she have a different last name?"

I squinted and covered my face to hide my non-existent tears. "She's been missing for two years."

She stood and reached over the counter. "You poor dear. Maybe… Let me check something." She patted my hand and bent to look at the monitor again.

I felt a sudden calm knowing my nervous demeanor fit the lie perfectly. "We think she was abducted. We got a tip that she might be in Atlanta. I followed the leads to a nightclub. Then I saw her being dragged into a van, and I followed her here. Please help me. She's is real trouble."

"Looks like they've got a young woman in the emergency department whom they've been unable to identify."

I fake gasped. "Is she alive? Is she unconscious?"
"Says she doesn't know her name. Maybe you could identify her."
* * *
The tech pulled open the door, and there she lay. All smiles. Golden hair. Perfect complexion. Barely old enough to drive and too young to be a prostitute.

A nurse and a police officer stood nearby. Each gave me a wary eye, but I only glanced at them before I trained my eyes on her.

I put on the full act. Face crinkling. Lips quivering. Choking on tears. I lifted my hands, rushed toward her, and said, "Hanna. It's me. Michael. We've been so worried. Are you okay?"

She scooted back on her bed and sat up.

Please keep your eyes on me. Don't look at the officer.

I rubbed my face, smiled, and gave her a tiny wink. She smiled back like a little girl who'd just joined one of her favorite games.

"Michael." Arms outstretched. Instant tears. Eyes on me.

She wrapped her arms around me and held me as though I were her long lost brother.

I heard the clap of leather shoes behind me. "Who are you? And who let you in here?" The officer's voice boomed with my quickening pulse.

I kept the tears and smile going to hide my fear. "My name is Michael Williams." I looked at Bliss with ongoing tears and added a nervous chortle. "I can't believe I found her." I grabbed her hand. "I'm so glad you're okay."

Looking at the officer, I whispered, "We thought she was dead. She disappeared after cheerleading practice two years ago. I blame myself. I was late to pick her up. When I got there…"

The nurse was in tears. The officer rubbed his chin. Eyes narrowed. "Let me see some ID."

I reached for my wallet and remembered locking it in my glove box like always, but this time, I'd forgot to get it out. "Officer, I'm sorry. The excitement of maybe finding her and actually finding her has been too much." Bliss grabbed my hand like any long-lost sister would. "I must've left it at the hotel."

The officer frowned. "I'll have to check it out."

"Thank you, sir. I want to catch the creep who snatched her. Our whole town was looking for Hanna. It was all over the news in East Tennessee."

"I'll give you a minute or two." He nodded to the nurse, and she followed him out the door.

My throat dried. I'd just lied to a police officer and worse, my lie could result in false hopes getting back to her family and me going to jail.

This idea wasn't a cheap high school prank. It was a crime. I had to think fast.

Bliss interrupted my racing thoughts and sent them to light speed when she touched my arm. "I'm going to have a baby."

"You're pregnant?"

She bit her lip and smiled. Her blue eyes and bright smile belonged on a six-year-old at a birthday party. But her face changed. Eyes darkened. Smile disappeared like a match blown out. Her touch became a squeeze. "You've got to help me. He'll kill it." She gripped tighter and clenched her teeth. "He'll kill me."

The six-year-old had become a street-savvy twenty-something. No nonsense. Eyes pleading and threatening at the same time. "You'll help me, or you'll go to jail with me."

"I'm here." I tugged my arm, but she held tight.

"You've got to get me out of here." She hopped off the bed, opened a cabinet, and pulled out a plastic bag. Her clothes.

She grabbed her IV bag, handed me the clothes, and said, "Help me into the bathroom. I'm going to change. You stand here. When I'm ready, I'll open the door. Then you go ask the nurse to show you the nearest restroom. She'll say it's okay to use the one in the room. You tell her I'm in there. When she points you down the hall, I'll sneak out."

She grabbed my arms. "Don't mess this up. When you go past the nurse's station, there's an unmarked door, frosted glass. It opens to a tiny hall and leads right out the back of the building. It's where the nurses used to sneak out to smoke. Go out that door and wait for me."

"How do know all this?"

I saw the six-year-old girl smile and the twenty-something glare at the same time. "In this business, the ER and juvie are just part of it. You learn to get along."

She grabbed the bag of clothes from my arms and went into the restroom.

CHAPTER 19
Emma

One of the cops shoved me into the backseat and slammed the door. He was built like a linebacker—a retired linebacker with huge muscles and a gut to match. He muttered something, and the other cop, scrawny and much younger, ran back toward the ER.

The linebacker cop slid into the driver's seat then tilted his mirror to meet my gaze. "Remember me?"

Oh no. He was off-duty cop at SinS.

He showed his corncob teeth, and his face shook with a silent laugh. "Oh yeah. You remember. I work for Donny in my off time." He winked. I cringed. "You're the girl Bobby's been talking about. Don't worry. We're not gonna hold you. We'll get you back to your daddy as soon as possible."

Footsteps smacked the pavement as scrawny cop came running and hopped into the car. "Thanks. I had to go bad."

"No worries. I ran a check on our little friend. Looks like she's clean." He turned toward me with a sickening grin. "Don't know how you got mixed up with Mason Morales, but we may have just saved your life by catching him. Who knows what might've happened to you?"

I wanted to ask about Bliss, but I couldn't ask him. I'd ask scrawny cop if the big guy disappeared, but I couldn't see that happening. I felt certain Donny's boy, the linebacker cop, would keep his eye on me until the merchandise had been safely returned.

Donny's boy smacked the steering wheel and started the car. "Looks like the night's over for us. I'll drop you off at the station, then take little miss innocent home."

"Don't we need to process her or ask her questions about Morales?"

"You think too much. She doesn't know anything, and if she did, she ain't gonna talk unless we got somethin' on her, which we don't. So, what's the point. If you want to handle all the paperwork, fine, but she hasn't committed a crime. If the detectives want to talk to her, they know where they can find her."

"They do?"

"I told you. I ran a check on her."

Scrawny cop climbed out of the car at the station. "Sure you don't need me to come along?"

"You can if you want, but it's on my way home."

The door closed, and there I sat with my self-appointed arresting officer, prosecutor, judge, and jury. He tilted the mirror again. "You were smart to keep your mouth shut. Don't know if you'd hoped to do anything stupid, but it's good you didn't." He smacked his thigh and laughed. "Because you were a good girl, you get your life back."

We stopped a couple of blocks from the station. He turned off the phone on his dash and plucked a flip phone from his pocket. As he punched the buttons with his thumb, I said, "I thought you were taking me home."

"Home?" He chuckled. "Is that what you call it? You in a hurry to get back? Got a hot date?" He glared at me in his mirror. "You might stay healthy if you'll *always* be a good girl and keep your mouth shut."

I recognized the hum of Bobby's van and blinked as his headlights hit the rearview mirror. *No more nights off for me.*

"Looks like it's time to go home to Daddy."

Bobby opened my door, gripped my arm, and yanked me out of the car. The cop unlocked the handcuffs and got back in his car without another word, and drove away.

Bobby waited until the taillights disappeared, then he smacked the back of my head and gripped my hair. The van door slid open. Roberto reached to pull me up, then Bobby shoved me inside. I slammed into Roberto and we fell onto the futon.

No Mason. Thank God. Maybe I'd never have to see him again.

Roberto helped me sit up, then he closed the door. My gentle giant. Even if Bobby wanted to kill me, I felt sure Roberto would stop him.

Bobby climbed into the front seat and hit the gas, throwing me off the futon. "Where is she?"

"How am I supposed to know? The cops grabbed me. Remember?"

He tried to spin around and smack me again, but Roberto blocked him with a quick hand. In his smooth, deep voice, he said, "Watch your driving. I'll watch her." His face softened, and he looked at me. "She ain' goin' nowhere."

I felt comfort and fear at the same time. Roberto protected me, but he could easily crush me. "Last I knew, Bliss was still at the hospital."

"Well, she isn't there anymore."

"What? She's not there?"

I felt a warmth and a chill like I'd never felt before. *Michael? He saved her.* Somehow I felt it. "The police probably took her once she was released."

"Nope. She's gone, and the police are on the lookout. You'd better pray she's sitting at home and not out yacking her jaws or on the run."

"*I'd* better pray? What'd I do?"

"You took her to the hospital."

"You think I drove? You *know* it was Mason."

Roberto gave me a warning look.

Cool down. I would never win an argument with Bobby. I knew it, and Roberto's eyes knew it as well. I swallowed my pride. "You're right. It's my fault. I'll do everything I can to bring her back."

Bobby almost screamed. "You'll do what you're told, exactly what you're told, and nothing more."

I had already thought I was in hell, but apparently, hell has many layers, and I was only scratching the surface. Could my living nightmare get any worse?

CHAPTER 20
Michael

As I walked down the hall, my thoughts raced and heart sprinted, outpacing the beeping monitors. *Breathe or you'll need that code cart.*

A door opened beside me, and I jumped. Bliss clutched my arm and pulled me through the doorway into a short hall.

She leaned against the wall, panted and held her stomach. Sweat dripped from her limp hair.

I leaned to see her face. "Are you okay?"

Her narrowed eyes and clenched teeth answered for her, and I was glad she didn't have a weapon.

She poked my arm. "You almost walked right past the door." She drew a deep breath, closed her eyes, and blew through pursed lips. "Now, get me out of here."

I grabbed her hand and started to run to the end of the hall, but Bliss waved her free hand furiously. "Slow it down."

I tightened my grip. "I'll go as slow as I can, but we need to move."

One flight of stairs, and we slipped out the door. Thank God the backside of the hospital wasn't well lit. Not a soul around but the smell of cigarette smoke lingered.

What I'd done hit me. I'd lied to police and snatched a prostitute from the emergency room—a pregnant prostitute—a crazy, adolescent, pregnant prostitute. I was nuts. Flat-out crazy.

But this beautiful, desperate girl was in trouble like none I'd ever seen. And even more, her unborn baby was in danger. The police would take her to jail. Her pimp would bail her out, drag her to a clinic, force her through an abortion, then put her back in the club, on the streets, or in a dumpster.

She and her baby didn't matter to her pimp or anyone else. She was a nameless whore. A cheap thrill. An object. To them.

Not to me.

She was one of God's children, a scared little girl in a precocious body. And if I didn't help her, who would?

No one. Because no one could see her. She was invisible. In and out of the overcrowded, no-time-to-fix-anything, uncaring system.

But she was visible to me. And I couldn't prevent my stomach from churning as I looked at her soft blue eyes.

She moaned. "How far do we have to go?"

"I can see my Explorer from here."

I wanted to run as fast as I could, but walking hopefully kept us unnoticed—invisible. Invisible would be good. *Dear God, let us be invisible.* I held her hand, and we walked like a normal couple—a twenty-five-year-old in khakis and a polo with a sixteen-year-old in skinny jeans and a skin-tight top.

I hit the fob and climbed into my Explorer. When I started the engine, I remembered Sam and Kyle. "I can't leave my friends."

"Who?" Bliss said. Her eyes wide, fear swept over her face.

"I brought my friend Kyle and his wife, Sam here. I can't leave them."

My phone buzzed in my pocket. It was Kyle. *Where are you? They've checked Sam out and are ready to send us home.*

I started to text that I would pick them up out front, but I imagined hospital surveillance capturing us. No way. "I'll pick you up across the street behind the ER."

* * *

Kyle scowled at me, then stepped up to my window. The security light silhouetted him. It's probably best I could no longer see his face. He wrapped his knuckles against my window then opened the back door for Sam. "Why are you picking us up out here? And who's your friend?"

He stuck his palm in my face and shook his head.

What happened to the Kyle I used to know?

He ducked his head through the window, poking me in the chest as he looked at Bliss. Thank God it was dark, and she was wrapped in my jacket with her head down.

"She just needs a ride home." What else could I say?

Kyle spit his whisper into my ear. "You. Have. No idea what you're doing."

I gripped the steering wheel and glanced in the rearview mirror. Sam sat in silence and stared out the window.

No one said a word. Kyle tapped on his phone as mine buzzed in my pocket. I could only imagine the fiery darts Kyle was blasting at me with his thumbs. But Sam's silence was the most profound message. Silence and Sam just didn't go together. If she'd been that ill, they would have kept her. Something else was wrong.

As Kyle rounded the Explorer, I heard Sam's door lock. Kyle pulled the handle, jerked it, then smacked the window. "Come on, Sam. Don't be like this."

No response.

Kyle tossed his hands and turned away.

Sam broke the silence. "Don't be like what?"

I'd never heard such a shrill sound.

Bliss squealed and pulled my jacket over her head.

Shaking sobs came from the back seat. *This can't go on forever.* I killed the engine, climbed out, and walked toward Kyle. "What happened in there?"

"What happened in the ER isn't the problem." Kyle patted my shoulder. "I'm sorry I snapped. Sorry I was such an idiot. And sorry I've ruined everything. But I'm not going to give up. Sam means everything to me."

"You need to tell *her* not me."

He nodded and sniffed. Shadows and streetlights mingled on his face as he glanced at their cozy, brick townhouse. It should have been the perfect starter home, but it obviously wasn't starting perfectly.

He shook my hand and pulled me into a quick guy hug. "You're a good guy, Michael. I haven't always been the best friend, but you've always been there for me."

"I'm *still* here, Kyle. Still here."

As he stepped toward my Explorer, headlights flashed across his face, and his eyes widened. "It's her! Why did you bring her? What's she saying to Sam?"

Kyle ran to the Explorer opened my door and hit the unlock button. Click. Sam locked her door. They traded clicks until Kyle pounded the glass. "Sam, please. I'm sorry. Can we go inside?"

Finally, Sam unlocked her door but didn't open it. Kyle took the hint, opened the door and reached for her hand. She stood and shoved her hands in her pockets then marched up the brick walkway with her head down. She gripped the wrought iron rail, climbed the steps, opened the solid white door, then slammed it behind her.

Kyle stood alone under the porchlight. I expected Sam to turn out the light and lock the door, but the door opened and she stuck her head outside. "Thanks for everything, Michael." She waved at Kyle to come inside. He gave me a quick wave and dashed inside.

I took a deep breath and climbed back into my car. Mind racing—whirling through the mess I'd created.

Bliss had taken off my jacket and sat facing me. Despite the pain in her eyes and sweat beading on her face, she smiled and winked.

I can't remember feeling more awkward.

She twisted toward me and lifted her head. Still panting and obviously fighting pain, she arched her back, and popped her perky chest. "What should we do now?"

Awkward feeling. Instant sweat. And pounding pulse.

Her words and movements felt so scripted and forced. This scared, determined, childish, street-smart girl-woman had flipped into full-on hooker mode, even in her pain. It's as though being alone in an SUV with a man triggered some over-powering hypnosis.

Drugs, beatings, whatever. Something had programmed her to be the answer to a man's fancy.

I might have imagined being tempted by such a moment under other circumstances, but I was repulsed, ready to open my door and heave onto the street. She was sixteen years old, pregnant, in pain, on the run, yet ready to offer herself to me on cue.

"Bliss, I don't..." I didn't even know what to say. I didn't want her to feel rejected. *God, help me.*

I held out my hand, palm up. She smiled and placed her hand on mine. She started to inch toward me, but I gripped her hand and stared into her eyes.

"You don't have to do anything for me. Let me help you."

She withdrew her hand, pulled her knees to her chest. Tears streamed as she nibbled her lip and stared out the window, a scared little girl once more.

I didn't know who was more lost. What was I to do? One of the things Dad said still burned in my mind. *There's no such thing as a child prostitute. Think of them as fallen angels. And grace is the one thing that can fix their broken halos.*

Then I remembered that website he'd mentioned. *Fixmyhalo.com.*

I pulled away from Kyle and Sam's and drove to a Chic-fil-A drive-through. The dining room lights went out right after we ordered. "Looks like we got here just in time. You hungry?"

Bright eyes and girlish smile, she nodded. "Peach shake and fries."

I needed something strong, but lemonade would have to do.

Bliss cradled her shake and curled her feet under her. I parked at the restaurant. I was not about to park on the street with an under-aged girl who was dressed to kill. Blue and red flashing lights would have found me for sure.

I pulled my phone from my pocket, went to fixmyhalo.com and touched their *contact us* button.

I touched the phone number, and held the phone to my ear. As late as it was, I fully expected a recorded message, but a woman answered.

Thank God.

CHAPTER 21
Emma

We flew around the final corner and swerved into the lot behind Hell's Outhouse. Bobby hit the brake and skidded to a stop. He burst out, slammed his door, and dashed around van. As he flung open the sliding door, I felt like a little girl bracing for Gramps's belt, tightening every muscle.

Roberto blocked the door. "Don't touch her. You know it wasn't her fault. And she knows what she has to do."

Bobby jammed his finger into Roberto's chest. "You my boss now?"

I closed my eyes, waiting for Bobby to pluck me out of the van and slam me against our humble hell hole. But Roberto was a wall.

"I know who's boss, and you know she's worth more healthy, smiling, and pretty."

Bobby took two steps toward the back door and opened it.

Roberto grabbed my hand. As he helped me out of the van, Bobby jumped in between us and gripped my wrist.

"Listen up, princess. Romeo saved you this time because he knows what I can do when I get pissed off." He jerked my arm. "So, don't make me mad again—ever."

He let go of my wrist, and blood rushed back into my hand. Then he gently brushed my cheek, pushing loose strands of hair behind my ear. "I don't ever want anything to happen to that beautiful face."

His smile was more terrifying than his scowl. He was a sticky fly trap, and I was his fly. His sweetness had sucked me in, and his grip would never let me go.

Emma crawled back into her grave.

Selene smiled. "I'm yours, baby. You should know that by now." As he opened the door, I added, "You know I would never cross you, Daddy."

I called him Daddy. For the first time. *Please, God, for the one-and-only time.* If Bobby was Daddy, then Emma was truly gone—forever. *Please don't be gone.*

CHAPTER 22
Michael

It was too late to find the safe house, too awkward to go to Mom and Dad's, and too ridiculous to think about a hotel. We were close to the church. I could park there. If anyone saw the Explorer they'd just think Dad was in his office preparing for tomorrow's sermon.

It didn't take long for the windows to fog. Too stuffy to sleep, I rolled the windows down part way.

My phone buzzed. *Mom.*

She used complete sentences and perfect grammar even in her texts. "Are you guys okay? How is Sam?"

At least I'd finally gotten her to keep her texts short. "Are you coming home?"

Nuts. I had to make up something fast.

The last time I'd lied to my mom, it was something stupid like skipping class or pretending be sick so I wouldn't have to go to church. But I wasn't about to tell her I was sleeping in my Explorer with a pregnant teenager.

If I had, she probably would have thought I was lying.

There I was for the first time in my life, alone in my Explorer with a girl. Bliss had fallen asleep leaning against my shoulder. I lay her on her side and crawled into the backseat.

Dear God, please don't let a curious cop check us out.

I texted Mom. "Sam is fine. It's late. I'm going to crash here." Mom would undoubtedly spy on my location with her app, so I added another lie. "Phone's about to die." Then I powered off my phone.

* * *

I awakened to cars humming past the church and the sun climbing the steeple. Stiff shoulders. Aching back. I yawned, rubbed my eyes, and stretched.

I peered over the front seat. No Bliss. My heart skipped a few beats then the door opened beside me. Bliss stuck her smiling face inside and slid across the backseat beside me.

"Good morning." Her bright eyes and shining face seemed so out of place.

I faked my best pre-coffee smile.

She offered her patented bounce, clap, and smile. "I had to go potty. That building was unlocked, so I went inside and found a restroom."

"The church?" She nodded and I asked, "Did anyone see you?"

She shrugged. "Don't think so." Her eyes scanned the parking lot. "There's nobody here."

Deep sigh. The dashboard clock read seven forty. The worship team would arrive for sound check any time. I really needed to use the restroom, but I wasn't about to go inside. I'd sooner wet myself than get caught in the church parking lot with Bliss.

I stopped at a rundown gas station off the main drag, one of the few that still had grungy bathrooms on the outside. No obvious cameras. Perfect.

I drove past, parked on the street and dashed into the tiny scum closet. It looked as dirty as I felt. Years of neglect clung to the walls. I left the door cracked rather than have to touch the grime-coated door knob.

As I stepped outside, the smell of exhaust and gasoline were like a cool mountain breezed compared to the stench I'd just sucked into my lungs.

Now that I could breathe, we could find this safe house.

* * *

I double-checked the address as I eased down the long forgotten street, looking for the house number. Scattered porch lights Aside from a few broken-down cars, the street was empty.

Bliss curled up on the seat. Worry in her eyes, she nibbled her lip.

The old brick house didn't look like much, but it was one of the few without a cracked or boarded window.

Bliss trembled as I opened her door and took her hand. She tugged against my grip.

"It's okay. This house is safe."

I wasn't exactly convinced, and her eyes seemed to know it. She jerked free and crossed her arms. No more scared little girl. Her eyes were those of a street-smart, don't-mess-with-me psycho.

Raising my hands, I backed away, and she shut the door. I felt as empty as that street. Nothing felt right. I looked at the house again. It seemed quiet and empty.

I turned to the girl in my SUV. Scared-little-girl again. Knees pulled to her chest, staring straight ahead.

I slid behind the wheel and stared with her. An older woman in a housecoat sat on a porch halfway down the street. Hair a mess. Face crinkled. She puffed on her cigarette and watched us. What did she see but a young man and a prostitute sitting in a car? Nothing more. I couldn't bear her eyes boring through me, and I wondered how many others would see us together. Would it get back to the police, or worse yet, get back to her pimp?

My palms began to sweat as I held the steering wheel. I glanced at Bliss, at the old house. Who in their right mind would suggest this place to anyone? I couldn't just drive around town with her. I had no idea where else I could take her, but I couldn't leave her or force her to go in there.

The little girl beside me said, "Don't make me go in there."

Before I could respond, the teenage psychopath beside me snarled, "You can't make me go in there."

"I'm not gonna make you go in there."

She sniffed, faced forward again.

"We'll find something better."

As I started to turn the keys, I heard a screen door creak then slam shut. A forty-something woman stepped out of the house and trotted down the steps. She stopped beside my Explorer and I rolled down Bliss's window.

She smiled at Bliss, then focused on me. "Are you Michael?"

"Yes, ma'am." I lowered my head and tipped my invisible hat.

She smirked and angled her head back toward the house. "I know the place doesn't look like much, but every dream has to start somewhere."

"Looks like a bit of a nightmare from here," I said.

"Wouldn't you like to come inside and take a look?"

Bliss stared at the floor. I wanted to see the inside, but it seemed more important to let Bliss feel some sense of control, so I frowned and shook my head. "I'm sorry. She's not ready."

The woman placed her hands on the window and squatted until she was eye-level with Bliss. "What's your name?"

In barely a whisper she said, "They call me Bliss." She glanced at the woman.

"They called me Summer because of my blond hair." She flicked her brown curls. "Not *my* color. The color *they* gave me. Everything was fake." She grabbed her breasts and gave them a squeeze. "Everything."

A tiny little sound came from the girl beside him. A giggle?

The woman's face softened, and her warm smile grew. "I thought I was lost forever. No coming back. I was wrong. I'm back and stronger than ever."

She stretched out her hand. "My name is Natalie. *My* name. No one's ever going to change it again. The only thing fake about me is these babies"—she popped a quick check—"and I'm not having surgery to change them. Now, hold my hand." When Bliss reached for her hand, Natalie said, "*They* called you Bliss. But what is *your* name? Who's that little girl in there waiting for her chance to break free?"

Bliss bit her lip and shook her head. "No one uses their real name."

"Natalie is my *real* name—the name my mother gave me. What did your mother call you?"

Bliss chuckled. "She called me a lot of things."

Natalie whispered. "Your name. You can say it. It's your first step to finding yourself."

Bliss looked at me. Tears trickling. Her face splotchy red. "Can we go?" I didn't hear a sound but read her lips.

I leaned past her and said, "Natalie, thank you for trying."

As I spoke, the front door swung open, and loud heels clunked onto the porch. A fierce-looking woman with smooth dark skin, alluring eyes, and eye-catching curves walked across the porch and down the steps. Form-fitting jeans. Snug but comfy-looking, deep-purple dress T-shirt. And her walk could melt any man.

As she approached my Explorer, a huge smile stretched across her face. "Bliss! What you doin' here?"

Natalie backed up, hand on her hip. "They were just about to leave."

"Leave? She ain' even come in yet."

"Tawnya!" Bliss shoved open the door, almost knocking Natalie over. She stormed past Natalie and tackled her friend. "We thought you were dead."

"Good." Tawnya's voice was big and bold. She looked like no nonsense. I felt no surprise that a woman with that stout of a personality would have everything it took to escape the life. She squeezed Bliss in a hug you'd expect when greeting a soldier returning from combat.

She said it again. "Good. Meant everyone to think I's dead so Bobby would leave me alone. Lettin' him think I's dead is my one chance to live. 'Cause if he knows I's still alive, I'd be dead." I was drawn in by her big eyes and wealth of expressions.

Bliss held on tight until Tawnya finally nudged her. "You gotta see inside. You of all people should know by now it's what's inside that counts." Tawyna looked at Natalie. "You stay out here with Mr. Clean. I'll show her around."

Natalie opened the door and slid onto the seat beside me.

I must have looked scared to death because she asked, "You okay?"

I felt like I was seeing an older version of Bliss. Instead of looking worn and discarded, Natalie was vibrant and thriving. She'd somehow crawled out of that gutter and found a new life helping other girls find theirs.

"So, Michael. I assume that's your real name. How did you get hooked up with Bliss? And why did you bring her here?"

I looked at her tight lips and narrowed eyes and saw thick walls of mistrust. "I'm not proud of my story," I said, "but I don't deserve your judgment."

Eyes wide, Natalie said, "Ha. You've been judging me since you turned onto this street. Before you even saw my face. And here you sit like some shining prince rescuing the long-lost princess and dumping her in a different dungeon."

"I don't deserve that. I'm no prince, but our little princess deserves more than this. Tell me you can't see that."

I wanted to start my Explorer, floor it, and never look back. But I couldn't. As crazy-messed-up as it was, Bliss had my heart in her hands, and I would do whatever I could to help her. Face any judgment, deserved or otherwise. Ignore any unfounded suspicions. Whatever I needed to do. But there I sat with a self-appointed judge and jury and no other realistic options. I couldn't take Bliss home. I wasn't about to turn her over to the police. And I wasn't sure if I could leave her here. It wasn't exactly a dream house.

Natalie broke the silence. "Sorry, I judged you. But you understand? Don't you?"

"All men are jerks?"

"Something like that. When you've been used and abused as much as I've been, you can't help but think men are all the same. It feels forced and unnatural to think otherwise."

I could feel her eyes on me as I stared ahead. Her eyes bored through me, and so did the eyes of the woman down the street, sitting on her porch. I chuckled inside as the woman puffed her cigarette and glared at me. I couldn't help wondering what was she thinking as she saw me with another woman in my Explorer.

Natalie asked, "What makes you different, Michael?"

I didn't want to look at her. Afraid my eyes would dip into the cleavage peeking over her otherwise tasteful V neck. Afraid her eye daggers would cut through me if I did. "I'm no different—no better than anyone else."

"That's what makes you different."

I turned toward her, and she smiled. "Because you don't see yourself as better than anyone else, someone like Bliss means something to you. Other men look at her as an object to be used. Women look at her as an object to be scorned."

I swallowed to hide my tears. "When I first saw her, I saw an innocent girl trapped in a grown-up body, trapped in a world she'd been forced to embrace. She deserves better."

"Other people only see what she's become, not where she came from or what's been stolen from her."

The screen door swung open and banged against the house.

"Careful! Are you gonna buy us a new door?" Natalie shouted as

Tawnya and Bliss darted out the door, hand-in-hand.

Bliss slipped away from her and ran up to my Explorer. "I'm going to stay with Tawnya."

Natalie patted my thigh. "Thanks." She opened the door and slid out. She closed the door behind her and leaned against the open window. "The world needs more men like you."

Warmth rushed through my face. I didn't feel like a hero. I felt empty. Had I rescued the damsel in distress, or was I simply dropping the princess off at a new dungeon like Natalie had said?

It didn't matter. It was out of my hands and time to move on.

Part of me wanted to see the inside, but my fear wanted to run and hide, forget about last night. Forget about the bachelor party. But I couldn't imagine forgetting Bliss. Even more, I couldn't imagine forgetting Emma. Her hazel eyes still owned my memories.

I waved one last good-bye to Bliss and her new crew then started down the street. Doors locked. Eyes scanning the street for anything suspicious.

I couldn't get out of that neighborhood fast enough.

As I drove toward the house where the woman had been smoking in her house coat, the front porch was empty.

My phone buzzed with a text. I glanced at the screen. Kyle. "Where are you? Call me."

Always something.

Phone still in hand, I rolled past the older woman's porch. No sign of her, but the garage beside the house slowly opened revealing a sleek, silver van with tinted windows. My heart skipped a beat, and sweat poured at the sight of that van. I swiped my thumb across my phone and touched record. I held the phone to my ear as I drove past, hoping to capture the tag number, hoping against hope it was the same van I'd seen at the airport.

I kept moving. Not about to stop and let those guys recognize me and hunt me down.

I turned at the first intersection, parked in an empty spot, and played back the video. Then I dug through my old emails, found the message I'd sent myself from the airport, opened the video and... boom. It was the same van.

I watched the new video again. *House number?* There it was—above the garage door. I dialed 911, then paused. I expected the police would do a drive-by or knock on the door and ask some questions. Either way would alert those scumbags. The place would be deserted within hours. Gone without a trace.

I asked Siri, "Who do I call to report child sex trafficking?"

The phone brought up the number for the National Human Trafficking Hotline.

I tapped the number.

* * *

As I finished the call, my phone buzzed in my hand. *Kyle.* I answered, "What's up?"

"I'm scared." Obvious fear in his shaky words and cracking voice.

Kyle was never one to get scared. "If you're scared, I'm terrified. What's going on?"

He was sobbed and didn't say a word.

"Kyle, what's wrong. Is Sam okay?"

Long Pause. Deep breath. "I really screwed up. Sam's pregnant."

"Screwed up? It's a little fast, but that's great. You're gonna be a dad."

"She's pregnant, *and* she has Chlamydia."

"Chlamydia?"

"VD."

"I know what Chlamydia is, but how?"

"You and I both know how. I never should've let Jordie plan my bachelor party. I got so drunk, I don't even know what happened. I just remember waking up at home."

CHAPTER 23
Emma

I lay awake with my eyes closed. I was in no mood to see anything. Even though Bobby hadn't tossed me back into my old room, everything around me would only remind me I was in prison—a beautiful prison but a prison nonetheless.

Bliss was gone. I wanted to be gone too.

I need some pills. Bobby, where are you?

He was evil, but he wasn't stupid. He'd only give us enough pills to fake our way through each job but never enough to end it all. I thought about the stash I'd had and wondered why I'd waited until now when I had no pills. I'd made the mistake of sharing a few with the other girls. That dirty cop must have taken the rest.

I'd have to find another way. I wanted to sleep and never wake up.

I'd finally managed to nod off somehow only to wake at the sound of doors slamming, then my door flew open and banged against the wall. Bobby flung a young girl into my room and shouted. "Keep her in here, and keep her quiet."

He slammed the door, and I could hear him sliding the bookcase in front of it. Only one reason for that. Trouble. Big trouble. I smiled because trouble for Bobby would mean a few quiet days for me. No jobs. No johns. Nothing.

Except for my new little friend.

Dark hair. Dark eyes. Dark skin. She was a beautiful, terrified Indian girl about ten or eleven years old. Bobby was a bigger scumbag than I'd thought. Bliss was bad enough. I'm sure he'd picked her up around fourteen or fifteen, but this girl. She was a baby.

I patted the bed. "You can sit beside me if you want."

She settled onto the floor and leaned against the wall. Her slender arms shook, and tears dripped down her cheeks.

I slid off my bed and sat beside her.

She sniffled and stuttered. "Where am I?"

"This is nowhere, baby girl." I lifted the loose strands of hair that shielded her eyes and tucked them behind her ear. "It's certainly no place for a sweet girl like you. What's your name?"

She shook her head and buried her face in her hands. Her tiny sobs and her tiny body expressed everything I felt. I was that little girl on the inside, crumpled on the floor, pouring out my tears, wishing that life gave a damn about me. Wishing that someone, anyone, cared about me. *Bliss.* That messed up split-personality head case had been my only real friend, and now she was gone too.

A whisper broke my trance. "They call me Veshya."
"They?"
Her tear-glossed eyes looked into mine. Her lips shut tight, and she shook her head violently.
"It's okay. You don't have to say any more."
She stared at the floor and said, "My mother called me Cali."
"Cali?"
She nodded. No smile. No expression.
"Cali is a pretty name." I saw a tiny smile and a hint of life in her eyes.

I wrapped my arm around her, pulled her close, and wished there was a god who could make it all go away. But even if there were, he certainly didn't care about me or sweet Cali.

I was my only hope. As I squeezed Cali, I knew I was her only hope as well.

* * *

Cali and I huddled together on the floor. What a strange picture. Two unlikely souls forced together in a love-starved world where real love could never be found. I stared at the huge bed—the most comfortable thing I'd ever slept on. A California King for nobody's princess.

My stomach rolled as I imagined what these sick dogs would do with my new friend. I wanted to grab her and run, but there was no way out, not alive anyway.

Candy and Tawnya had both thought the key and the back door were their tickets to freedom. As much as I wanted to get out of this hell, I wouldn't give Bobby the satisfaction of scaring me or killing me.

Everything was quiet. Too quiet. I pulled open the door to Bobby's office. A bookcase blocked it from the other side. I pressed against it, but it seemed to be bolted in place. I rushed to the back door, looked through the peephole, and saw nothing but darkness. I unbolted the door and opened it. A metal cabinet blocked the door, and it wasn't going anywhere either.

I'd never felt claustrophobic before, but being walled-in and having no windows felt like the world was closing in on me, slowly squeezing what little life was left. I'd thought I was hopeless before, but this new feeling took me even lower. I couldn't find Emma in there anywhere, and Selene had locked herself in a closet and swallowed the key. I was no one. Nothing.

Cali's small voice drew my attention. "Are you scared too?"

At least I had someone to share my fear. She wasn't Bliss, but Cali was my new friend. I'd never thought of fear as a way to make new friends, but we connected with that one shared emotion.

"Yes, I'm scared too, kiddo."

She looked at me funny. "Kiddo?"

"It's just an expression, a nickname."

"Kiddo." She smiled, and I grinned at her sweet accent and delicate voice.

* * *

The quiet didn't last long.

Tires squealed into the lot behind my room. Heavy doors slammed shut.

Through the other door, I heard Bobby rummaging through his desk and the loud click of his gun as he loaded a round.

I held Cali tight and somehow felt good about being locked in my room.

A door rattled as someone's fist pounded it.

Roberto said, voice low, "It's Donny."

Donny's voice echoed. "Where's the girl you promised?"

My already-racing heart kicked it up a few notches. I squeezed my little friend a little harder. She was my live teddy bear for the moment. I needed someone to hold, because I knew Donny was talking about me. He was after me. He had fancy cars, clothes, and money, but he also had a harsh reputation, bigger bodyguards, and bigger guns.

My hope for escape shrank even smaller.

Bobby's sounded breathless. "Donny! I'm not holding out on you. I'm just too hot right now."

I looked at Cali. No idea why she was here, but Bobby's words told me she was what made him too hot. So young. So rare. So innocent. The police, FBI, someone was surely hunting for her. My friend might just be my ticket to freedom.

My door rattled as something crashed into Bobby's bookcase.

Donny's voice boomed. "You're hot? Look at me. You've got bigger problems. The cops are pussycats next to me. You promised the girl. I'm here to collect."

"Donny..."

Their voices grew too quiet for me to hear.

A few minutes may as well have been an hour.

Finally, the door outside Bobby's office opened again. Car doors opened, but no engine noises. Then muffled voices outside moved toward the other door, and I heard them outside my back door—the door that led to the bar.

"What's this?" Donny asked. "Move this shelf. Now."

I heard a power screwdriver.

I grabbed Cali and dashed to the closet. Holding her shoulders firmly, I said, "You have to hide in here and stay quiet. Not one sound. Not a sneeze. Not a cough. Nothing. Understand?"

She nodded.

I lifted her over my head and nudged her onto the top shelf. I handed her a blanket. "You hide here. If I don't come to get you, you *only* open this door after it's been completely quiet for a long time."

I waited while she did what I told her, then closed the closet and turned to face the door. I don't think I'd ever felt so useless—so nothing. I tossed a prayer not really believing anyone was listening. I expected no miracle but hoped Selene would come back so the nothing I'd become could hide, or better yet, die.

No time.

The door swung open, and Donny charged through, followed by his goons and a production crew.

Where was Bobby?

Goon number one stepped aside, and one of his girls poked her head through the wall of men crowding into my room. She grabbed my arm, pulled me into the bathroom, and slammed the door behind us.

"You Selene?"

I nodded.

"It ain't good, honey. Donny's mad, and he's no fun when he's mad." Her overdone makeup and spray-spackled big hair were a bit much, but the fear in her eyes warned me more than her words. "Donny's likely to take out his frustrations on you."

"He's gonna beat me?"

She smirked. "You wish. You'd be so much better off. Let me put it this way. He brought that whole crew out there to make sure he gets his money's worth out of you." She looked me up and down. "By the look of you, you ain't never been rode as hard as what's coming tonight. You ain't gonna ever be the same."

She clutched my cheeks as I started to cry. "Better play it cool. Tears will only make them work you harder. I say act numb like they're playing with a rag doll. It'll go a lot faster, and you can just pretend you ain't there." She handed me two pills. "You're gonna need these. If you're still awake after the first few sets, I'll slip you some more. Now let me fix your hair."

Selene wouldn't be able to get me through this night without help. I needed those pills to take my mind anywhere but here. Thank whoever for the pills. Two wouldn't be enough to deaden my mind, but they might be enough to bring Selene back.

CHAPTER 24
Michael

Kyle kept talking. I didn't want to hear it. My mind raced through that night. The girls. The booze. Jordan's smirk as I shook hands with one of the strippers. I wish I'd smashed his face instead of running out the back door. Maybe things would've ended differently.

"I'm sorry," I said. "None of this should've happened."

"I'm the one who trusted Jordan."

"I shouldn't have left you there."

"Jordie wouldn't have let you spoil his plans either way. I think he was jealous of what Sam and I had."

"Had? What are you talking about? You guys will get through this."

"Yeah, but will we ever be the same? It's not exactly the way I wanted our marriage to start."

I listened to him sobbing through the phone. I wished I were with him. "You'll make it through this."

Silence.

"Sam's not speaking to me." I heard a door open in the background. "She's coming. Maybe you could come over. She might talk to you."

* * *

I can't say I'd ever seen Sam with no makeup at all. Eyes swollen from tears. Hair frizzy. She wore one of Kyle's T-shirts over her yoga pants as she handed me a cup of coffee then slid onto a large cushion on their oversize window sill.

Their cozy townhome had been hers before they married. A gift from Mom and Dad. Way more home than the two of them would have been able to afford.

She cradled her coffee and stared out the window. "Thanks for coming."

I didn't know what to say. "Thanks for the coffee." I wasn't sure she should be drinking coffee since she was pregnant, but I wasn't going to tell her that.

My eyes must've said enough. "It's herbal tea. Supposed to be good for pregnancy."

"Gotta think of what's best for the baby."

New tears. "That's why I'm still here."

I pulled a chair closer. She patted the plush cushion that filled the window sill, inviting me to sit beside her.

"Michael, I haven't said anything to Mom and Dad. Most of my girlfriends don't know anything, only my best, most-trusted friend. I'm talking to you because I trust you and because I can't talk to Kyle right now. I can't even look at him. There's too much to process."

She wiped fresh tears. "I feel such a mix of emotions. Betrayed. Lost. Empty. Excited. But most of all, I just don't know what to think. Kyle seemed like the one thing I'd really gotten right. So genuine, always loving, always there when I needed him, even when I just pretended to need him."

Her eyes melted my soul as she stuttered between sobs. "If I can't trust him. I don't know if I can trust anything. He was my rock."

"You have every right to be upset."

"Upset?" She pointed at her blurred, reddened eyes, flushed cheeks, and pale lips. "This is way beyond upset."

"Okay. You have every right to go completely nuclear. No one can erase what's happened, and the effects will go on for the rest of your life. But I know Kyle, and I know he loves you."

Those reddened eyes narrowed and burned into mine. "I'm not sure that's going to be enough."

I opened my mouth, but Sam cut me off with her outstretched hand. "Don't... don't try to say anything to explain away what he's done."

Too paralyzed to talk or think of talking. I waited for her to breathe and take a few more sips of her tea. "Does that mean it's over?"

I should've just kept my mouth shut or never come over to start with, because she poured out even more tears. The cup rolled out of her hands. The last few sips of tea splattered onto the cushion and the floor. She kicked the cup across the room and buried her face in her hands.

I sat perfectly still. Afraid to move. Afraid to breathe. And not about to say a word.

I would never have recognized her when she looked up at me. Swollen eyes. Frizzy hair. No hint of the smile or bright eyes I was accustomed to.

She sniffed, drew a deep breath, then thrust her finger toward her belly. "It'll never be over. I'm pregnant, and this baby will be my forever reminder that Kyle betrayed me."

I took a deep breath, but she interrupted.

"I don't care if he was too drunk to know what was happening. He wasn't drunk when he got to wherever it was. He wasn't drunk when he decided to take the first drink." Her eyes burned into me. "And he wasn't drunk when he chose to let Jordan plan his bachelor party. Do you really think he didn't know what could happen—what would happen?"

"Call me naïve, but I had no clue. Maybe—"

"You *are* naïve, Michael. Kyle isn't. He played Mr. Nicey Nice for you and me, but he wanted Jordan to plan that party. He wanted Jordan to be his out, his excuse, so he could have one last hoorah before the chains of marriage clamped around his manhood. And it makes me wonder how many hoorahs he'd had before."

"Are you guys going to be okay?"

"That's what he called you over here to find out, isn't it? He didn't want someone to console me. He wants to control me, rein me in, and keep his precious little wife faithfully by his side. Well, I can't answer you right now, Michael. Call it buyer's remorse. Doesn't matter. Right now, I can barely think. But one thing I can tell you. Kyle had better keep his distance and keep his mouth shut until I cool off."

* * *

I walked across the glossy hardwood past the classic staircase—the kind that's perfect for group pictures—with a wall you would expect to grow with photos as the family grows. Chic gray with white wood trim and crown molding. The house was the only thing left that was perfect. I met Kyle in their tiled kitchen with granite tops and backsplash. All stainless appliances.

I looked back through the house. Sam still curled up in the window. Still staring outside.

Kyle looked like a little kid waiting to hear what his punishment was going to be. "What did she say?"

"Give her some time and space. You try to get close or say anything, and you're apt to die. You'd better say your prayers, lots of them, because this could end it all."

"Not what I wanted to hear."

"You think she wanted to hear 'pregnant' and 'Chlamydia' in the same sentence? I'd say the best thing you've got going for you right now is that she's still here. That means there's still a chance you guys can make it." I'd never really felt any hate or disgust for Kyle before. But as I looked through their home at Sam, and knew what she'd hoped for, what she'd deserved, what she'd fully trusted she had found in Kyle, I wanted to punch him in the gut and shove him out the back door.

"I can't believe one night could screw up the rest of my life."

"Maybe that's your problem, Kyle. It's not just *your* life."

CHAPTER 25
Emma

Two pills and a few minutes later, and Selene was back. Until that night, Bobby could throw whatever he wanted to at her, she could handle it and give it right back.

Until that night.

Two pills wouldn't be enough. Two personalities wouldn't be enough.

The pain. The groping. The smacking. Pinching. Shoving. Hitting.

Forced sex. It was all more than even Selene could bear.

The only consolation were the blinding lights. At least I couldn't see who or what was coming at me. And I couldn't imagine why anyone would want to buy such videos as these beasts were making.

After I don't know how many rounds, Donny's girl pulled me into the bathroom, dropped four pills in my hand, and said, "It's best if you just pass out. Nothing here you want to ever remember."

I barely remember taking the pills. And I don't remember anything else until I woke up in darkness. My head throbbed. Pulse pounded in my chest, in my ears, and in all the places screaming in pain. I felt torn—literally torn. I was afraid to stand, afraid to use the toilet, and, most of all, afraid to look in the mirror. So I lay still and stared into the blackness.

My throat was dry and sore. My skin sticky. My hair matted. I wore no clothes. No blanket covered me. I imagined the lonely, uncaring, forever-far-away god looking down on me, ignoring my pain as he had my whole life.

No more tears. All that was left was emptiness, loneliness, and the one remaining longing—to be done with it all. If this was my life, I wanted it over. No one cared for me. No one ever had. No one ever would.

And in that darkness, I no longer cared either.

Next time, four pills would only be the start. If I ever saw Donny's girl again, I'd snatch the whole bottle and down them all. I chuckled inside wondering what kind of video they could make with a dead girl.

Enough of the drugs hung on, and I fell asleep again.

* * *

I awakened to a hint of light from the bathroom. My heart jumped as I imagined Bobby or worse coming through that door. I dug my heels into the bed and started to scoot back. As I sat up and reached to pull the blanket over my shoulders, I realized someone had covered me while I slept.

The bathroom door slowly opened. I gasped and held my breath until a tiny silhouette stepped into the light.

Cali. What a relief.

She walked toward me and handed me a glass of water. Such a simple act. But I couldn't remember the last time anyone had done even a simple kindness for me—anyone except Bliss.

I flipped on the lamp, and Cali climbed onto the bed and nestled beside me.

She gazed at me with brown puppy eyes. "I heard you scream." Her tears melted my heart. I could only imagine the world she had come from and wondered why was she'd gotten stuck in this hell with me. But I smiled and felt a glimmer of hope for her because she could still cry.

She touched my face. "Are you hurt?" Her tiny voice and soft hand were a soothing salve.

I shrugged. "They can't break what's already broken." I wrapped myself in the sheet, held that pint-sized angel in my arms, and felt a warmth like never before. Her tiny heart beat next to mine. I realized how much I loved her and felt fresh springs of hope as I cried my own tears.

I don't ever remember being held the way I held her. Not by my mother. Certainly, not by my Puritan grandparents.

I stroked her long, dark hair and wondered if Mandy had ever even had the chance to hold me in her arms. I remembered thinking it strange how Gramps and Grams always kept an eye on her and made her leave me alone. They let me think she would hurt me—that she was some awful person and not a good role model. I suspect she didn't even get to hold me as a newborn, at least not long enough.

As I held Cali, I thought *this must be what it feels like to be a mom.* And my mom never got that chance. Mandy did everything she could to get away from Gramps and Grams. I guess she had to get away from me as well. I must have been a daily reminder of her pain, and she wanted to escape just like I did.

I pulled Cali close and kissed the top of her head. *I'm not going to run away like Mandy did.* Thoughts of ending my life turned to thoughts of saving Cali's.

They can't break what's already broken. I had nothing to lose. When you get to the place where you want to end your life, what else do have to worry about. If I couldn't escape, death while trying would be my plan B.

I kissed her again and rubbed her head. "Cali, I'm going to do everything I can to protect you," *but I can't make any promises.*

There are no promises in hell. No protection. And no escape.

With Bliss gone and Cali so young and so innocent, now more than ever, I felt a burning desire to get out. If I didn't escape, I could see myself rotting in a dumpster. No one would know or care. I pictured Cali beside me, eyes open and unseeing, and desire turned to desperation.

When it was just me and no one else cared, I'd lost heart and stopped caring as well.

But Cali changed everything. I cared about her. I cared about Bliss.

And even though no one else cared about me, deep down, I still cared about myself.

I grabbed Cali's shoulders and looked into her eyes. "I don't know how or when, but I'm going to get us out of here."

Her eyes widened and she swallowed.

"You have to do everything I tell you. I'm going to keep you hidden just like we did last night. And when the time is right, I'll get you, and we'll get out of here."

"All right." Those two words, so simple, so trusting.

I had to at least pretend it was possible. After all, Bliss had somehow managed to escape.

I thought of Tawnya and felt a sudden chill. Maybe Bliss wasn't the only one who had escaped.

As I held Cali, hope held me.

CHAPTER 26
Michael

When I left Kyle and Sam's, I just drove around until time for church. I didn't go. Couldn't. Wouldn't be able to focus anyway. And I wasn't sure I could look at Dad as he spoke. Didn't feel like going home, going to church, or anywhere, but I stopped at the house to shower and change once I knew Mom and Dad would've left for church.

I felt bad letting Mom worry and hoped I wasn't a distraction for Dad as he preached. More than that, I hoped and prayed Bliss would be okay and somehow find a decent life—maybe even get married and have a family. I couldn't stop thinking about her and the girl in the silver van. After I left the house, my plan was to drive until I'd lost track of time and didn't know where I was. I needed time to diffuse and not think about anything.

My phone buzzed. I didn't recognize the number, but my gut told me to answer anyway.

A coarse voice said, "Michael Williams?"

"Who's asking?"

"Agent Randel Myers, FBI. I'm calling about a silver van you reported."

My skin tingled, and a chill rushed through me. "Did you find the girls?"

"I like your enthusiasm, but we've not been that lucky. The girls and the men you described are nowhere to be found, but that van was definitely the one you saw. Your ID and location were enough to enable us to get a search warrant. Do you know a woman named Velma Jameson? Turns out the van belongs to her."

The woman on the porch.

I could still see her. Cigarette. Scowl. Drab housecoat. My pulse kicked up. I swallowed and cleared my throat. "I don't know her, but there was a woman on the front porch where I saw the van."

"Front porch? The report says you saw the van at the airport."

"I saw it again this morning. I recorded it on video as I drove past. The woman was sitting on the front porch with the van beside her house."

"What did she look like?"

"Mid-fifties, maybe sixty. Brown hair with gray streaks. Heavy-set. About five foot two."

"Sounds like her. You think you could identify her in a lineup?"

I was too intimidated to ask what they were holding her for since they hadn't found the girls. "I know I could."

"That's a start. We've got very little on her except a few things we found in our search, but if we bring her in, ID her, and hold her for a few hours, we might get her to squeal and lead us to the others."

* * *

I'd never been inside a police station, and I didn't want to be there now. The blend of cut stone and huge windows surprised me. I walked through the open two-story atrium to an expansive information desk. I had imagined a much smaller building. Maybe fifties-style brick. Peeling paint around the window trim. Tiny halls. Walls and blinds stained from past years of cigarette smoke. Desks crammed together and piled high with papers and folders. But it was pristine and felt strange.

Why hadn't the FBI taken me to a field office? Instead, there I was in the same precinct that covered the hospital where I'd helped Bliss avoid the police. How I prayed none of those cops were there or that they wouldn't recognize me. Maybe they hadn't noticed me for Bliss. I could hope, couldn't I?

I kept my head down and thanked God I'd changed clothes.

A police officer ushered me into a little room with a few chairs and a large window with the blind drawn. I sat alone for a couple of minutes that felt like a half hour. Even though I was on this side of the window, my pulse surged in my ears, and my face felt warm. What was I thinking coming to a police station?

The door finally opened. "Michael?" A clean-cut man in his late thirties shook my hand. "I'm Agent Myers. Thanks for coming. Agent Lett couldn't be here. She and I have been following a local sex-trafficking ring for some time. You might be able to help us bust it wide open."

A voice from the hall said, "Agent Myers?"

He excused himself for a second, held the doorframe and stuck his head out. I only heard low rumbles followed by footsteps. "Thanks Kravitz. Talk to you later."

"Always something," he said, then turned down the lights, and opened the blind.

There she was. They could have brought in a hundred women. But there was no mistaking this one. She was a cross between a prison matron and a Pitbull.

"That's her, number three."

He spoke into a speaker. "Number three, step forward."

I'd never imagined a sex trafficker being an old woman. She looked like she'd lived a rough life. Worn out. Indifferent. I knew she couldn't see me, but she stared at the glass between us. As an officer ushered them toward the exit. Each of them left, but she stood there. Stone-cold.

I saw myself. Staring. Indifferent. When I left that party, I was just like her, sitting on life's front porch and looking the other way.

No more.

"Agent Myers, please let me know if I can help in any way."

"You've done your part. Thanks."

"No. I mean thank you, but I want to help. Those men who smuggled those little girls, they need to be stopped."

He gave me his card. I didn't expect I'd ever hear from him again.

CHAPTER 27
Emma

The room was quiet. Too quiet.

It had been almost three days. I tried both doors. Tried to find some kind of tool to help. But it was no use. We were trapped until someone rescued us or discovered our remains.

The mini-fridge, bathroom, and DVDs kept us alive, but they would only last so long. We enough junk food for maybe one more day. The isolation was welcomed, but the waiting had become terrifying. My mind ran ever scenario—every awful scenario.

I'd heard nothing. No Bobby. No Roberto. Not a peep from any of the other girls. No one. Cali and I remained holed-up in our room. The walls felt closer by the hour, and the air was stifling.

I imagined police swarming, taking me to jail, and sending Cali to who knows where. I feared Donny and his boys would come back with more cruelty and more cameras. I even had the crazy thought that Bobby loved me somewhere deep down inside his blackened heart, and he would swoop in and rescue us both. I almost slapped myself for that thought.

No way.

No one was going to save us. I was our only chance. There was no one else. No prince charming. No cosmic do-gooder. No one.

Then the thought struck me. *This is it. The end.* Trapped, only to be found after it was too late.

My heart skipped a beat as Cali hopped onto the bed beside me. She held a doll she'd grabbed from the closet.

All of us were still little girls inside. Sometimes a teddy bear or a doll were our best escape—a retreat into lost childhood.

Cali gently stroked the doll's hair. When she looked up at me, her dark, saucer eyes melted my heart. There she sat, a kind, loving mother to her little doll. She caressed it, loving that doll like every child deserves to be loved. She cradled that worn-out toy and rocked it in her arms.

Her life had never been her own, still wasn't, and may never be. But she'd stolen a moment for herself and found joy. She wriggled closer and leaned against me as she tickled her doll's tummy.

I lost myself as I watched her. An imaginary mother with her imaginary child in her imaginary world. Wouldn't it be nice? We all need moments like that.

Sirens broke the silence. Cali squeezed her doll and my hand.

I listened for any sign of Bobby, one of the girls, anyone beyond the barred door. But I heard no scrambling, no slamming doors, no voices.

The place was as empty as I felt.

The outer door rattled. "Police. Open up."

Everything inside me stiffened at the shouting and pounding, then I jumped at the thump of something heavy slamming against Bobby's office door—the outer door. I heard glass shatter and the door crash open. Footsteps and voices filled Bobby's office.

I wanted to scream, but terror seized me. What if it's not really the police? What if it's Linebacker Cop and some other dirty cops? What if it's Donny and his brutes? And even if it is the police, I'll either wind up in jail or back with Bobby or worse.

I looked at Cali—both of us wide-eyed and trembling—and I motioned for her to stay quiet. I needed to think and listen. Her lips trembled, tears streamed, yet she still managed a hint of a smile.

I stared at the door. Would the police check behind the cabinet? Would they tear down the door and find us? Part of me wanted them to, but I couldn't trust them any more than I could trust Bobby.

If they released me to him, he would kill me, and if he didn't kill me, he'd sell me to the highest bidder.

I had no good choice. I was a slave to fear and afraid of everyone but the little girl beside me. Then I felt a sudden chill. *The guy from that party and the ER. Michael.*

I felt no fear as I thought of him. Goose bumps. Tingling. Mouth dry. Heart pounding. Mind racing. Maybe he could help us. Maybe I was just hoping or dreaming.

I shook it off and lifted Cali onto my lap. I wasn't going to be anybody's damsel in distress. No one had ever looked out for me except me, and even though I'd done a lousy job, I was the only hope for me and for Cali.

I whispered in her ear. "I'll find a way out of here for both of us." Then it dawned on me. I could hide us both the way I'd hidden Cali, but we would have to do it in near silence.

It seemed like the police were there for an hour. I got a chuckle imagining Bobby's office completely trashed.

Finally, the voices faded. Engines started. And cars drove away.

As soon as everything was quiet, I grabbed Cali and said, "We need to clean up this mess, so it looks like no one has been in here today."

I snatched up our mess and crammed it under the bed. Wrappers. Bottles. Everything that wasn't part of the decor. Bobby would think Donny took me. Donny would think Bobby did it.

I knew Bobby would have someone watching the place—expecting the police to come—hoping they wouldn't find Cali. He wouldn't worry about them finding me. I'm not worth anything, but this little girl, she would break everything wide open. She'd be all over the news, and so would Bobby and maybe even Donny.

And I suspected, as soon as the police were gone, Bobby's watchdog would be here to inspect the damage and move the girl to a new location—*if* he could find her.

I picked up Cali and carried her into the closet. I lifted her as high as I could. She was so tiny, I think I almost could've tossed her onto the top shelf. She pulled herself up and hid under the blankets.

I ducked into the corner behind the closet door, pulled out the ridiculous stack of shoe boxes and hid behind them. I laughed at myself and all the other girls. We didn't have much to care about, but we sure took care of our shoes and those crazy expensive *costumes*. Ha. There wasn't enough material to even call it underwear. We put more value on those things that advertised our flesh than we placed on ourselves.

I slumped to floor, crumpled behind the tower of shoes, and cried silent tears.

No one plans this life. No one chooses this life. We become someone else because the life empties us until all that remains is the objects we've become. Lifelike robots. Void of emotion. I was done and undone with no realistic way out. But I was determined to get out for Cali and me.

She deserved what I'd never had. Someone to love her. Someone to hold her. A mom. A real mom.

I had no idea what real love looked like. Never knew it. Never saw it. And no longer saw any point in dreaming about it. I was garbage, ready to throw myself away, but when I looked at Cali, I felt something I'd never felt before. I wanted to hold her, never let her go, and never let anyone hurt her. I think I felt what a real mom is supposed to feel.

I listened and waited, hoping I could somehow get Cali out of there and somewhere safe.

CHAPTER 28
Michael

I lay on my bed staring into the darkness. Thoughts flying, I closed my eyes and prayed for sleep, but I kept seeing that woman on her porch and that van beside her house. Why hadn't they gotten rid of the van?

Maybe they'd heard a BOLO on a police scanner. Maybe they were hiding out, looking for another vehicle. Maybe they had only borrowed the van. Maybe maybe maybe.

I grabbed my phone and checked the time again. Amazing how time crawls when you can't sleep. I distracted myself with Facebook then checked my email.

Agent Myers. *Got a lead. Call me.*

Just after three o'clock in the morning. Wide awake, I sat up and called.

"Agent Myers here. Thanks for calling."

It was a little unnerving that he answered so quickly and just started talking. I hadn't even said "hello."

"Thought we had a lead on the girl. Found a receipt from a local club at the old woman's house. Checked with the club's owner and staff. Of course, everyone claims to know nothing, but one of the guys seemed overly nervous, so we followed him. We caught him selling drugs, arrested him, searched his apartment and his phone. Found some back-and-forth texts with a contact called Bobby. I suspect this Bobby is Bobby Salinas, a small-time hustler and pimp.

"We checked out his last known address—a cesspool for sex and drugs. But everyone had cleared out. Someone at the club must have tipped them off."

He finally paused to breathe, but the silence lingered, and I felt a wave of nausea. Did he think it was me, that I was the one who tipped them off? How could he think that?

I took a deep breath. "What do you need from me?"

"We'd like you to sit with a sketch artist and describe the girl and the men you saw."

* * *

The police station was not a place I wanted to frequent. I wore a baseball cap and kept my head down in case I saw one of the cops from the ER.

An officer led me to a quiet room. *Out of sight. Thank God.*

I had no idea what to expect, only knew what I'd seen on TV. Then the door opened and a short, stout fifty-something woman shuffled through. No eye contact. Her hair looked like it hadn't changed since high school.

She seemed frazzled, panting and wiping her forehead as she balanced her tools, sketchpad, oversize, over-stuffed bag, and suitcase of a purse. She heaved everything onto the table and sank into the chair across from me.

"Becky Pols." She picked up her sketchpad and pencil.

"Michael Williams."

"Thank you for coming. We couldn't do our jobs without people like you."

I felt flushed and nauseated. There was nothing special about me, except that I seemed to find myself in the middle of other people's problems and I can't leave well enough alone. "I was picking up my friends at the airport."

"I'm sure the perps didn't expect anything unusual either, but thank goodness you were there or we wouldn't even know they existed. Describe what you saw."

"She had long brown—"

"Not the girl. What you first saw."

Nausea grew into a lump in my throat. Why were they asking me these questions? "I'm sorry, but don't you guys have all of this on surveillance video?"

"Of course, but there are things the camera doesn't see the same way an eye witness does. Please. What did you see?"

"I thought it strange that a fifty-something white man would be walking with a little girl from India. He didn't seem like the grandpa type. And she looked scared as he tugged on her elbow."

"What made you suspect she was scared?"

"She never looked at him. No smile. She stared at the sidewalk. I would expect a girl in an airport with her grandpa to smile, laugh, look around, and look up at him now and then. When she finally glanced at me, her eyes widened. She looked up at the man holding her hand then back at me with a tense stare."

"And what did you do?"

"You should already know what I did. It's in the video and all the reports."

"You think I read every report?" She stared at me as if she'd like to stab me with her sketch pen.

"I pulled out my phone, acted like I was making a call, and I recorded everything on video." *The video you should've already watched.*

"Smart. Like you seemed to know what you were doing, and you knew they were committing some kind of crime."

She scowled as she began her sketch.

Like you seem to know what you're doing? The already cramped room felt smaller and hotter. And I felt trapped.

She drew in silence for ten minutes—minutes that felt like hours.

The door knob rattled, and the door opened. Agent Myers. He stared at me as he held his flip phone to his ear. "He's sitting right here." He nodded. "I'll ask him. Thanks, Flo."

"Michael, thank you for coming willingly."

Willingly? Are they questioning me? "Of course. I want to catch the bad guys and rescue those girls."

"I'm sure you do. Do you know why we asked you to come to the station?"

"No." Heat rushed into my cheeks, my scalp tingled, and I clenched my teeth. "I reported a crime. Now I feel like a suspect."

He smirked and raised an eyebrow. "Not exactly a suspect, but can you explain your affiliation with Bobby Salinas?"

"I know no one named Salinas, and the only Bobby I knew was a kid in middle school."

He leaned across the table and folded his hands. "Then maybe you'd like to explain why you were captured on surveillance helping one of his girls escape police custody when she was in the ER."

I lowered my face into my hands and pictured myself in handcuffs, tossed into a cell with a sex-starved giant. I shook my head and swallowed my fear. "I didn't want to do anything wrong."

"But you did, and now you're going to explain."

"The young woman called herself Bliss. I have no idea what her real name is—."

"So, you were soliciting a no-name prostitute and didn't want to get caught."

"No! I've never…" I let the words stop. What could I say? It didn't have to be true. They could make me look guilty. It would be my word against the FBI and the police. "I wasn't soliciting her and never had. She was scared, and I was trying to help her."

"Thin ice. That's what I'm seeing here Michael. I think when we catch the guys trafficking these girls, they'll tell us you've been working with their rival, Bobby Salinas."

I heard a little alarm in my head from watching too many crime shows. *Shut your mouth and ask for an attorney.*

But as soon as I ask to speak to a lawyer, Myers would assume I was guilty or trying to cover up something else.

I lifted my head, looked him in the eyes, and said, "Do you actually believe I'm connected to any of these guys?"

He smiled. "In my job, everyone's a suspect, and I had a little help from one of our men in blue who told me he'd seen you with one of Salinas's girls in the ER."

I bit my lip. Inside I was on fire and trying not to explode. I took a deep breath. "I helped a young girl in trouble for the same reason I wanted to help the girl at the airport. She was in trouble, and no else was going to help her." I looked squarely in his eyes. "You know what would've happened to her if I'd left her alone."

He opened his mouth to answer, but I stopped him.

"It wasn't a question. You *know* exactly what would have happened. Her pimp would have posted bail, and as soon as he found out she was pregnant, he'd have forced her into an abortion. She asked for my help to protect her and her baby."

"Well, aren't you just a saint?"

If he was trying to make me mad, it worked. I pounded my fist on the table, pushed away, and stood. "Are we done here? 'Cause I am."

He said the magic words that never work. "Calm down." Then he motioned for me to sit again. "Michael, I was testing you. I'm sorry. It's obvious you're not working with Salinas. A real psychopath wouldn't show such emotion."

"I just wanted to do the right thing."

Agent Myers said, "Why? What's your motivation?"

"Do you really need to know all this?"

"Only curious."

I told him about the bachelor party and about running into Emma and Bliss in the ER. I didn't use any names. He actually yawned at one point but pretended to be interested.

When I finished, he said, "So, you were basically in the wrong place at the wrong time."

"If that's how you look at it, but for Bliss and the little girl at the airport, I'd say I was in the perfect place at the perfect time. There would be no chance for either of them if I hadn't been there at the right moment." A chill ran up my spine. When I spoke the words, the reality of those two moments hit me. I felt a sense of purpose like I'd never felt before. "Agent Myers, I want to do anything I can to help these girls. What I saw for both of them isn't life. It's a cruel existence. It's slavery. They deserve a life of their own—with their own choices, their own dreams."

"Noble thoughts. And good words for me to hear. It's too often these stories end badly, largely because no one cares."

I pictured the handcuffs falling off and the sex-starved giant disappeared. Agent Myers shook my hand. "Thanks for your honesty and for the sketch. We'll compare it to our database. Hopefully it'll give us a hit." He stood and shook my hand. "We're all done for now. I'll call you if we need anything more."

"Please do. Thanks."

As he opened the door and motioned for me to leave, I said, "You're not going to arrest me for helping Bliss leave the hospital and escape the police?"

"Not my jurisdiction, but I'll put in a good word with Detective Kravitz. Maybe he'll forget about it." He winked. "What happened to Bliss anyway?"

"She's in a halfway house for girls who've escaped the life."

"Sounds good. I wish more stories ended that way."

Bliss's story wasn't over. It was just beginning. And then I thought about Emma and the little girl. What about their stories?

CHAPTER 29
Emma

I heard the outer door to Bobby's office open and shut. *He's here.* I knew it would be Bobby. He wouldn't be able to stand it. He'd have to come to see what was left, and to get me—and the girl.

At least two sets of footsteps. Furniture shuffled. Doors opened and shut. But no voices. I imagined Bobby and one of his boys, hopefully Roberto, peering into hallways and rooms, afraid police might still be there waiting for them.

I reached up to the shelf where Cali hid, patted her leg and motioned for her to remain still and quiet. I pointed to the light switch to dampen her fear, then I turned off the closet light and wriggled into my hiding place. Then I heard the power drill and knew he was coming. He was freeing the bookcase to get to my door. Cali and I were the only things left worth anything. The wall vibrated behind me as Bobby and Roberto pulled the bookshelf away from the door.

"Selene, princess, are you here? It's Daddy."

I wanted to throw up at the sound of his voice and his soft, squishy words. He was not my daddy. He was not my anything.

I couldn't think, my heart beat so fast. The closet was dark and cramped. I couldn't breathe, but I could sense him coming closer, the closet door bursting open. And I imagined his grip on my wrist like I'd felt a thousand times. He would own me again, and I would be his submissive slave.

No. It's not going to happen. Emma was back. I was that feisty kid again, the one who'd stood up for herself. The one who ran a thousand miles away to find a new life.

Even if my defiance cost me everything, it would still be my life.

I willed my heartbeat into control and slowed my breathing as I waited.

The closet door opened. The light flipped on, and I heard Roberto's voice—warm and gentle. I couldn't understand how or why he worked for Bobby. "There's no one here."

"Check everything. She's got to be here."

"What if Donny got here before the police?"

"Are you saying he was, because you were supposed to be watching."

"I can only watch one side of the building. Maybe he came in the other side."

Bobby screamed a string of expletives. Then it happened. Roberto pushed back the clothes, placed his hand on the mountain of shoeboxes, and saw me—eye-to-eye. My warm, gentle giant. He looked at me with a mix of love and sadness and tossed words over his shoulder. "They're gone. There's no one here."

Bobby's footsteps tore through the bedroom and out the door, slamming it behind him.

Roberto leaned down and whispered, "I'll leave the door open for you." He kissed my forehead. "I'll always leave the door open for you."

My heart beat like it was brand new. Fresh air in my lungs. Wind in my sails. Yet fear still surrounded me, clung to me. I didn't know where to go, who to call, or what to do. When you're on the edge of a cliff and the mountain behind you has crumbled, you really don't have a next step. Any move I made could plunge me into a new canyon.

I couldn't call the police. I had no friends, no family, no skills that I'd want to use. I was free yet still a slave, and fear was my new master.

"God, if you're there, I've never seen you, never heard your voice, never known you, but I need you. I've got no one to turn to and no place to run."

CHAPTER 30
Michael

"Michael, Agent Myers here. We need your help again if you're willing."

"Sure, what's up?"

"I told you we'd staked out Salinas' place after our search. Well, we think we've got him."

"What do you need me to do?"

"I want you to ride with me to see if you recognize anyone."

"I've only seen Morales, Bliss, Emma, and one other guy."

"Maybe you can ID the other guy."

* * *

In the daylight, the place didn't look like much. A grungy bar in a grungy neighborhood with a "rooms for rent" sign stuck in a window. Agent Myers parked in a nearby driveway with a view of the backdoor.

A stakeout. I'd imagined being on a stakeout. Sitting for hours. Pulse-pounding anticipation. Junk food and energy drinks. Waiting like a lion ready to pounce.

Agent Myers took a bite of his pastrami. "Pretty exciting, huh?"

I kept my eyes on that back door and nodded.

I heard him chuckle. "You don't have to stare at that door. You'll hear if a car pulls up."

It seemed like forever. Then it happened. Tires crunched on some loose gravel in the parking lot behind the bar. Two men climbed out a black van. It may have been the same van I saw at the bachelor party. The bulky guy was the bodyguard from the bachelor party. Definitely the same van. I recognized the other guy too. He was the ladies' man I bumped into as I left that house. He had to be Salinas. "There they are."

Myers peered across the street and the parking lot. "Salinas is the short guy. You recognize the other one?"

"Both of them were with Morales at the bachelor party." Myers didn't react. Didn't move. Didn't do anything. "Are we just here to watch?"

He nodded and we watched until they came out. Neither of them looked happy. They hopped in their car and drove away.

"That's it?"

He didn't answer. He just opened his door and hopped out. "Come on. Let's check it out. We could notify law enforcement, but it's better that we don't. They'll be back. I wanted you here to ID the other guy. Now that they're gone, let's check it out."

As we crossed the street he slipped on a pair of disposable gloves.

The back door was unlocked. Once inside, Myers headed straight toward another door directly opposite our entrance. "It's locked." He spun and scanned the room. "It doesn't make sense. Why would they lock this door, but leave the outside door unlocked."

The place had been ransacked. Papers strewn across the floor. Desk askew. Sofa pulled away from the wall. A lamp on its side.

I kept my hands folded to avoid touching anything. "What do suppose happened?"

"I suspect they were looking for something important and didn't find it. Maybe someone saw us and warned them, or someone else got here first and took whatever it was."

Myers started to pull off his gloves then stopped. I followed his gaze to the desk. A drill and four screws lay on top of the strewn papers. He pointed at the drill and scanned the room, stopping when he noticed the bookshelf wasn't flush against the wall. "They used this drill. Why else would it be on top of everything else?" Gloves back on, he pulled the shelf further from the wall and exposed another door.

"None of our earlier reports noted this door."

My pulse quickened as he placed his hand on his gun, motioned for me to stay put, then he eased the door open.

* * *

Emma

I thought Bobby was gone, but I heard footsteps again. Roberto must've told him, and they were coming back. I felt paralyzed. I dreamed of Bobby bursting through the door and ending my nightmare. One shot to the head, and I'd be done forever. No more running. No more abuse. No more anything.

Then I heard a whimper above me.

"Cali." I whispered. The shelf over my head bobbled as she slid off and huddled beside me.

Tears streamed as she whispered, "I need the toilet."

I held her close. "Can you hold it?"

"I can try."

* * *

Michael

I heard a whimper. Myers must have, too, because he lifted his finger to his lips.

He pointed toward the sofa and mouthed "sit down." I tiptoed to the sofa and eased onto it. He walked toward the back door, opened it, and slammed it shut. Then he turned around and leaned against the door. Arms folded. Gun drawn.

He raised his hand as if to say, "Sit tight." Then he watched the bookshelf.

* * *

Emma

The door slammed.

They're gone. I took a deep breath and patted Cali on the shoulder. She wiped her tears then scampered out of our hiding place toward the bathroom.

I curled into a ball and buried my face in my hands. *What's next? Nothing good.* I wanted to scream—to run. I wanted someone to save me, but that was a fantasy. There was nothing to do but hold on to the tiniest thread of hope or wait to die.

Get a grip, Emma. Selene awakened. *What's your problem? What can they do to you now? What can anyone do to you?*

Huddled against the wall, I could hide from everyone but Selene. She was the same steel-hearted diva she'd always been. Unflappable. Detached and in control.

But I was not Selene. I was little Emma, hiding like I'd always done. I was that naked girl, alone in a cornfield.

Even Selene couldn't save me this time. She faded like fog in the sun as I imagined Bobby or Donny or the cops barging through the door.

They can do whatever they want. My life is over.

It had never been my life anyway. And this girl was done running and had no place to gone. Done putting out. Done with putting on ridiculously-expensive, next-to-nothing clothes only to take them off for some schmuck who only got it when he paid for it. I was tired of hiding bruises, dodging police, popping pills.

Tired of living.

The toilet flushed, disrupting my pity party. Then I heard a familiar voice.

"It's her. That's the girl I saw at the airport."

Michael?

A deeper voice said, "You're sure it's the same girl?"

"One hundred percent."

I remained still and hidden. My heart pounded out of my chest. My pulse raged in my ears. Face hot. Dizzy. Nausea. Instant sweat.

I heard Cali's tiny footsteps, then the closet door flung open. She swung around it, wide-eyed and drenched with sweat and tears. Her tiny frame was shaking. Lips trembling.

Michael shouted, "We're scaring her. Put your gun away."

Gun? He's here with the police? The usual warped routine flashed through my eyes. Arrested. Groped. Drug-tested. Locked up then released to Bobby to do it all over again.

No! Selene screamed in my mind, and I agreed with her. *It can't happen again. I can't go through any more of this.*

Suicide by cop seemed like my best way out.

But what about Cali? I couldn't risk her getting shot. I'd do anything to save her.

I pulled her close and held my breath, waiting for them to burst into the closet. Instead, I heard tires squeal followed by a loud thud. I pictured the outside door slamming against the desk. *Bobby.*

Could it get any worse?

Cali squeezed me tighter and buried her head in my chest. I thought my heart would stop. Shouting and shooting jolted my already-frazzled nerves and blurred my thoughts. I imagined a hail of bullets and blood spatter. As crazy as it was, I imagined my boudoir destroyed. Bullet holes and blood on the walls. Broken mirrors. Pillow fluff floating in the air. Why did I even care about something so ridiculous? It wasn't even mine. Never had been.

The gun shots rang in my ears even after the shooting stopped. I held my breath and listened. Then the closet door swung open.

There stood Roberto. "I came back for you, but Bobby followed me. I waited when I saw him, but he said there was an FBI agent inside, and Donny wanted him dead."

"Where's Bobby?"

"Dead. The agent shot him."

For the first time in a long time, I felt something other than fear. I felt a wave of peace. With Bobby dead, I felt hope. "The Agent?"

"Dead." Roberto stood over me like a tower of strength. He was my gladiator, a sturdy warrior, and no longer Bobby's slave.

I stretched out my hand, and Roberto pulled me up. I wrapped my arms around him, and he rested his chin on the top of my head. In my twisted world, he had been my steady rock. Yes, he'd done Bobby's bidding, but he had also looked out for me. I'd pictured myself in his arms so many times. And I never felt used when I was with him. Holding me. Keeping me safe. No expectations. No judgment.

Cali wrapped her arms around me and held onto my waist. We stood together in that strippers' closet like some freak-show family. Strange as it may sound, I'd never felt more like I belonged.

But my happy moment disappeared at the stern words, "Come out with your hands up."

Michael? He'd probably heard that phrase a thousand times in every cop show he'd ever seen and dreamed about saying it since he was a kid.

I whipped around Roberto and out of the closet. Michael barely stood, bracing himself against the wall between my bed and the bathroom. Sweat-soaked hair. His trembling hands held a gun.

We locked eyes and I stepped toward him. "Put down the gun."

He took a step back, eyes looking past me at Roberto. I could feel my gentle giant behind me.

"It's ok. Roberto isn't going to hurt anyone."

"Agent Myers is dead." Michael glanced at the body then me as he aimed the gun at Roberto. Michael gritted his teeth and tightened his grip, but not enough to keep the gun from shaking.

I pressed toward him, unable to ignore the blood spattered against the walls, the bodies, their ashen faces, blood-soaked clothes, and the raw meat smell. I pushed Cali behind me, hoping she wasn't looking. Michael was unrecognizable. Pale. Terror in his reddened eyes.

I shouted over his glazed stare. "Is Roberto holding a gun? No. Did he shoot the agent? No. Roberto doesn't kill people. He protects people. He came here to protect me from you."

"Me? I didn't hurt anyone?"

"You're the only one holding a gun."

Michael tossed the gun onto the bed.

Roberto moved behind me. He could snap Michael in two, so I spun around and lay my hands on his chest then slid my fingers up to his face.

His shoulders softened. His hands opened. But he still looked past me and stared at Michael.

I whirled toward Michael, keeping a hand on Roberto. "I'm not going to jail again. Bobby's dead." I thumped my chest and added, "I belong to no one but myself." I stepped into his space and opened my arms, ready to hug him.

But his eyes widened. He glanced at the gun as Roberto pushed past me. I fell onto the bed and grabbed the gun.

I looked back to see Roberto squeezing Michael like an old raggedy doll. Michael's face contorted with pain—his eyes trained on the gun in my hands.

I didn't know what to do. I wasn't going to shoot him. I didn't want to aim it at him or anyone—except Donny. I would have no trouble blasting a hole through that creep's face—his and every one of his goons.

But Michael wasn't Donny. He was like me, caught in a world where he didn't belong.

I shoved the gun into my purse and nudged Roberto. "Let him go. Maybe he can help us."

CHAPTER 31
Michael

This is it. I never imagined my life ending this way. I felt a strange giddiness as darkness surrounded me. I was floating and falling.

I awakened to fiery pain in my spine. My head pounded. I was lying on the floor in that bizarre room. Roberto must have knocked me out.

"Michael?"

I forced my eyes open. Emma was leaning over me. I felt drawn to her. Her eyes. Her hair. The sensual fragrance of her lingering perfume.

"Michael, you've got to help us."

I rubbed my head and sat up, but the room spun and so did my stomach. I swallowed the salty taste in my mouth and concentrated on not throwing up. Emma's hand rested on my shoulder.

"Are you okay?"

All I could do was look into her eyes. A federal agent lay dead against the other wall. Her pimp lay dead behind her. Bullet holes scattered across the walls. Glass from the broken mirror mixed with blood on the carpet and the bed. Was I okay?

I shook my head. Then tears streamed. My lips quivered. I wanted to run, hide, scream, do anything but face the reality around me. *I'm going to jail. I'm going to die.* My mind raced through a hundred terrible scenarios.

Emma grabbed my other shoulder and shook me.

I closed my eyes and wished it was all a terrible dream.

Smack.

My face stung. I opened my eyes as she reloaded her hand for another slap. Her eyes bore through me. She owned me with that frantic, determined look, and I would do whatever she said.

Roberto's giant hands gripped my shoulders from behind and plucked me off the floor like I weighed nothing. The little girl from the airport had climbed onto the bed who knows when. She looked at me with those same eyes and that same fear I'd see at the airport.

A sudden chill rushed over me like a whisper. *It's not about you.* I didn't hear any voice. No light from heaven. Just a feeling and a sudden understanding and determination that I had to do whatever I could to help that child.

I lifted my hand to signal that I was fine.

Roberto let go.

I stepped past Emma and sat on the bed beside the girl.

Emma said, "Her name is Cali. You've got to help us."

I focused on the girl. "Cali. What a pretty name." *How strange to find this lovely little girl in such an ugly place.* "My name is Michael. I'm going to do everything I can to help you." I looked at Emma. "I want to help you, too, but first we need to get her to the police."

Instant scowl. "The police? Are you nuts? We aren't going anywhere near the police. You know what they'll do to her?"

I didn't even have time to shake my head.

"At best, they'll dump her into the system, and she'll never have a chance. Or worse, that dirty cop—and who knows how many others Donny's got on his payroll—one of those dirty cops will slip her back to Donny."

"Surely, we can find one decent cop or a social worker."

"You know any?" When I looked away, she said, "Didn't think so."

I sighed and shrugged. "So, what should we do?"

Emma's hand balled into a fist. Teeth clenched. Eyes wide. "You need to think fast, Michael. You're the one on the outside. This is the only world I know. You've got to have some idea where we can take her."

Bliss. The thought gave me a new set of chills. "Do you have a smartphone."

Roberto handed me his phone. I opened his maps app, typed in the address, and handed it back to him. "I mapped the address where I took Bliss."

Emma's face brightened. The first smile I'd seen in days. She surprised me with an intense hug, and she held me nose to nose, eye to eye. She owned me, and I think she knew it. She hugged me again, kissed my cheek, and grabbed Roberto's phone.

Roberto snatched his phone and headed toward the door as Emma stomped her foot and shouted. "We're not leaving him here?"

Roberto hadn't said a word until now. "Someone's got to be here when the police come. It can't be us. Grab the girl and come on." Roberto looked at me. "We were never here. You and the FBI came in and found Bobby."

As he spoke, Emma pulled the gun out of her purse, wiped it clean, and stuck it Agent Myers's hand.

Roberto cleared his throat and stepped toward me. "Bobby knocked you out, shot the agent, and the agent shot him. You came to and called 911. Give us about ten minutes to get away, then you can call the police."

* * *

Ten minutes feels like forever when you're in a strange room with two corpses. I'd never experienced the raw-hamburger smell of fresh death. My pounding head spun. I couldn't stay in that room. I went into

Bobby's office and lay on the sofa until it was time.
Then I called 911.

CHAPTER 32
Emma

"Let's get out of here."

We sprinted toward Bobby's car, probably not the smartest choice. The police would certainly be looking for it, but we had no other choice. We weren't about to steal the agent's car, and we weren't about to stick around get arrested.

As we headed down the street, I got my first daytime look at the blind and uncaring neighborhood. An older woman tending her flowers. A mother rocking her baby on an old porch swing. Toddler chasing invisible butterflies. Two guys sitting staring under the hood of a rusted Mustang, smoking. Every one of them found something else to look at as we passed, as though they knew who we were, where we came from, and they chose to look the other way.

I tried to look the other way too, but the toddler chasing butterflies looked at me. Big smile and wave. It only lasted a second before his mom grabbed his wrist, but smiles are contagious, and I caught his.

Roberto rested his hand on mine. He didn't have to say a word. His gentle touch said enough. I'd thought my life was over as I'd waited for Bobby to burst through the door and give me his worst. If not Bobby, Donny would have snatched me up and squeezed out every video he could and plaster my pain all over the internet.

But Roberto's hand told me my life was not over, and new life was about to begin. Bobby was behind us forever. His blood, mixed with the agent's, would be too much for Donny to explain. He wouldn't want anything to associate him with Bobby or that place. That agent's blood in my room may have been my ticket to freedom from the Don.

As Roberto held my hand, I thought maybe this moment truly was what freedom felt like.

I squeezed Roberto's hand, and he smiled. I pretended I was seventeen and starting over. Windows down. Grams's old Falcon screaming down the highway. The past behind me. Blue skies ahead.

I hadn't even been gone a year, but I'd endured more in those months than anyone deserves in a lifetime. I would continue to chase after freedom, cling to it, and relish it. But I couldn't relax just yet. Too many loose ends.

It was too soon to crank the music. Winding our way through Atlanta, my ears were piqued, listening for sirens. We had miles and years to go, and life might never be normal—whatever normal was, but we had our start. The wicked witch was dead, and we were on our way to the Emerald City.

I looked over my shoulder. Cali lay sound asleep on the back seat. It had already felt like a long day, but the sun was overhead, and shadows were scarce. How could she sleep, especially after all that? I was so jealous.

When I looked up, I met eyes with the driver behind us. Shaved head. Chiseled face. Narrow eyes. I recognized him as one of Donny's goons. If I remembered him from when I was high, he would certainly remember me. The free-spirited seventeen year old disappeared, and Emma wanted to run and hide once more.

I flipped around in the seat. "We're being followed."

Roberto glanced in the rearview mirror.

"Why aren't you going faster?"

"If I speed up, he'll know we saw him."

The light was green, but Roberto slowed. As the light turned yellow, he tapped the brakes then, when the light turned red, we zoomed left.

As I held on for dear life, I glanced out the rear window. The swift turn jolted Cali into the door, and she sat up.

When she popped up, that goon's eyes popped wide open, and a chill shot through me. Of course, Donny had his boys watching our hell hole, waiting for Bobby to sneak off with their merchandise. And here we were cruising through town wearing a bullseye.

Donny's goon slammed on the gas, and his black van tilted through the turn. Tires squealing. Horns blaring.

"Cali, get down." As I climbed over the seat, Roberto hammered the pedal, and I flew into the back seat and tried not to squish Cali. I wrapped my arms around her trembling body. Fresh tears. "Did you see that man?"

Why did I ask? Her tears answered. One glimpse was all she had needed. I pulled her head to my chest and stroked her hair. "Do whatever you need to, Roberto. We've got to get away from him."

His eyes met mine in the rearview mirror, and he said, "Pull up the seat."

Bobby had apparently converted the backseat into bench seat with a hidden storage compartment. Perfect for smuggling drugs, cash, maybe even a little girl. But in this case, a shotgun and a bag of xannies. Bobby's very own secret stash. *I'll pocket those later.*

"Know how to use it?" Roberto asked.

"Yes." And I wanted to. I grabbed the cold steel and the wooden stock. Hands trembling. Heart pounding. I tried to picture those college boys running for their lives through the cornfield.

"Keep the gun down and lower that left window. When I turn this baby around, you shoot. Understand?"

I answered with a pump.

The van was on our heels. Roberto gunned it. *God, don't let us draw any more attention.* Thank God, it was midday and normal people were at work.

As Roberto accelerated, I imagined bumping the curb at eighty and flipping off the road into a pole, but Roberto seemed to know what he was doing. He went just fast enough to open a gap between us and the van. As we swerved into a traffic circle, he tapped the brakes, spinning us sideways, then he slammed the brakes.

As the van roared toward my open window, I raised the barrel. As much as I wanted him dead, I couldn't do it.

My head slammed the rear window as Roberto slammed the gas. The silver van took the turn impossibly fast, struck the curb, flipped, and rolled.

Warmth surged through me. Twisted elation mixed with tears. That creep's cold stare flashed across my mind. I was a single-use, throw-away object for him. Who knew what they had in store for Cali, but the store was closed, and she was no longer for sale.

It took a few blocks for my heart to slow down. After about twenty minutes, Roberto glanced at the GPS on his phone and said, "Almost there."

CHAPTER 33
Michael

I walked outside as spoke to the 911 operator. Sirens screamed before I had finished the call. There were more cops and more flashing lights than I'd ever seen. I guess "a Federal Agent has been shot" is a magic phrase.

Cops in bulletproof vests bolted past me with guns drawn and eyes wide. A hefty fifty-something in a cheap suit marched toward me. He spoke in a tired-from-talking voice. "You Michael Williams?"

"Yes."

"Detective Kravitz." I could barely see his eyes for his eyebrows, but he glared at me. "What exactly were you doing here?"

"Agent Myers brought me here to stake out the building and watch for any signs of the girl I'd seen at the airport."

"The girl you saw at the airport? She a prostitute?"

"She was a little girl, an Indian girl." *Don't these people talk to each other?* "She looked terrified, and the whole scene felt out-of-place. Agent Myers thought she might be here."

"Was she?"

I hoped my nerves would cover for the lack of any poker face. "No sign of her, but we saw two men go inside. We waited until they left. The door was open, so we went in. No one was there, but the two men came back and started shooting."

"Describe."

"It was a blur, really, and it doesn't help that I got knocked out."

"Why do you suppose they didn't kill you?"

"I wasn't a threat. I'm not exactly a big guy, and I didn't have a gun."

"What do you remember?"

"The smaller guy pulled a gun and started shooting. Agent Myers shot back. They both went down. Next thing I remember is waking up on the floor."

As cops and investigators flooded the parking lot and the building, my thoughts and fears spun. Too many voices. Sirens. Lights. Occasional shoulder bumps as officers passed in and out of the building.

Kravitz raised an eyebrow. "Is that right?"

My gut lurched at his tone. I was a suspect again. My stomach rolled and, despite my best efforts, I slumped against the nearest police car and heaved my guts onto the pavement.

The detective stepped away and one of the investigators whispered in his ear. He glared at me and pointed to the officers standing outside.

"Keep an eye on him. Don't let him leave."

He rushed through the door, and my thoughts rushed after him. *What did they find? What did I miss? Did I leave fingerprints on something I shouldn't have touched? Do they think I killed the agent? Breathe, Michael.*

Kravitz waved a couple of officers closer as he walked straight toward me.

"Mr. Williams, can you explain the blood all over Agent Myers' hand but none on his gun?"

Heat surged through my face. I faked another heave. "I have no idea. I told you, I was knocked out. Can we talk after I see a doctor?"

CHAPTER 34
Emma

The lonely street was no yellow brick road. No street lights. Aging houses with brick porches and faded siding. Roberto slowed and stopped in front of the address Michael had directed them to. It looked like so many of the trash pits where had Bobby dumped us.

I choked on exhaust as I rolled up the window. Roberto's hand rested on mine. I could barely see his gentle stare in the darkness. I leaned into him, resting my head against his chest. I didn't want to leave him for a second. My protector. I certainly didn't want to go into that house.

I could still see every nameless face, their wagging tongues, sneers. The sting of their laughter and scowls. Their sweat and slime. Pinching, grabbing, groping. Their disgusting odors—everything from diesel fumes to urine. It didn't matter. They were all pigs. We were their fodder to devour and discard.

I knew this house wasn't the same. Same style. Same porch. But the trees were smaller, and someone had given this house some attention. Flowers lined the front of the house. The walk had been power washed. But to the terrified, naked-in-the-cornfield girl inside me, they were all the same and no place I ever wanted to enter again. Everything inside me wanted to run. But I didn't. I had to go into the house for Cali.

CHAPTER 35
Natalie

What seems like the end of the road is often a new beginning. These girls come to me desperate. I try to give them a fresh start.

It's not easy. It's never easy.

They've forgotten what hope is. Some have never felt it. Some are here because someone else hoped for them. That was Bliss. She had buried herself inside that little girl who'd been raped repeatedly by her step-dad then sold for sex by her "boyfriend."

But she's no longer anyone's property. She's free, or at least working on it. The real woman was still deep inside but trying to find her way out. Still calling herself Bliss, she couldn't or wouldn't remember her name.

I watched her and Tawnya. They had an obvious bond. Bliss clung to her like a big sister. On that night that changed everything, they sat together on the sofa in the front room. Normal stuff. Girl talk. Enjoying doing nothing.

But their eyes widened at the sound of a car rumbling down the street. Their faces made it obvious that it wasn't just any car. They knew the car by the sound. Hands clasped, they peered between the curtains.

Bliss screamed. "It's Bobby's car."

I wanted to call 911 so badly, but my history with a few of the local cops, one in particular, had killed my trust. I imagined those filthy scum listening to the dispatch and jumping on the chance to come screw with me and my girls. I wasn't about to let them ruin another dream.

"Come with me, ladies." I would house anywhere from two to eight women. Bliss made seven, not counting myself. The girls knew the drill. The girls hurried through the front room and into the kitchen. We had a secret door in the pantry. And it wasn't the first time we'd had to use it.

Everyone knew the drill. Tawnya stretched out her hand for Bliss.

But Bliss was glued to the window. "Emma's getting out!"

"Don't even think about it, baby girl," Tawnya said.

Bliss wriggled her hand free and dashed to the door and onto the porch. It wasn't the first time this kind of thing had happened. Some of these girls found twisted comfort in the cycle of abuse and protection they'd received from their pimps. And there Bliss ran, right back to his hand.

I turned off the inside lights, flipped on the outside lights, and watched through the front window. It wasn't unusual for a pimp to use another girl as bait. And the bait was holding a little Indian girl by the hand.

I wanted to throw up as Bliss ran toward them. She threw her arms around the woman, who stumbled backward. Even in the dim light, I could tell they were sobbing. Shoulders shaking. And a hug that could've lasted forever.

I cracked the door to listen and get and get a better look.

Bliss said, "Come inside." I immediately bristled. Skin on fire. Mothering instincts on high alert.

I stepped to the edge of the porch. "He's not coming in here."

CHAPTER 36
Emma

Cali looked at me with wide eyes and shook her head. She didn't want to leave the car. She didn't want to leave me. I understood her fear and was terrified for her. Strange world. Strange people. She'd finally met someone who cared, and I was passing her off to strangers.

I barely knew this girl, but I felt a pit in my stomach, a gnawing emptiness. I wanted to hold Cali forever and never let go. I wanted her to be mine—my little girl to love and to raise to become something special. I wanted her to always know she was loved. I swallowed bitter tears as I wondered how my *mother* could've passed me off on Gramps and Grams.

Roberto laid his hand on mine. "You should take her inside."

I couldn't stop the tears. I'd never felt real love, and now I was giving it away.

I shook my head and stuttered between sobs. "Maybe you should check it out first."

Roberto climbed out of the car. My heart raced. I didn't want him to leave—not even for a second. I wanted him to get back in the car, and the three of us could run away and somehow become a family.

Cali slid over the seat and into my lap. Roberto stopped in front of the car and stared at the house. The curtains opened just enough for someone to peek outside. As the porch lights turned on, I couldn't see a face. Maybe it was Bliss. Then it hit me. Bliss would likely be terrified to see Roberto.

"Cali, we need to go with him." I hopped out of the car and held her hand as we joined Roberto.

My heart jumped into my throat as the door swung open. I imagined a raging lunatic with a shotgun. Then Bliss burst through the doorway and rushed toward us. She buried me in a hug that almost knocked me down.

I cradled her face in my hands, and her eyes shined. I asked, "Why did you run?"

With a giddy, school-girl smile she said, "I'm gonna have a baby."

I felt a mix of joy and yuck. Who knows who the sperm donor was? And why would she want to be saddled with some schmuck's kid? Didn't matter. Bliss was beaming, and couldn't help but reflect her smile.

She was messed up but clever. Not a chance Bobby would've let her stay pregnant, let alone have a kid. So, she ran. I hugged her again.

"Michael helped you escape?"

She nodded. "He brought me here."

I couldn't help looking at her still-flat belly. "Do you know who's it is?"

She did her innocent hip twist, finger to her lips, and toe tap. "I'd like to think it was the groom from that bachelor party where we met Michael."

"You did it on purpose?"

She couldn't hide her blush or her smile. "He seemed like a nice guy."

Wow. He bought you for sex, and you think he's a nice guy. Maybe she was as dumb as I'd thought. "You didn't use a condom? Bliss! Really?"

Her smile turned to tears. "I can't stay in the life anymore."

The door swung open again, and a forty-something blonde stepped out. Even in the dim porch light, I could see her scowl. Elbows out. Fists on her hips.

Unfazed, Bliss said, "Come inside."

The blonde nodded toward Roberto, who stood behind me. "He's not coming in here."

Her stern tone meant business, and I wasn't about to cross her. "Roberto, you want to wait in the car?"

CHAPTER 37
Michael

"Looks like a grade II concussion, but your CT is clear."

The doctor's words gave me some relief. At least there was evidence that I'd been knocked out. But I feared his report wouldn't be enough for Kravitz.

The police escorted me out of the ER in silence. Headlights had replaced sunlight. The heat of the day left the night air thick and stale.

They drove me to the station and ushered me into one of those rooms like I'd seen in movies. Blank walls. Big window you can't see through. I imagined officers watching my every move. Did I look nervous? Guilty? What were they looking for? What were they waiting on?

I sat in silence, staring at the blank walls, the wrong side of the window, and the clock. I'd never felt paranoid before, but crazy fears were running away with what was left of my brain. And sleep deprivation didn't help.

Even the clock was behind bars. Caged up so inmates couldn't smash it. The cruel face of time stared me down as seconds, minutes, and hours ticked by. Nothing. Not a guard to talk to. Not another prisoner. Just me, alone with my exhausted and terrified reflection in the one-way glass.

Then it struck me. They're holding me to wear me down and coax me into a confession. What did they think I was going to confess to? I didn't do anything, and they wouldn't find my prints on either gun or any gunpowder residue on my hands. But my first introduction to Detective Kravitz didn't leave me feeling any sense of comfort. I imagined him grilling me for hours until I'd be burnt to a crisp.

The days, weeks, and years flashed before me. College. Grad school. New job. I was going to be a premier software developer, eventually start my own company. But not if Kravitz had his way. My life, just starting, felt like it was over.

Then the door opened. Two cops. Zero smiles. No handshake. They grabbed the two chairs opposite me. I winced as the chairs screeched across the floor. One officer, built like a retired linebacker, flipped his chair around and straddled it. The other, a scrawny guy who couldn't hide his smile with his forced glare, tossed a stack of papers and photos in front of me and leaned into my face. His giddy smile made me wonder if I was his first interrogation.

Officer Congeniality tapped on one page. "Doc says 'patient *states* he was knocked out.' Did you know it's hard for a physician to definitely prove someone was actually knocked out? They basically take your word for it."

My stomach rolled as he continued.

"You didn't even need stitches, but lucky for you, you at least had a little goose egg."

He tapped the back of my skull, and I winced. I wanted to scream. I wanted to smack him. But I kept cool—on the outside.

Inside, I was picturing myself in handcuffs. Ankles chained together. Walking down an eerie prison corridor. Dim lights. The only noise, the ringing in my ears. I imagined sitting alone counting days until days no longer mattered. And dreading my turn to lie down, stare at the surgical lights, and take the needle.

"Williams!" The linebacker cop smacked the table. "Are you listening?"

I nodded.

"Killing an FBI agent is a capital crime." He kept talking as the door opened and Kravitz joined the party. "We're not talking time or life in prison. We're talking the chair, so you'd better start talking."

As Kravitz stepped toward me, my head throbbed. My eyes ached and burned. Vision drifted sideways. Ears rang. And the room fell silent and dark.

I opened my eyes to a dusty floor pressing against my cheek. Patent leather shoes stood sideways in front of me, and Officer Congeniality's face leaned into mine. The knot on my skull pounded as though I'd slammed into a concrete wall.

I closed my eyes and opened them to the ceiling rushing over me and faces of paramedics bouncing above me. A gurney vibrated beneath me, and its wheels squeaked in rhythm as my world went dark again.

* * *

"You're back." The doctor smiled. "I didn't expect to see you again—at least not so soon." He looked up. His crinkled brow told me the police were behind me, waiting their turn. He looked past me and spoke sternly. "I told you he'd lost consciousness. Concussions are serious business." He shook his head. "But I guess you respect your own medical judgment over mine. There'll be no more questions for this man today. His mind needs to rest. Unless it's a matter of life or death, you need to give him a couple of days before pressing him."

CHAPTER 38
Emma

Bliss dashed up the steps and grabbed the woman's shoulders. "They're okay. I swear. Selene... Emma is my friend."

The woman said, "What about Roberto? Doesn't he work with your pimp?"

I moved toward them, not brave enough or stupid enough to climb the steps, just brave enough to say, "Bobby's dead. Roberto is with me. And we don't work for anyone."

The blonde stood her ground and maintained tight fists. "Dead? What happened?"

"FBI shot him. That's how we escaped."

"You expect me to believe everything's fine because you tell me your pimp is dead, but you're here with his minion?"

"I'm not here for me." I tugged on Cali's hand. She was clinging to my waist and hiding behind me. "We need a safe place for her." She stuck her head out—too scared to smile. She looked up at me, and I knelt in front of her and kissed her forehead. "I want you to be safe and never have to see those bad men again."

The blonde shuffled down the steps. The porch light revealed the tears winding down her cheeks. She squatted beside me and whispered. "I don't know what to do with a little girl."

I nodded toward Bliss. "You think you're taking care of big girls here? Most of them are still little girls trapped in women's bodies. Childhoods stolen. They've got no idea how to be big girls." I looked into Cali's deep brown eyes. "I imagine this little girl has seen more than most of your big girls, and she needs you."

"What about you?"

"I don't know about me." Those words stung as they rolled off my lips. I didn't know about me at all. I'd lost myself if I'd ever known myself. Tears streamed, and my voice trembled. "I think she'll be safer with you—and safer if Roberto and I run. Hopefully the creeps who were selling her will think she's with us."

"You're not scared?" the blonde asked.

"I'm terrified, but I'm used to it. She shouldn't have to be."

This total stranger pulled me close and wrapped me in a hug. She knew my pain. I could feel a deep, inexplicable strength in her arms as her heart beat with mine. She looked into my eyes. "I've lived with the same fear. You and I are so much alike. I will do everything to keep her safe."

She turned to Cali and held out her hand. Cali's hand was so tiny in hers. "My name's Natalie. What's yours?"

"Cali."

"Cali. That's a pretty name. I promise to keep you safe, and Emma will come see you as often as she can."

I could see it in Natalie's eyes. I knew she meant well, but we both knew her safety was beyond our control.

* * *

I've been through a lot, and I've seen my share of tears. But I've never cried like I did when I left that girl behind. I waved, but I couldn't look. I felt like I did that day Gramps tossed me in his truck and forced me into that clinic. They sucked the life out of me—that tiny life no one wanted except me.

I was young, but I knew the game. As much as I despised Johnny Paul, having his child would have meant emancipation, welfare, Medicaid, an apartment, school, freedom, and a life of my own—away from Gramps and Grams. Away from Nowheresville. And she—I like to think the baby was a girl—she would've been my shot at redemption. And she would have been my daughter, whom I would have loved the way a child should be loved.

But to my grandparents, my little girl was a blight. She would've been the living evidence of even more shame, and they were willing to kill to hide that shame. I never got to hold her, name her, even bury her. She was "clump of cells" and a "medical procedure."

But I was her mother.

And now I felt like Cali had been ripped away from me too. But she was going to be hidden and safe. Why hadn't I hid my baby girl from Gramps? How had he even known? I suspected Johnny Paul's dad had figured it out and told him. Doesn't matter. They were all dead to me.

But Cali was very much alive. And I wanted to keep it that way.

CHAPTER 39
Michael

I'd never had a hangover, but, when my phone woke me from a dead sleep, I felt instant, skull-splitting pain. I reached for my nightstand, but the table wasn't there. I saw stark, gray walls. The hospital. A tiny pulse of light blinked from inside a plastic bag by the window. My phone. I wanted to grab it, smash it, make it stop, but I couldn't move. My head throbbed. Finally, a nurse clomped into the room. Every footstep rattled my brain. She grabbed my phone and silenced it.

Our eyes met, and she mouthed "sorry" and trotted out of the room. I wasn't awake enough to speak. After she closed the door, my eyes fought to stay open, but sleep won.

* * *

Have you ever had one of those dreams where everything's right in the world? I was having that kind of dream. A sun-drenched valley of wildflowers. A winding, untamed stream. Warm breeze. Distant, snow-capped mountains. And a perfectly clear sky.

In the distance, I saw a beautiful young girl with long, golden hair wearing a simple white dress dotted with flowers. She twirled in carefree circles and waved at butterflies. Young and innocent. And when she looked at me, she smiled. It was Bliss.

She slowly waltzed toward me. As she grew closer, she grew taller. When she smiled, I no longer saw Bliss but Sam. I felt her hand on mine. Soft and warm.

"Michael."

The voice startled me. I gasped, opened my eyes, and sat up. Thank God, my headache had finally dulled. I blinked to take in the sight. It was Sam seated at my bedside. "I didn't expect to see you." My voice came out raspy, and I cleared my throat. "How did you know I was here?"

"I needed some alone time to think, so I sent Kyle on an errand. I tried to call you to apologize for getting you stuck in the middle of our mess, but you didn't answer. I don't know why, but it made me nervous. Everything has been so… wrong since we got home. I checked your location, and it said you were here at the hospital." She leaned back in her chair, sighed and smiled. "When I realized you were in the hospital and weren't answering your phone, I feared the worst. I'm glad I found you. I'm glad you're okay."

I swallowed my tears. My throat ached and I couldn't find any words. As I looked into Sam's eyes, I wanted to go back to my dream, to that carefree girl dancing among the flowers.

But that girl was gone forever, and so were my dreams. I closed my eyes to hide my tears. I felt her gentle hand wiping my cheeks.

I opened my eyes and said, "I'm a murder suspect."

"What?" Sam shrieked.

My head throbbed. "Remember the silver van at the airport? They found it, and an FBI agent brought me along on a stakeout to see if I recognized anyone. It's a long story, but suffice it to say, he got shot. I got knocked out. And the police want to pin it on me."

"How could you kill anyone if you were unconscious? How could they think you'd kill anyone period?"

"It doesn't make sense. I know someone has to be guilty, but this detective doesn't seem to care who it is or if they've even got the real killer. Either quick justice looks better than no justice, or there's something going on that I don't understand."

"So what happened?"

"We were searching the building where this pimp kept his girls. The agent thought he may have had some connection with the girl from the airport. The dirtball surprised us, blasted the agent, and the agent shot him. They both died."

I told her the whole story. Roberto. Emma. The girl from the airport. All of it.

When I finished, she said, "No reasonable jury would ever convict you." I'd seen that look on her face a thousand times. It was the you're-the-sweetest-guy-I-know look. I blushed even though she hadn't said a word. Even though I'd let her down in the worst way, she still looked at me like I was some kind of hero.

Her soft hand pressed against my cheek, and she leaned toward me and kissed my forehead. As sweet as it was, I was sorry that was all I would ever get from Sam. I was the nice guy—the dullsville guy and nothing like Kyle.

"If Kyle were more like you, we'd never have gotten into this mess."

I reached for her hand and held it. So tiny compared to mine. So vulnerable. And decorated with her stunning ring. I couldn't help but think *what a beautiful lie.* Kyle had married the most perfect woman I could imagine. He didn't deserve her, and she didn't deserve what he'd done to her, or what he'd taken away. But I knew Kyle, and as reckless as he'd been, I knew he loved her, and he wished he could turn back time and set things right.

I gently squeezed and stroked the back of her hand with my thumb. "Sam."

She blushed. "I think I should go."

CHAPTER 40
Emma

Windows down. Wind in my hair. I was free like never before. Free, but empty, unable to see anything but Cali's sweet face, her tears, and her arms that begged me to stay.

Roberto held my hand as he drove. "You okay?" His smooth, Latino accent soothed my nerves.

I guess my tears had given me away.

"Why are you crying? You're free. Bobby's dead. Donny ain't gonna mess with you no more." He pumped his biceps. "He can try, but it won't do no good. And he ain't stupid."

I chuckled and wiped my tears. "I'm not afraid of Donny or anyone else. What can they do to me that's not already been done? Nothing."

"You crying for Cali?"

My gentle giant knew my heart. I dreamed of wrapping my arms around her like I did when she was afraid. I wanted to hold on to that moment forever.

But it was never going to happen.

We were headed south on US 41. I could hardly wait to leave Atlanta behind us. Roberto gripped the steering wheel as a semi barreled toward us. The truck swerved just in time to miss us. If it hadn't, we would've certainly died. I crushed the fleeting thought of grabbing the wheel and forcing the car into the next semi.

But my stubborn heart would not let go. As much as I wanted to die, I couldn't stop thinking about Cali.

Roberto squeezed my hand. "You thinking about the girl or yourself?"

"What do you mean?"

"You did the right thing leaving her. She needs people who can help her."

"You're saying I can't help her?"

"What do you think?" I heard the sarcasm in his tone, and my skin bristled. Selene was ready to pounce on him if Emma flinched.

Roberto continued. "You ready to have a kid? Be a mother? Would you even know what to do?"

"I thought you were on my side?"

"I'm right here. I'm on your side, and I won't let you beat yourself up when you did the right thing."

The right thing? What was the right thing? When Gramps and Gram took me in, they did it because it was "the right thing." But I'm pretty sure I would have been better off with anyone else. Maybe the same was

true for Cali.
 Maybe I was the *right thing* for Cali.

CHAPTER 41
Michael

Detective Kravitz burst through the door as soon as Sam left.

"All better now?" He grabbed a chair, scooted next to my bed, and sat.

I pressed the nurse call light. "I haven't see the doctor yet this morning."

"I have questions that can't wait."

I glared at him. "I've got nothing to hide. I was unarmed and unconscious."

He scowled, and a wicked smile stretched across his face. "The gun was wiped clean." He leaned in, his hot, ashtray breath in my face. "You know something you're not telling me. You're protecting someone. I suggest you forget about it and protect yourself." He stood as footsteps approached my door.

The nurse popped in. "Is everything okay?"

Her smiled faded when Detective Kravitz edged past her. "I didn't think you were allowed to question him until he is released by his doctor."

"I was just checking on our star witness. Gotta make sure he's healthy enough to tell the truth."

CHAPTER 42
Natalie

Cali's smooth black hair barely touched her shoulders. She had mesmerizing dark eyes. She was dainty and flawless. No wonder the creeps wanted her. She would've been their gold mine. And they would have mined her until she was spent.

But little girls aren't meant to be mined. They're meant to be loved. I could do that much, but I had no clue what else to do to raise a child, and I was too old to start.

It had been a long day, and I desperately needed sleep, and so did Cali, I'm sure. But she was wide-eyed and staring at the street.

The air was strangely cool for a midsummer evening, so she drew close to me, and we sat on the porch swing. She lay her against my chest, stretched her arm across me, and fell asleep. I gently stroked her hair and hummed. My grandma used to do the same. She was the only solid human being in my long line of trash, but when she got too old, too forgetful, life discarded her.

As I slid my fingers through Cali's hair, I couldn't help but love her like Grandma had loved me. I lost myself in the moment. Swinging back and forth. Cool breeze in my face. The warmth of her tiny frame on my lap. All my worries on hold.

Until headlights rounded the corner and immediately went dark. A chill shot up my spine. I lurched from the swing. Cali awakened with wide eyes. I scooped Cali into my arms and dashed into the house.

Bliss had fallen asleep on the sofa but awakened with a jolt as I flung the door open. I handed Cali to Bliss and skootched them toward the kitchen, then I slid off the porch into the bushes and peered down the street. The rumble of an engine and tires grew closer and slowed. I caught a glimpse of the vehicle as it passed a neighbor's security light. A large dark SUV. No markings, but I saw the dim flicker of a cigarette.

My already-racing heart flipped into overdrive when the vehicle stopped a few houses down and the engine stopped. I patted my pocket to make sure I still had my phone. Momentary silence and stillness. Then, doors opened and shut. I imagined four huge thugs wearing black and toting guns heading straight for us. Everything inside me wanted to scream, but I waited.

Nothing. No footsteps. No voices. No flashlights.

I couldn't stand it. I could feel them coming. Outstanding warrants, drugs, who knew what my girls might had been hiding, but none of it would matter if we were all dead. I took a chance and called 911.

I whispered to the operator, "There's a large black SUV driving slowly with its headlights off. It stopped. At least four people got out. I couldn't really see, but I heard all four doors open. I think they're coming." I rattled off the address. "Please hurry."

Who was I kidding? We were in a no-name neighborhood. If anyone did come, it would be to pronounce us dead and scrape up the pieces for the eleven o'clock news.

The *pop pop pop* of at least two guns exploded from the street. I crouched lower, every nerve in my body trembling.

"Were those gunshots?" the operator asked, her voice pitched higher than it had been before.

I wasn't about to respond, not with armed men *right there*.

"Stay on the line," she said. "Help is on the way."

I heard car doors open and shut and an engine start. "They're leaving." I almost shouted into the phone as I stepped closer to the street. The taillights sailed down the street, around the corner, and out of sight. Without thinking, I ran to where the SUV had stopped and saw a sedan with its doors open and blood-covered bodies hanging out.

A distant voice grew louder. The operator. The phone. I lifted it to my ear, but I couldn't talk.

"Ma'am." She somehow remained calm. "What happened? What do you see?"

I couldn't see anything through my tears. When I stepped closer to the car, I stammered, "Two men. Shot."

"Are they breathing?"

I tried to look, only took in unseeing eyes. More blood.

"Dead, I think. There's blood everywhere."

CHAPTER 43
Natalie

Squealing tires and sirens. I'd never seen so many police vehicles. Ambulances and Fire and Rescue followed. A bit much for our always-forgotten neighborhood. At least a dozen cops hopped out of their cars. Guns drawn. Eyes up and down the street.

One of them made a beeline toward me. Silhouetted by all the lights, but I could tell his suit was a little small, and he'd had few more donuts than your average cop. "You the 911 caller?" I nodded. He snatched my phone and held it to his ear. "Police on the scene. We'll take it from here."

Strange that he didn't give the operator his name. His walk, his demeanor—everything about him took me back to those awful nights watching for johns and cops. Standing in the cold, in the rain, in the dark. Dripping with sweat on July nights. It didn't matter where or when, every time I heard a siren or saw the lights, my stomach would flip, my heart would race, and I'd scramble to hide.

Real life is nothing like the movies. We didn't wear short skirts or fishnet hose. There were no pimps in gold necklaces and thousand-dollar sneakers showing off the girls. I'd wear jeans, sneakers, and a baggy sweatshirt. Anything less, and I would've been busted for sure. A bag of groceries was my favorite prop.

The johns knew the difference. They'd slow down, pull toward the curb, and watch for a response. Any self-respecting woman would move away from the curb, walk faster, or even run. But I'd breeze over to the car like we were old friends.

The cops knew the difference as well, and they'd be watching from a block or two away. The second I'd lean toward that car window, their lights would flash and the siren would whirr. In my mind, it was like some kind of sick guy code so the john could scoot away and they could bust the whore.

After more than ten years out of the life, I should've been free of those fears, but when I saw that cop and heard his tone, I felt a new, deeper fear—for myself and every one of my girls. I didn't dare look toward the house or think of walking that direction.

The cop handed me my phone and clicked on his flashlight. I'm sure he gave me a quick once over. I squinted at the beam in my eyes. Every time I thought I might catch a better look at his face, he'd shine that spotlight in my face.

"You want to tell me what you were doing out here and what you saw?"

I jumped at his tone.

My years in the clubs and hotels taught me how to think fast, how to act, and how to lie. I turned it all on. Instant tears. Stammer. Fidget. "Oh, my gosh! I was walking Ginger, my dog, when this SUV passed. She jolted after it and tore the leash right out of my hand. When they stopped, four men got out, and Ginger was going nuts. She must have sensed something was wrong."

I covered my face, sniffled, shook my head, and fanned my face. "One of them kicked her and she ran away." I looked around as if seeking my dog. "I don't know where she went. I have to find her."

"Could you forget your dog for a minute? Did you see their faces?"

"I couldn't, but I was afraid they had stopped because I was walking alone, so I called 911. While I was on the phone, I heard the gunshots. Thank goodness you came when you did. I think they would have shot me next, but I heard the sirens, and they did too, then they took off."

"Where's your dog now?"

Come on tears. Blubbering. I shook my head and folded my hands, pretending to pray. "I have to find Ginger. She hasn't come back."

Just as I felt like my ruse was working, he looked past me and asked, "Who's your friend?"

Oh, dear God! I wheeled around to see Bliss smiling into his flashlight like a living Barbie doll. I grabbed her shoulders and pulled her close. "Oh, honey. Did you hear the gunshots?" I whispered into her ear. "Pretend you're my cousin visiting from Iowa."

Bliss swooped around me and extended her hand to the cop. "I'm Agatha, her cousin from Iowa."

"You look familiar."

"I get that a lot. I guess you always look like someone."

I nudged her and said, "Ginger ran away."

Bliss gave a sad pucker then hugged me, hiding her face on my shoulder.

I imagined the cuffs coming out and feared that familiar sting on my wrists. Thank God it was dark and the cop had a crime scene behind him. When he glanced over his shoulder, I motioned for Bliss to head back to the house, then I stepped past him toward the crime-scene tape.

"Where are you going?"

"Nowhere. Sorry. I'm just so messed up right now. I can't think." I stood and stared at the shot-up car, the blood, the ambulances, and I covered my face and sobbed.

I had no idea if he was buying any of it, but at least Bliss had sneaked away and I wasn't in cuffs—yet.

CHAPTER 44
Michael

Kravitz screamed into his phone. "Who got shot?" He threw me a quick glare and bolted out the door, bumping into my nurse.

She twisted as he blasted past. Her gaze followed him down the hall. As his clunky footsteps faded, she rolled her eyes, stepped into my room and smirked. "I guess you're free to go. Officer Whatshisface is gone, and the doctor has released you."

She opened the cabinet and tossed me my phone as if she'd read my mind.

I stared at it, not sure who to call. A notification popped up. *Breaking News.* As a faithful news junkie, I tapped the screen.

Shooting Near East Side: Officers Down.

I relived the scene with Agent Myers and Salinas. Gunshots ringing in my ears. The burnt smell of gunpowder. And the blurry image the agent falling. Emma out of nowhere. Her bodyguard. Then nothing.

It was too fresh. Too real. One of those bullets could have easily blown me away—easily blown Emma away. She had enough of her life taken away already.

As I opened the article, I caught a glimpse of the address. The shooting had taken place on Kessler Street.

That's what I'd left Bliss. That's where I'd sent Emma. Had the cops had come for her? Why would there be gunshots? Police down? Where would she get a gun? Would she know how to use it? No way. It had to be one of Salinas's thugs.

If they shot the police officers, what would they do to Emma and Bliss? Even if I were thinking clearly, I could never get there fast enough. Somehow, through my brain haze, I remembered that forty-something blonde.

Natalie.

Thank God I'd added her to my contacts.

She answered on the first ring, panting. "Can't talk."

I heard sirens in the background. "Is Bliss okay? Is Emma—?"

She hung up.

I fired off a text. "I'm coming."

No response.

I called again.

No answer. No voicemail.

A thousand scenarios whirred through my mind. Emma and Bliss gone. Maybe Roberto had snatched them. Cops tried to arrest Emma. Bliss got shot in crossfire. Maybe Natalie wasn't who she claimed to be.

Whatever happened had to be awful, and my mind wouldn't rest, not until I'd seen Emma.

The faint voice of reason asked why I should care. She was just a prostitute.

She's more.

I hated that nagging, gotta-save-her feeling.

I threw on my clothes and flew out the door. As soon as I stepped outside, I remembered my Explorer was at home. No time for that. I hopped into a cab. "3316 Kessler. Please."

* * *

A band of yellow tape stretched across the street, and police covered the whole block. Pain gripped my chest as though I'd eaten ghost peppers on an empty stomach.

The driver slowed. Blue and red lights flashing. Spotlights on a dark sedan. News crew. "Where should I drop you off? Can't turn here."

"Around the corner is fine." I gave him forty bucks and hopped out.

These old neighborhoods, with no street lights and every third house empty, creeped me out. I trotted down the sketchy sidewalk, stumbling in the dark over cracked and uneven sections. Dogs barking. Doors opening and shutting. Silhouettes of gawkers between houses.

Then I saw Natalie across the street as I looked between two of the houses. I knew it was her. Spotlights from rescue vehicles lit up her side of the street, and I couldn't miss her big hair and big personality. Arms waving as she shouted something at... *Kravitz.*

I knew he came because of the shooting, but how is Natalie involved, and if Natalie is involved, is Emma involved? Bliss? Did one of them get shot?

Emma, I hope you're okay.

I had to get to that house. I had to know. Forget the ghost-pepper stomach. I was more worried about not messing my pants and not getting caught. Kravitz was already suspicious. I couldn't let him find me here.

I was still in the shadows. Thank God. I stayed out of the light as I backed onto the sidewalk behind me and headed further down the street, peeking between houses as I went. When I was more than halfway down the block, I figured I was close enough to Natalie's house. Maybe I could sneak through a side yard and across the street. And hopefully find Emma and Bliss.

I hadn't expected it, but tears dribbled down my cheek. It wasn't so much sudden sadness as emotional exhaustion. My life had been so simple, but there I was skulking through the dark to see if two prostitutes and a little girl were still alive.

The thought of caring and getting involved would have been

ridiculous only weeks before, but, at that moment, it was my only thought.

Deep, deep breath. I blew it out slowly. Stretched and jiggled my legs. *Come on, Michael.* I glanced up and down the street to gather my bearings. When I was almost across from Natalie's house, I realized how close I'd been to the smoking-housecoat woman's home. A chill zipped up my spine. All the police cars were in front of that house.

The police weren't there for Emma or Bliss. They must have been there for the old lady and those goons from the silver van.

I darted between the houses and almost impaled myself on a gas meter. I dodged a trash can and a scavenging cat. *Way to alert the neighbors.* Thank God for all the commotion and flashing lights. Maybe no one would notice the idiot stumbling over himself in the dark.

I ducked behind a parked car. I could see Natalie's house with the lights on and the curtains drawn. No movement on the porch.

Then, I heard footsteps on the street and saw a shadow walking my direction. I slid along the back of the car, hoping to hide beside it on the sidewalk, but I caught my toe on the curb, tripped over the sidewalk, and sprawled onto the grass.

"Michael?"

Bliss? I lay there feeling the sacrifice of my manhood and bruises on more than my elbows. Thank God it was dark.

"Are you okay?" Her hand on my shoulder sent my skin tingling. How I hated that war of emotions. I would never think of using Bliss or anyone like her, but I couldn't help the feelings any more than she could fight her looks or the impact of her touch.

"I'm fine." I groaned as I pushed myself off the cracked cement.

"What are you doing here?"

"I saw the news, and I had to know you, Cali, and Emma were safe."

"Cali and me are safe, but Emma left with Roberto."

My heart sank at the thought of Emma on the run, but what choice did she really have.

Bliss took my hand and led me across the street.

I couldn't help looking down the street. A flurry of cops and paramedics. Strange how black body bags reflect so much light. Amid all the commotion, I saw the silhouettes of stout man in a suit and a big-haired woman arguing. Had to be Kravitz and Natalie. *Keep him occupied, girl.*

Bliss tugged on my elbow. "Let's go inside."

As we approached the steps, a woman's voice shouted from inside. "Man!" Footsteps and silhouettes scrambled. Tawnya stood in the doorway, hands raised against the doorframe, hip cocked to one side. I didn't have to see her face to read the expression. "Y'ain't comin' in here. Ain't *no* man coming in this house."

Bliss stepped in front of me. "He's not a man. He's Michael." Her bouncy little-girl voice was pink Himalayan salt in my wound. And Tawyna's belly laugh didn't help either, but she opened the door.

Fifties-style home. Dark wood molding around the door frames. Ancient fixtures. Push-button light switches. Tiny doors. Tiny kitchen with one of those metal tables like my grandma used to have. Fresh paint. Some kind of auburn or acorn squash color. New carpet smell.

Bliss did a spin. Arms wide open. "Isn't it great?"

I fake smiled. Couldn't help but think of the house where we'd first met.

Tawyna stepped between us, pursed her lips. "It don't look like much, but it's better than anything these girls has ever seen. And we been working hard to make it look good." She nudged my shoulder. "You don't have to like it, but I ain't never seen you in here doin' nothing to make it better."

I don't know who was scarier, Kravitz or her. She must've seen the angst in my face because she burst into laughter. "I'm just messing with you." She stepped back, hand on her hip and waving finger. "You didn't do nothing."

I like this girl. She was captivating. A mix of guilt and nausea swished inside, and I couldn't look at her.

Her nudge got stronger, and she pushed me backward. "What's wrong with you? You can't look at me without seeing a hooker?"

I shook my head, and she shoved me onto a sofa. I buried my face in my hands—expecting a slap any second, but someone's backside bumped against my hands.

"Don't you touch him." Bliss to my rescue.

The sofa shook as Tawnya collapsed beside me then leaned close. "You gots a lot to learn, freshness. You look at me feelin' all guilty like you a big sinner, but you ain't even been with a woman, has you?"

Another shot to my manhood. I couldn't respond. *Let her think what she wants.*

Bliss crashed beside me and leaned toward Tawnya. "Leave him alone. What's he done to you?"

"Girl, it ain't what he's done. It's what he's thinking. He's one of them. You seen the way he looks at you—the way he looks at me. Probably the way he looks at anything with smooth skin, silky hair, anything close to this." Tawnya stood as she spoke and did a small twirl.

I'm a dead man. If that cop doesn't toss me in the shark tank, these girls are going to make me wish he had.

I folded my hands as in desperate prayer. "I wanted to help. That's why I brought Bliss here. Then I saw the news and…"

The door flung open and banged the wall. Pictures and lights rattled. Natalie's voice boomed. "What's he doing here?" She glared at Tawnya, Bliss, and the other girls. "You know the rules!" She spun toward me. "And you! You can't be here. Not now. The cops are on their way. They'll be here any second." She glared at Tawnya. "You know what to do." I guess Tawnya didn't move fast enough. Natalie stomped her foot. Veins popping in her neck. Face red. "Do it now."

Tawnya clenched my elbow like I'd never felt. I was the naughty kid in a fifties classroom, and she was the spinster teacher dragging me by the ear. I knew better than to say a word or resist. She pulled me through the kitchen into the pantry, pulled an over-sized trashcan away from the wall, slid a small rug with her foot, then lifted a trap door.

She stretched out her hand and smiled like a torturer inviting her victim into the dungeon. I peered over the hole at the rickety steps then worked my way down into the dark.

"There's a string to your right. Pull it."

As the light clicked on, I was surprised to see a finished space. Area rugs. A hodgepodge of furniture. A mini fridge. And a boxy TV. "You guys must come down here a lot."

"No time to talk, Romeo. Gotta get the girls down there to watch you."

I slunk into the Goodwill reject sofa, the kind you'd find at the end of someone's driveway. I felt years of dust poof into the air around me and wished I'd held my breath.

Bliss hopped down the steps. Did her best Vanna White and said, "Isn't it great? It's like playing hide and seek with TV and snacks." Her cutesy girl face turned serious. "But we can't use the bathroom—can't flush or use water until we get the all clear. Oh, and we can't really watch TV or make any noise unless…" She pointed up the stairs. "Unless that door's open."

She plopped beside me.

New dust cloud. I coughed and sneezed. She laughed.

What am I doing here?

You didn't have to come. You could have run—still could.

The trap door was open. I could make a mad dash, but Kravitz… With my luck, I'd crash into him, and they'd add assault to my list of charges.

Footsteps grew louder overhead, and the other girls flew down the steps followed by Tawnya. She pulled the door shut and shushed everyone with her threatening eyes and her finger pressed against her lips. She wagged her pointer at Bliss then me and mouthed, "Not one word."

She tossed a pen and notebook onto the coffee table and motioned for us to write instead of talk.

As she locked eyes with me, I thought *I'm not crossing you, girl. Not now. Not ever.*

And there we sat. Waiting. Glued to our phones in silence until Bliss said, "Where's Cali?"

Skin tingling. Heart pounding. I jumped to my feet. "Cali? She's here?"

Tawnya scowled and shoved me onto the sofa. "What part of shut up do you *not* understand? You want the cops down here?"

A silent nod seemed like my safest response, but I couldn't contain myself. I stood toe to toe and looked into her eyes. "I want to see her and know she's safe."

Tawnya lowered her chin. "Bliss was right. You ain't like no man I ever seen."

"I want to see her."

"Your girl is safe with me. And that's all you get."

A door slammed, and I flinched. Probably the front door and probably Natalie's signal that the police were there.

CHAPTER 45
Emma

Cars and semis stacked I-75, but Roberto and I were weaving in and out of traffic, flying. I imagined blue and red flashing lights behind us at any second.

"Don't you think you should slow down?"

Roberto eased off the pedal. He blinked, rubbed his eyes, then slammed another shot of his energy drink.

"Where are we going?"

"My cousin Ernesto lives in Miami," Roberto said. "He can get us legit jobs. We can stay with him and my Tía Mariela until we get a place."

I wanted to believe him, but my stomach knotted and I wondered if he was for real. Or was his plan to be my new pimp with new promises?

I wanted it to be true, this fresh start. But too many things could go wrong. I could only trust myself.

I couldn't change anything at that moment, and Miami was still hours away. Plenty of time to worry about what-ifs, but, for the moment, I chose to believe. I buried my doubts and lay my head on his shoulder. "A place of our own sounds nice."

I stroked his silky-smooth bronze skin and ran my fingers down his arm. Goosebumps rose on his skin, and I allowed myself to enjoy knowing I'd done that. As many times as he'd saved me from Bobby's fist, he surely loved me. But if he didn't, I'd sooner slit his throat than let him drag me back into the life.

Lightning filled distant clouds. The wind picked up, and Roberto gripped the wheel with both hands. Mist from the wet pavement flicked off of the road and dotted our windshield.

"Looks like it rained." I rolled down my window, inhaled that after-the-rain freshness, and tried to not think about the approaching storm. A bolt of lightning splintered a tree. Thunder shook the car, and I jumped out of my seat.

Roberto's eyes rounded. No energy drink could match the power of fear. He hammered the gas. "That was too close."

I held out my hand. "Roberto, let me borrow your phone to see how big this storm is."

* * *

I'd never seen so many apps and had no idea what most of them were since my Spanish is lousy. I meant to tap his weather app, but I touched the local news for Atlanta.

Police Officers Shot.

Something in the photo caught my eye. Then I read Kessler Street and recognized Natalie beside a police officer. I couldn't make out her face, but the hair, the sweater, the height—it was definitely her.

"What are you doing?"

"I can't find your weather app."

He snatched the phone. Swiped. Tapped. Handed it back.

I stared at the screen. The storm stretched from the Gulf across Louisiana and up the east coast. We would be in it for hours, but the storm didn't matter. None of it mattered anymore. I kept seeing Natalie standing by a cop and the headlines. *Police Officers Shot.* The article probably said nothing about Bliss or Cali, but I couldn't flip back through his phone to find the article without raising suspicion. *We've got to go back.* I had to know they were safe. I had to know Cali was safe.

I had to see her—to be with her. And deep in my gut, thinking something may have happened made me doubt I could ever willingly leave her again.

I glanced at the weather app and lay my free hand on Roberto's shoulder. "You really want to drive through this storm in the middle of the night?"

His phone vibrated in my hand. *A text.* I flipped it over. The text was from Ernesto. My heart thumped as I read *Do you have the girl?* I lay the phone face down on his thigh hoping it would vibrate again so he'd see the message and not know I'd seen it.

It vibrated again. He glanced at the screen.

I sipped his energy drink, finished the last of it and crumpled the can. "We should stop and get a bite to eat."

He gave me a look, and I gave him my little-girl pouty face. "Let's get out of the storm. I'm hungry, and it's crazy late."

He smiled.

I got him. He had no idea I'd seen the text. One thing the life taught me was to read a man's thoughts by the tiniest change of expression.

He took the next exit. "We'll grab some food then find a rat trap that'll take cash."

Gas. Mini Mart. Liquor store. Perfect. We stopped for gas. I pumped while Roberto went into the liquor store. He was nowhere in sight, so I snuck into the back seat, lifted it and grabbed Bobby's little stash of xannies. I was surprised he hadn't given me more since he liked what he thought they did to me. He said they settled me down, and I could go forever with just a couple of them. But I'd learned to hoard them, and had become a good faker. Learned it from Bliss. *No one uses their real names. No one shows their real feelings.*

She seemed like a ditz, but she was shrewd, beyond street smart.

She was a survivor. And I was too. I'd gotten so use to Bobby's demands, so used to becoming Selene, that I didn't need xannies for him. I'd built up my stash in case it ever got to the point of giving up all hope, but the cops had snatched them.

Time to use Bobby's stash—on Roberto.

CHAPTER 46
Emma

    Roberto slept in the backseat. No idea what hit him, I'm sure. Although he'd probably had enough tequila to knock himself out, my xannies made it certain. I'd thought of leaving him at a cheap hotel or on a bus to Miami, but I chose to believe he was still my friend—my prince. He had saved me from Bobby, after all.

    I had no choice but to knock him out. He already had plans to build a new life with his family. I couldn't see him agreeing to go back to Atlanta first. I used his phone to text his cousin. "Change of plans. Going back to Atlanta. Girl in trouble."

    I ignored the flurry of texts that followed, glad I'd silenced Roberto's phone even though the dings probably wouldn't have awakened him anyway. I chuckled at his face in the rearview mirror. Mouth hanging open, oozing drool and vibrating as he snored. I hoped he would wake up as my teddy bear and not a grizzly.

    Deep sigh. I pulled onto the interstate and hammered it. I couldn't get to Bliss and Cali fast enough. Going eighty-five should get us there in no time.

    I prayed they'd be okay.

CHAPTER 47
Natalie

When I was still in the life, my worst customers had been cops—one in particular, Sergeant Kravitz. That detective reminded me so much of that lowlife. He marched down the sidewalk silhouetted in the streetlights. Smoke trail following. I could already smell the blend of ashtray and cheap cologne.

I stood my ground on the front porch as I had so many times. I wished I had enough nerve to stand there with a shotgun. If I ever saw that douchebag again, I just might blow him away. But you can't always live out your dreams. I had to at least pretend to be a good girl.

As he plodded toward my steps, I said, "You need something else?"

"Mind if I come inside?"

"You got a reason, or you just want to visit?"

He clicked up the steps and past me. I flew to the door and held it shut.

He took one step back and glared at me. Even in the dim light of my front porch, I knew that look. I'd seen it a million times. That look said, "You're nothing. You're a cheap whore. You're not even worth the fifty bucks." On and on. That look said everything no woman should ever hear or feel. It stirred such a war in me. I fought to not lump all men into that same cesspool, fought to keep my cool. Good thing I didn't have that shotgun.

He pressed closer, and I felt pinned between him and the door. Shaking inside. I prayed the girls were all hidden and quiet, and prayed my anger wouldn't explode. I looked into his scowling eyes. "You didn't ask nicely."

He shrugged. "Pretty please?"

I wanted to slap him, but I stepped inside and held open the door. "I should've made you get a warrant."

"Nice place you got here. Lot of stuff. I'm guessing you don't live here by yourself."

"My sister and her kids are over here all the time. Always leaving their stuff."

He played it cool, but he was obviously looking for something.

"What are you hoping to find here?"

He gave me a fake smile. "Not looking for anything in particular, but a detective is always a detective. It's none of my business and not why I'm here, but it's obvious you don't live alone, and given the fact that I see no one else here at the moment, I get the feeling I should be looking for something." He stepped into me as though he was ready for a slow dance, and he looked down into my eyes. "What, or should I say who, are you hiding?"

I almost fell backward, bumping into the front door. He stepped closer still. Ashtray breath in my face. "Who are you hiding?"

I couldn't look at him. I couldn't even think. Too many times I'd been pressed against a door. Trapped. Unable to run or hide. Unable to scream because a hand would slap across my face as soon as I'd take that deep breath. Unable to be heard. And no one to care or react even if I could. I was there all over again in some dark room, cheap hotel, back alley, frat party. Didn't matter. They were all the same. They all left me ruined.

Drugs had helped. I could numb the pain, lose myself, forget or pretend I wasn't there. But I'd been clean for two years, six months, and four days. Clean or not clean, I could've downed a handful of downers. Anything to escape that feeling.

Then he pressed against me. Not with his hands. His chest in my face. Feet wide apart. Hands against the door. His sleeves slid down, and I saw a tiny SinS tattoo on his wrist. He lowered his head to my shoulder a drew a deep sniff. "I'm disappointed you didn't remember me, Natalie. Hurt actually."

My gut crashed into the basement. A quiver rippled through my whole body. Uncontrolled shaking. *Sergeant Kravitz. Old, fat, and gray.*

He laughed. I remembered that laugh. I remembered the why behind the laugh. He was always a freebie. He'd slap me around, cuff me, threaten to arrest me, do whatever he wanted with me, because he was a cop, and I was...

"Sasha. Isn't that what you called yourself?" He grabbed my chin and jerked it up until I opened my eyes. "Or is that the name they gave you?"

He let go and shoved me into the door. "You should think about going back to Sasha. Natalie's okay, but Sasha. That name says something. And you weren't all that bad..."

I was not Sasha. I had never been Sasha. Sasha was the name I'd hidden behind, the name my long-dead pimp had forced on me, and the name I'd hoped was dead and buried with him. I wasn't about to go down that road again.

I drove my fist into his throat.

Kravitz stumbled backward. Eyes wide open. He sucked in a deep breath. Big wheezing sound. Coughing. Sputtering. He clenched his teeth and came at me.

But I was ready. And I was not going to back down. I'd rehearsed this kind of scene over and over like J-Lo in *Enough*. I took a wide stance, gritted my teeth, and tightened my fists. Showtime.

He lunged at me and grabbed my throat with both hands.

I pulled my arms down and, with one movement, I thrust my knee into his manhood as hard as I could, then shot my arms up and out. Before he could react, I head-butted his nose.

He struggled to stay on his feet then grabbed my shirt at the neck. I clutched his wrist and pressed his hand and fingers against my chest. When I felt his nails, I yanked downward tearing my shirt and leaving traces of my skin and blood under his nails.

I stomped his toe with my heel and screamed in his face. "I'm not Sasha. My *name* is Natalie!"

He clutched his nose with his left hand, stared at the blood on his fingers, and shook it off as he fell backward, bumping my lamp and side table. I stepped toward him, and he reached for his gun.

My pulse was flying, but it didn't matter. I grabbed the lamp. Not one of your cheap nowadays throwaways. This lamp had a weighted base. I yanked it from the table. The room went dark as the cord jerked from the socket. The porchlight shined on his stunned face.

His gun clicked as he loaded a round. I cocked the lamp over my head and unloaded with all my strength, then brought it down on his skull.

I don't know which was louder, the clang of the lamp against his head or the gunshot.

CHAPTER 48
Emma

Several blocks away from where I'd left Cali, I could already see the flashing lights. Pulse pounding. Head throbbing. I thought the street would be clear by now. *Why are the cops still here?*

I slowed the car. *Think think think.* I couldn't handle another run in with the police, especially with Roberto in the backseat and who knew what in the trunk. I eased past Kessler Street. Police cars completely blocked it, so I drove around the block and parked a couple of houses down from Natalie's.

I stared at the mesmerizing lights and haze from all the exhaust. Thank God the police cars were at the other end of the block. That meant the shooting hadn't been at Natalie's house, and I could breathe again.

I trotted up to her house and took a look around. Everything quiet. Porchlight on. One lamp in the window. It looked like everyone had gone to bed.

Then I heard shouting. *Natalie.*

Through the window, I saw the lamp go out followed by a gunshot and a bone-chilling scream. Without a second thought, I sprinted to the house and burst through the door. I ran my fingers over the wall to find a light switch.

In the sudden brightness of the overhead light, I saw Natalie drenched in sweat. Tears streaming. Shirt torn and spattered with blood. *Oh, my God. She's been shot.* I ran to her, but she stopped me with her outstretched arm. "Stop. Don't touch me." She looked at the door and pointed. "You need to leave *now*. The police will be here any second. They're bound to have heard the gunshot."

"What happened? Are you okay?"

Tears and anger mixed into a blubbering scream. "I killed a cop, and you don't want to be here when they come. Now go."

I spun toward the door but it was too late. Cops were sprinting down the sidewalk toward the house. I looked at Natalie, not sure what to do. She'd buried her face in her hands. No time to think. I made a dash toward the kitchen. There had to be a back door.

And there it was. As reached for it, I felt a firm grip on my elbow.

* * *

Michael

Our already quiet room became dead silent at the sound of a gun and a scream. What in the world had happened to my boring life? I'd never been one to look for trouble, but it had certainly found me, and it was up to me to get out of it.

I jumped to my feet and gestured for the ladies to be quiet. Then I dashed up the steps, pulse raging. As I lifted the trap door and peeked into the pantry, I willed my stomach to stay put and thanked God I hadn't eaten for hours.

The kitchen and front room were dark. I plucked the string and left the basement in the dark as well. I prayed everyone would stay silent and perked my ears. The front door creaked open, and I heard thumping against the wall followed by light in the front room. I couldn't see anyone, but I heard soft footsteps followed by "You need to leave now..."

Natalie. Who is she talking to?
"What happened..."
Emma? What is she doing here? Who fired the shot?
Natalie screamed. "I killed a cop..."

As Emma darted through the kitchen, I shot out of the pantry and grabbed her arm before she reached the back door. Thank God, because I could hear police from every direction.

Her instincts held fast as she stayed silent and followed me through the trap door and into the dark basement. I prayed the cops wouldn't have thermal cameras as I pulled the door shut and turned on the lights. I whispered to the group, "Police are here. Not a sound."

Emma wiggled free of my grip and threw her arms around Tawnya.

* * *

Emma

I wrapped my arms so tight around Tawnya that she groaned. We sank to the sofa holding each other and dripping tears on each other's shoulders. I barely knew her, but I knew her well. She and I had lived the same life. Groomed. Grabbed. Groped. And garbaged. She had been the queen of Bobby's hell, and I was her unknown protégé. By watching her videos and listening to the other girls tell their stories, I learned every trick I needed to stay alive. I knew her pain, and she knew mine.

My quickened heart felt soothed in her arms. Breathing slowed. Pulse slowed. Tears slowed to a trickle. Her arms slipped free, and her hands gripped my face. She looked into my soul. "You're going to be okay. Don't know how, but I can feel it." She kissed my forehead and looked at me again. Eyes so deep, so intent and full of love. "My auntie used to say 'Love God with all that's in you.'" She squeezed a little tighter. "Emma, the love of God is real, and it's in you. I can feel it."

I laughed and cried and died a little as she said it. Gramps and Grams, our smug little church, everyone I could remember from my miserable childhood had pounded those empty words into my head. They spoke of the love of God, but I never saw it. It was never real to me.

Those words sounded so ridiculous, but as Tawnya said them, and as she wrapped me in her arms, those words felt good, and they felt real.

Doors opened and shut above us. Tawnya whispered, "What is going on up there?"

I surveyed the room. Bliss. Michael. Girls I'd never seen before. But, "Where's Cali?"

So much for my slowed heartrate.

Bliss raised her hand. How silly and how cute. "She hid in a closet upstairs."

I've got to go get her. Without a word, I tip-toed up the steps, tugged the string to turn off the light, and eased open the trap door. Kitchen lights were still off. I slipped into the pantry undetected. All the commotion seemed to be in the front room, and boy were they giving it to Natalie.

Dead cop in her living room. She might as well notify next of kin. I wanted to care. I did care. I wanted to do something, but what could I do? I wasn't even supposed to be there, and if they saw me, they'd surely find the other girls. Bliss was still a fugitive, and who knew about the other girls and even Michael? They probably thought he killed that agent, or at least they'd want to pin it on him.

I peeked at the side door. No one there. I stuck my head around the corner. An empty hallway stretched from the kitchen past a couple of rooms to what looked to be the main hallway from the front room. The hint of light in that far hall revealed stairs.

I slid through the kitchen and down the hall toward the back staircase. Shadows on the floor. Footsteps in the opposite hall. Sound of a door opening. Footsteps disappeared. The clank of lifting a toilet seat.

Holding my breath, I darted up the stairs like a kid sneaking cookies to her bedroom.

Where's Cali?

CHAPTER 49
Natalie
Ten Minutes Earlier

I can't say a felt the least bit of remorse knowing I killed one of the scum that had destroyed my life, but there was no time to savor a victory. Even in his death, he could destroy me again. As I heard the trap door close. I could hear the whir of sirens coming closer.

The last time I felt this scared, I was snatched off the street by a rival pimp and locked in a hellhole for days. I'd thought it was over. I'd wished it was over. After all these years and everything I'd been through and survived, I'd finally gotten to the place where I thought I could move on with a real life.

But sometimes life deals more than one lousy hand. Maybe this was my last deal, and it was time to fold.

No way. I've been through too much, and I've survived worse.

I grabbed my phone and called the one person who might be able to help. Agent Florence Lett. Flo, as I called her, had been a social worker before she became my probation officer. Eventually she had moved to the FBI. Even after all these years, we still kept in touch.

"Flo? I need your help. You still got that app that records calls?"

"What happened?"

"Do it now. Turn on the app and record."

I didn't give her a chance to hesitate or hang up. She knew me, and she knew I would only ask if I were in big trouble. "Are we recording?"

"You bet."

"Leave it on 'til I hang up or the phone dies. And mute your end."

I set the phone under the side table and slumped onto the floor and closed my eyes.

Knock knock knock. "Police. Open up."

I lay still as the door opened. Footsteps flooded around me.

"Oh, my God. Kravitz is down."

"Check his pulse."

"Was he shot?"

"I don't see an entry or exit. Just a bloody nose and blood on his hands."

"What about this woman?"

"What about her? She's breathing. He's not. Come give me a hand."

Footsteps scrambled around Kravitz. I could hear the thud thud thud of chest compressions. I swallowed silent tears as they worked on him but neglected me. Not a finger to check my pulse or shake me to see if I'd respond. I was truly dead to them.

"He's one of us, and we're not going let him go easy."

My heart kicked into high gear at the thought that he might survive. That man had kept me trapped in the life so he could abuse me and get his piece of the profits. I'd wanted him dead more than I'd wanted to live.

But these girls had changed me. They'd taught me that hope lives even in the deepest darkness. Even when you can't see, it's there. As much as I'd hated Kravitz, I wished there was another way. I wished it didn't have to be me or him. I wished we both could live peaceful, descent lives, but I couldn't see any light in him. Only bitter darkness.

As the officers performed CPR, I choked on my own spit. I coughed, gagged, and vomited on my new carpet. Still no one noticed or no one cared.

The door opened again. More footsteps. The thud of equipment dropping on the floor beside me. I opened my eyes to a petite paramedic leaning over me.

"You okay?" I nodded and she continued. "What happened?" She plucked a wipe out of her bag and cleaned my mouth.

"Hold it right there," a big voice said from the doorway. "This is a crime scene. Don't touch anything you don't have to touch. Do your jobs with as little impact as possible."

"I guess I can't clean anything up except your face." Her eyes were kind, and my heart smiled. It's hard to maintain kindness when all you deal with is hurt. I hadn't seen too many paramedics or cops who didn't seem jaded.

She glanced at my chest. "Your shirt is torn. Are those scratches?"

Thank you, Jesus. Keep recording, Flo. I laid the cards on the table. Huge tears. Sobs. I acted like I was going to heave again. "He attacked me and shot at me, so I hit him with the lamp."

The paramedic paused and glanced at Kravitz. "Why would the detective attack you?"

"He was dirty. He remembered me from my old life. I guess he thought I was a threat."

She muttered. "Looks like you were." She checked my pulse and blood pressure. Her eyes weren't as soft as they'd been. I guess she'd seen and heard enough over the years that the stories all sounded the same. Maybe I oversold it with the tears. Nonetheless, Flo was still listening. These officers might not be like Kravitz, but they would see him as one of their own and want to pin responsibility on me. That's why I wanted Flo to hear and record.

I lifted my head to see Kravitz. While the medics did CPR, his buddies did their best to clean him up, but no one scraped his fingernails.

God, let them find my DNA.

The medics were on the phone with the ER. They shocked him at least three times. Nothing. But they weren't going to give up on a cop. They lifted him onto a board and kept working on him as they hauled him out to the ambulance. The cops followed—all except the big-voice officer.

He said, "Good work everyone." He motioned to the officers. "Stay with Kravitz and keep me informed. I've got a few more questions here. If I need any help, I'll call."

The room cleared. It was just me and the officer.

"Well, what's your story?" He didn't sit, didn't squat. He stood over me, looking down on me like they all did.

"I haven't got a story. I'm going tell you the truth. That's what you want isn't it?"

"Don't get smart with me. I've worked with Detective Kravitz since he was a sergeant. I know who you are, what you are, and I know you've got your side of the story. Now spill it."

"You don't want the truth."

"Talk."

"Kravitz recognized me from his years on the street. I'd been one of his girls."

"His girls?"

"He worked with my pimp and several others. He shielded them from the police in exchange for favors. I was one of his favors. But unlike most of the girls, I made it out. I knew enough to keep my head down and my mouth shut, but when he saw me tonight, he knew I would connect him to those guys who shot your fellow officers. They were working for Donny, and they'd lost some pretty hot merchandise that he wanted them to retrieve. They followed the trail here and so did the officers who got in their way."

His lips twisted. His brow furrowed. And he rubbed his chin. "What kind of merchandise? Drugs?"

"Girls." I watched his eyes, watched for any reaction, and I listened as sounds of the police cars and emergency vehicles faded.

CHAPTER 50
Emma

I passed the closet at the top of the stairs and the one at the end of the hall. I suspected Cali would've chosen the closet in the corner bedroom, farthest from the front door.

I tiptoed, hoping the floor wouldn't creak. I didn't want to scare Cali or alert anyone downstairs, although they were making enough noise to cover a squeaky floor.

I slowly opened the narrow door. It squeaked, and I stopped. It wasn't opened enough for me to squeeze through, but I stuck my head inside and whispered. "Cali, it's me, Emma." I flicked on the light. Poor thing had been hiding in the dark. How much of her young life had she spent like that?

I scanned the shelves overhead. Nothing. Of course, not. She'd had no one to lift her. Then I felt her tiny arms wrap around my waist. I pulled her out of the closet and slunk to the floor with her in my arms. I stroked her face, lifted her hair out of her eyes and tucked it behind her ear. Wiped her tears with my thumbs and kissed her forehead. *This little girl is never going to be bought.*

"You are going to be safe. I promise you. I'll keep you safe." *Or die trying.*

I held her on my lap in that cozy bedroom. Her soft cheek against my chest. Her tiny hand caressing my arm, touching my hair. I hadn't had too many moments where life felt like living, but this moment was one of them. I anticipated the police would eventually search the rest of the house, but what could they do to an innocent girl? Besides, we would hear them coming and hide.

Nothing else mattered. When I thought I might've lost her, I realized Cali had become everything. And if those few minutes were all we had, they were worth a lifetime.

How I wanted her to be mine, but even more I wanted her to be *her*, to be free and able to live her own life.

We held each other and listened for the police or Natalie. The voices faded. Footsteps faded. And the sounds of doors opening and shutting slowed and eventually stopped. I waited several minutes. Not a sound. Maybe they weren't going to search upstairs after all.

I gently hoisted her off my lap, gave her another peck on the forehead, and whispered, "I'm going to check and see if they're gone."

No one in the hall, the other bedrooms, or on the stairs. I inched down the stairs praying I could be silent. Once I reached the main floor, I peeked around the corner into the front room and spied a detective in a suit and tie standing over Natalie. I cringed at the sight of blood and vomit on the floor, and hoped the detective couldn't hear my breathing. I leaned against the wall and listened.

"So, you're trying to tell me one of my finest officers is a bad cop and you're a charm school graduate?"

"No, sir. I paid my dues and Detective Kravitz reaped the rewards. When he saw me, he saw a threat to his façade. He'd become somebody. Maybe he'd given up his bad habits, buried his skeletons, but he ran into one of those skeletons tonight and decided to bury her as well. But this girl didn't want to die, so I defended myself. I didn't want to kill him, but I didn't want him to shoot me either, so I grabbed the lamp and struck him as hard as I could."

I leaned against the wall in silence, exhaling slowly, praying I wouldn't be heard. I listened as the detective paced the floor and cracked his knuckles.

Finally, he broke the silence. "You said something about a young girl. What about her? Where's this girl he was supposedly smuggling?"

"I don't know."

"You don't know?" He raised his already-tense voice. "You'd better give me something besides a lame story of self-defense."

The chair squeaked across the floor, and I imagined Natalie standing toe-to-toe as she shouted back. "For the love of—he shot at me."

"My officer, from point-blank range, shot at you and missed? Why don't I take you downtown and have your hand dusted for gunpowder residue? I imagine you killed him then fired his gun to make it look like self-defense."

As the tirade continued, my legs felt like numb noodles from standing so still. My hands tingled. I must have been hyperventilating without realizing. The room felt like it was spinning. My face warmed, and I had to fight to avoid throwing up.

Rather than pass out and give myself away, I slid along the wall toward the back hallway. I would sneak back up the stairs and hide with Cali until it was over.

But a tiny hand gripped mine. *Cali.* She looked up at me, and I melted as usual. Jitters gone. Tingling gone. Problems still here.

I'd been through this drill before. The detective was taunting Natalie to rattle her emotions, hoping she would crack and forget her script. But it wasn't a script. Natalie was telling the truth. And I'd heard enough.

As I knelt beside Cali to whisper in her ear, I heard the detective say, "You show me this girl, or I'm going to show you your new home on death row."

CHAPTER 51
Natalie

It wasn't the first time I'd been threatened by a cop, but it was the most pathetic. He had nothing, and we both knew it. All he could do was threaten me with Cali. Why was she so important to his case?

Then it dawned on me. He must be in up to his neck with Kravitz. He was pressing me because he was desperate, which meant I was in deeper trouble than I'd imagined. If he didn't find the girl, he'd find a reason to kill me. Flo wouldn't be able to help me if I was dead.

Flo, I hope you're still there.

I pretended to see a spider, took off my shoe, and smacked on the floor as though I were three spiders, a tiny one, a big one, and another tiny one. I gave each one three stomps. Hopefully someone in that basement—surely that nerdy Michael knew some Morse code.

Then I looked up at the detective. "I'm sure the FBI will be curious as to why you're so interested in a little girl you say I've made up. The FBI knows she's real, and they know Agent Myers was killed while he was trying to find her. *If* I knew where she was, I'd be talking with the FBI and no one else. And if the FBI is on this case like I know they are, they've probably followed Kravitz and you here."

I smiled at the sweat on his forehead. I sat up and held out my hands as though I were eager to get cuffed. "I'm ready to go downtown when you are."

He sneered. He wanted me dead same as Kravitz, but he needed the girl even more.

What's a young Indian girl bring these days anyway? Ten grand? More? With these guys, it was more than the money. It was power, and they had to let the cops on their payroll know who was in charge. For Kravitz and this detective, finding the girl was about staying alive.

I shook my closed hands to torment him. "Cuff me and let's go."

He lifted his hand. I expected him to reach for his gun, but he reached across his chest and pulled out his Taser.

"Fun and games are over. No one's going anywhere."

I backed against the chair and stood. "Try anything, and I'll scream, and those other officers will come running."

He laughed. "Will they?" When he turned toward the window, I tried to make a run for it, but he shoved me into the chair, and it scooted across the floor and into the wall. "It's just you and me. I'm sure we can work this out between the two of us."

Out of the corner of my eye, I saw Emma and Cali hiding in the hallway.

I should've been terrified to see them vulnerable and exposed, but I felt a strange sense of calm like I would feel on a steamy summer afternoon when the sky grows dark, but there's enough breeze to expect the storm to blow over before it starts.

I screamed. "Flo!" I didn't shout. I screamed. I wanted everyone in that house and all the neighbors to hear. "He's going to kill me. Send help now."

He laughed. "Nice try." Then he pressed the Taser against my neck. "You know they make us endure these things before we get to carry one." He spit his words into my ear. "I'd say it's the worse pain I've ever experienced."

He pressed the Taser harder. He shoved his knee between my legs and clamped my right hand against the chair. "But you know, it's even worse when it zaps your jugular. I imagine one of these little probes spearing right through that sucker. Pssshh. You'd be spewing blood everywhere. I'd have to get a new tie. Wash my face. But we wouldn't want to do that, now would we?"

I blinked and tried to swallow—tried to breath.

"Now where's the girl?"

CHAPTER 52
Michael

S-O-S on the ceiling. I looked at Tawnya.

Her neck veins bulged. "She's in trouble."

Startled faces surrounded me. Every one of these women had seen and experienced more hurt than I'd dare imagine, and those stomps reawakened every fear and every ounce of resolve. They jumped up and stood ready. Tense lips. Clenched fists.

I looked at Bliss. On her feet and ready to fight. "You've got a child to think about. You stay here and call 911."

Tawnya gave me a *you-crazy* look. "Man, the cops are already here."

"What else are we gonna do?" I asked.

"We gonna stop talking and kick some butt." She whirled me around and shoved me toward the stairs. "Let's go."

I flung open the trap door and charged out of the pantry and through the kitchen.

Another cheap-suit detective stood over Natalie. I could only see her feet and hands. He had her pinned to a chair. His elbow cocked like he was holding a gun to her head.

As he looked over his shoulder toward me, a shadow flashed across the porch. I expected a flurry of police storming through the door, but the door slammed open and Roberto half-charged, half-staggered through the doorway wielding a shotgun.

The detective shouted. "One move and she's dead."

Unfazed, Roberto looked past him and at me. "Where's Emma?" He pumped the shotgun and leveled it at the man's face.

As the detective started to hold up his hands, Natalie reared back and planted her foot in his chest, sending him tumbling toward me. Instinctively, I caught him. No idea why I didn't just let him fall.

He whirled behind me. His chest against my back. His left arm wrapped around my chest. Hand gripping my throat. Cold steel pressed against my temple.

Roberto stepped toward us, blinking as though trying to wake up, his gun wavering. I expected lights out at any second.

Then I heard a shrill scream. I'd never expected such a powerful sound from such a tiny person. Cali stepped out of the hallway. Her face swollen with tears. Eyes shut tight. Mouth wide open, unleashing an ear-busting cry.

The detective's grip loosened, and his gun eased off of my skull. I remained still despite tension in every muscle. I was afraid if I twitched, it would be the last twitch I ever made.

Roberto stepped closer to the detective. Rubbed his eyes with one hand, sniffed, shook his head, and once again lifted the gun barrel toward the detective's face.

"Not one more move." The detective's gun and grip tightened.

"You think I care about that guy? Where's Emma?"

"Who the—?"

Tawnya's voice boomed behind me. "Ain' got no time for this."

Bam.

She smacked the back of that detective's head with an iron skillet.

His head clunked against mine. My ears rang. *Hello again, concussion.*

Then he fell to the floor.

Cali stopped screaming.

Roberto stood over him, prodding him with his shotgun. No response, but he was still breathing. Roberto stepped back, aimed the shotgun at the detective's head, and pressed the butt of the gun into his shoulder.

I heard the subtle click of the safety and braced for the blast.

But Cali dashed toward Roberto and wrapped her arms around his massive thigh. Her tears dribbled onto his leg, and he lowered the shotgun, patted her head and stroked her hair.

Emma flew out of the hallway behind Cali and cradled Roberto as he slumped to the floor. His eyes fluttered then drifted shut.

Despite the intensity of the moment, I chuckled. "Did you drug him?"

Emma nodded. "We were on our way to Miami." She pulled Cali close and kissed the top of her head. "But I couldn't leave Cali—not after I saw the news."

CHAPTER 53
Emma

Still holding Cali, I collapsed on the floor next to Roberto. I ran my fingers down his cheek and touched his sweet face, his soft lips. He was my prince after all. I'd deceived him. I'd drugged him, and he still fought for me. The way he stood against that cop, I knew he would even die for me.

Cali leaned over him like a kitten climbing onto a sound-asleep St. Bernard. She patted his cheeks and whispered into his ear. Then she kissed his forehead and his cheek and hugged his neck.

A sudden warmth rushed over me, warmth on the outside, a startling and refreshing coolness on the inside. I can't explain, but I felt a whisper deep inside. *This is love.* Real love.

I felt it like I had that first time I held Cali when she rescued me from that hopeless, used-up-and-worthless feeling. But this time, it felt like forever, like it would never leave, like I would never leave her.

Joy mixed with tears. All the darkness that had been my life for so many years, for all my years, all of it poured out in those tears. As she held me, I felt strength like never before. As though this tiny human was somehow empowering me.

But as good as it felt, there lingered a mountain-sized shadow of doubt. It was too good to be true. Was there really any such thing as love? Or is it something we all chase and never capture?

"The FBI will be here soon." Natalie's voice broke the trance. Back to reality. Back to the cesspool we live in. "Don't run off. And don't hide. The FBI aren't interested in your stories or your past, so don't worry about going to jail. They're coming for Cali."

I squeezed her tighter. "What do you mean? They can't take her?"

Natalie cocked her head and frowned. "Well, we can't exactly keep her?"

"Why not?"

"Are you kidding? Why would they trust us with a kid? I can barely manage these girls, and they're supposed to be adults."

Who knew I had even more tears? No more joy. Only tears. This was love, and love was going to be ripped right out of my arms. But it would never leave my heart. No matter what, I'd hold this little girl there forever.

I carried Cali to the kitchen. I decided to be a mom, even if only for one glass of milk. I set her down at the table, poured that glass of milk, and dug through the pantry, where I found a half-empty package of cookies. "Milk and cookies." I set a handful of cookies on a plate and placed it before her with the milk.

She smiled. Eyes no longer swollen. No more tears. She munched those cookies as if she hadn't eaten all day, and I realized she probably hadn't with everything that had happened.

I laughed at her milk mustache and felt like a mom if only for a second.

The doorbell rang. Who rings the doorbell hours after midnight, especially when the door's still open?

"FBI."

I pulled up a chair and sat beside Cali. Insides quivering. Hands shaking. Lips trembling. Tingling all over. She lay her head in my lap and fell asleep. She was my sprout of life after years of endless winter. As the agents poured in and voices rose, I felt like that sprout was about to get plucked.

But no one came into the kitchen, so, I hung on to the moment as long as I could.

By the sounds, I'd say there were at least a half dozen agents in the front room. I tried to pick out one voice. Finally, I heard Natalie's voice, and it was coming closer. "Come with me. I'll take you to her."

Two FBI agents walked in with Natalie and another woman. A smaller, less buxom version of Tawnya with a tight weave. She stretched out her hand and smiled. "Emma?" As she shook my hand, she said, "My name is Florence, Agent Florence Lett. I've been working this case since your friend Michael first called it in. It's nice to meet you."

Nice to meet me? No one had ever claimed it was nice to meet me. So many years and so much mistrust, but her smile and her handshake felt real. I wanted to trust. I wanted to hope, but all of my thoughts were wrapped in the fear that this woman or someone else was going to take Cali away from me.

I couldn't speak. I was still trembling, trying not to throw up.

"Please don't be nervous." Her voice was a soft as her hands.

"I'm scared." Understatement of the century.

She sat across from me, took my hand, and said, "There's a lot to process here. Two police officers murdered just down the street. Another in this house. A detective knocked out—almost dead. The ambulance will be taking him away shortly, then he's mine. And... Well, you get the picture."

"I only care about Cali. What happens to her?"

Her eyes did that what-you-talkin-bout thing. "You sure you aren't thinking about yourself too? You want Cali to stay with you?"

I stared at my folded hands—folded and still shaking. My throat ached from holding back tears. I couldn't look at her. Cali touched my arm as she scooted her chair close to me. For that split second, I was a world away with her. Walking through a valley of flowers. Just the two of us. No police. No murders. No men. No drugs. No worries.

The agent's voice kept me in the cold reality. "That is what you want, right?"

I nodded. And the tears won. I couldn't stop them. Cali climbed onto my lap like a salt bath pouring over fresh wounds. The tighter she squeezed, the more impossible the thought of losing her.

I scooted back in the chair and started to pull her off my neck, but Florence stopped me. "She's fine. Stay right there. Relax. Hold onto her. And listen. What I'm about to say is important, and I need to see your eyes. I need to know you are paying attention. You too, Cali."

I swallowed my tears again, pulled Cali close, and relaxed as best I could. Cali lay her head on my shoulder and kissed my neck.

Florence continued. "It's not unusual for two people to form an extremely tight bond when they've shared a traumatic experience, or, in your case, more than one. You and Miss Cali been through some serious stuff." She paused and looked at each of us and everyone else in the room, Natalie, Tawnya, and Bliss. "You need each other."

I almost smiled.

Florence touched my hand again. "You know I was a social worker long before I became an agent. And before that I was a foster kid." She looked at Natalie. "Bet you didn't even know that."

Natalie did a raised-eyebrow smile, and Florence went on. "So, even though nobody really knows your pain but you, believe it or not, the FBI—at least this agent feels your pain. So." She smacked the table. "Here's what we gonna do." She pointed at Cali and me. "We are going to process each of you." She held up her hands in a *don't panic* gesture and added, "You might be apart for a few hours, a couple of days at the most. But, and this is a big but, I"—she pointed at herself with both hands—"am going to do everything in my power, and I got a lot of power, to keep you together."

I climbed out of my seat, Cali clinging to my neck, her legs wrapped around me, and wrapped that agent in the biggest hug. Never in my life did I think I would ever have reason or desire to hug a federal agent.

Everyone was crying.

Florence whispered in my ear. "I know you've come a long way, girl. You stick with Natalie. She's been through it all, same as you, and she can get you through it." She squeezed my neck and patted my back like a proud coach, then she surprised me with a quick kiss on the forehead.

Natalie squeezed her way in for a hug. "Thank God for Flo. She's the real deal."

Florence spun around and surveyed the kitchen and the front room. "Michael Williams, come here please."

The two FBI agents escorted him into the kitchen and set him at the table.

CHAPTER 54
Michael

Agent Lett glared at me with one eyebrow raised. "I understand you were under investigation for the murder of Agent Myers."

My throat tightened at those haunting words. "Detective Kravitz had some questions, but no charges were made."

"Oooh. Good answer."

I don't know which was more intimidating, the question or the sarcasm. But I felt worse than the last kid picked for dodgeball. I was on one side by myself with no balls, hunkered down waiting to get pelted by everyone else. My hands shielded my face.

"Mr. Williams?"

I lifted my head, and Agent Lett smiled. "It's okay. You're not a suspect. You did the right thing, the one simple thing a lot of people would never do or even think to do. You called the National Human Trafficking Hotline, and we went to work immediately."

She hung her head, held her fist to her lips, and sniffled. "I only wish we hadn't lost Agent Myers." She looked me in the eyes. "He trusted you."

I tensed as she gritted her teeth, but she shook her head and waved off my fears. "Don't misunderstand me. He trusted *you*. It's rare for an agent to ask anyone outside of law enforcement on a stakeout. He saw something in you, and if you hadn't been there, we would've had to guess what happened, and we would have lost this young lady for good." She pointed her open hand at Cali and didn't even try to hide her tears. "This girl is here because of you. One finger. Eleven buttons. And a few words. I'm sure it didn't seem like much at the time. And I'm sure you never expected to witness the you-know-what storm that ripped through your life, but you're here. You made it. And the drama is over. The end."

She slammed both hands on the table, stood, and extended her hand. Firm handshake and a grateful smile. "If you hadn't done your job, I couldn't have done mine. Thank you."

My eyes felt misty, but I'd cried enough, and I'd survived more in these few weeks than all the rest of my life. I held on to her handshake. "Kravitz was going to send me down the river."

Agent Lett released my hand and shook her head. "He was a dirty cop. It's too bad it took Agent Myers's death to flush out him and his partners." She nodded toward the cheap-suit detective Tawnya had knocked out. FBI agents cuffed him while a paramedic checked his pupils and asked him to follow his finger.

Agent Lett continued. "Kravitz threatened you in order to displace suspicion from himself, but we knew better. Sorry you turned out to be bait. That part was unintentional, and we didn't figure it out until Natalie called me tonight."

I held out my hand again. "Agent Lett, thank you."

She smiled and shook it. "I'm sure the police will want statements from everyone, but that's up to them. The FBI is done with you—for now."

* * *

I waited in the front room while Agent Lett talked with Emma and Cali. I figured it might be the last time I'd ever see any of them. I don't know what I expected or wanted. A last good-bye? A hug? Even a wave or eye contact would mean something, but I wasn't ready to leave.

I sank into the sofa and pulled out my phone. I could at least pretend to look at it so it wouldn't be so obvious I was watching Emma. She was no longer a nameless dancer in a meter-maid costume. No longer a prostitute. She was a fighter. A survivor. And I could see something in her eyes I hadn't seen before. Hope.

Determination I'd seen. Smarts, wit, gumption. A lot of amazing qualities. But hope was brand new, and it looked good on her.

I gave up staring at my phone. I decided it was okay to be obvious and stare at her. She wasn't on a stage baring it all or in a private room. She was relaxed at a kitchen table, smiling, and talking.

My phone vibrated in my hand. It was almost dawn and Kyle was texting me. "Sam lost the baby, and she wants a divorce."

There were so many things I wanted to say to Kyle.

Sorry for your bad luck. I just beat a murder rap.

Sorry, Kyle. Don't you remember? It's not all about you.

My heart breaks for you. I just broke up a sex-trafficking ring.

Those were a few of the things I *wanted* to say, but I couldn't help but be that one steady friend to him. He would never send that text to Jordan or anyone else. He sent it to me because he knew I would always be his friend. Sam may leave, but I'd be there. Jordy would forget about him unless he needed a favor, but I'd be there.

I had to be there, especially now.

Kyle. I'm sorry.

I'm happy to talk to Sam, go out to dinner, coffee, whatever you need.

I'm here for you.

I will always be your friend.

Phone vibrated again. *I can always count on you. I'll call tomorrow at a decent hour.*

I looked up, and Emma was watching me. Those hazel eyes still worked their magic even though they were bloodshot. Her smile—alive and natural. Nothing forced. Nothing fake. She was somehow able to overcome all the pain in her past and find a way to smile.

I couldn't imagine saying good-bye.

CHAPTER 55
Emma

One thing I learned in the life was how to read men. They act all cool and sophisticated or tough and invulnerable, but after you've been used in so many ways by so many men, reading their thoughts becomes natural.

And I read Michael like a single-panel comic. I caught his eyes, but he tried to play it cool. He yawned and pretended to stare at his phone.

I cast my thought toward him with a wink and a smirk.

I was way past tired. The way you get when you're slap happy and ready to collapse. It's why they used to show all the B movies after midnight—everything's funny when you're that tired.

But I wasn't delirious. I was juiced on adrenaline. As Florence spoke, I kept glancing at Michael. Giggling to myself as he'd look away. Each time I looked at him, his blush faded and his smile grew.

And Michael wasn't looking at me like other guys. No. The naïve dork that tried to shake my hand at a bachelor party was not studying every curve, not dreaming about what he'd like to do to me or get from me. He was looking *at* me, not through me. He saw me, a person of worth.

To other men, I'd looked like a score, like a wad of cash. But Michael's tender heart, his soft smile, and the gentleness in his eyes made me feel like a priceless treasure.

That's how every woman should feel. That's how every person should feel.

Every time I took money from a john or a jane, they took a piece of me. Bobby sold little bits of me until I felt like there was nothing left. Selene kept me alive by burying me deep inside.

As I watched Michael lay down his phone and smile at me, I pictured Selene waving good-bye, and Emma crawling out of her grave.

Cali leaned against me and gave me another unrelenting hug. How in the world she was still awake? She squeezed tighter, and I realized it was my cue to listen to Florence.

She cleared her throat. "We've already worked it out for you and Cali to live in the same shelter. I can't make any promises beyond that. The rest will be up to the two of you."

"What happens to Roberto?"

She sighed. "I get what you see in him—a protector, a hero. But he's not who you think he is. He's going down for racketeering and human trafficking. If I know our boy, and I do, he was gonna flip you over to a new gang in Miami. My buddies over there used his phone to confirm his connections. You saved yourself by drugging him and coming back to Atlanta. If I didn't know better, I'd say somebody's watching over you."

I smirked. *No one's ever watched over me.*

Then I caught Michael's eyes again. He blushed, and I chuckled.

"We should probably get going."

Florence's words made it all suddenly real. Since that fateful sip of beer on the beach, I hadn't been going anywhere. My life hadn't been my own. I'd been surviving and wondering if it was worth it. I'd become like Bliss—buried any thought of getting out—only been thinking of getting along, getting stoned, getting through to the next Monday morning. The day everyone else hated had been my only free moment. Playing cards with the girls or being silly, hoping Bobby would stay passed out.

I pried Cali's arms off my waist and held her hand. "Let's go."

Michael stood and stepped toward the door. It looked as though he was going to play the gentleman and open the door for us, but he stood in front of the door. "May I talk to Emma for a minute?"

My insides quivered like that first time Johnny Paul spoke to me. But I didn't feel the acid crawling up my throat or that brash taste I'd developed at the sound of his name. No. This moment felt fresh and real.

Michael was like a middle school boy working up the courage to talk to a girl for the first time—fidgeting with his hands, rocking side-to-side, barely making eye contact.

I stretched out my hand. He stared at it awkwardly as if he'd been hoping for more than a handshake, but I said, "You never shook my hand." His mouth curved into a half smile, and we shook.

But I didn't want to let go. I held his hand and gently squeezed, hoping he would say something. I could tell he didn't want to say good-bye, and I didn't either. "I'm not letting go until you say something."

His face flushed, and he didn't say anything. I let my hand slip free and turned toward the door.

"Wait." He stepped in front of me and tentatively raised his hands toward my shoulders. But he didn't touch me. I guess he was afraid I'd been touched a few too many times and wasn't sure how I'd respond. I stepped closer until his hands slid over my shirt. I looked into his still moist eyes, and he said, "I don't want this to be good-bye."

Florence said, "It doesn't have to be. Exchange numbers, email, something. Now can we get going. It's almost time for me to get out of bed and go to work, and I ain't slept yet."

I nibbled my lip, giggled inside, then pecked him on the cheek. Sounds crazy, but that was actually the first time I ever kissed a guy on the cheek, and it somehow felt more intimate than any kiss I could remember.

Florence gave Michael her business card. "You want to reach her, you reach me—in the daytime." She tugged on my arm. Michael stepped aside, and we left. But it was not good-bye.

EPILOGUE
Emma

It turns out Cali wasn't really her name. I did some research, and they'd called her Khaalee. Sounds the same to me, but it's not really a name. It essentially means empty or worthless. Every time they said her name, they were calling her worthless, reminding her of her place.

Not anymore. Now, her place is with me, and she's worth more than anything in this world. I asked her if she would like a new name. She smiled like it was Christmas morning.

I've grown accustomed to calling her my princess. That's what she is to me. We looked up the Hindi word for princess. Thought that might be a good name. Raajaakumaaree seemed like a bit much. We looked up the Hindi word for queen. Raanee. That made a lot more sense, and we could spell it however we wanted.

Ronni is eighteen years old now, or so we think. The State Department never found any original documents for her, so they guessed at a birthdate. *Happy New Year.* That's right. They picked January first. Most creative.

Her full name is Ronni Emma Williams. Michael insisted on Emma, and Ronni agreed.

Michael and I married about four years after that horrible night. He did *not* have a bachelor party, and Jordan was *not* in our wedding. But Kyle was.

It took several months, but Kyle finally gave up living for himself and devoted himself to Sam. They never divorced, but they were separated most of that first year.

Roberto and Mason are still in prison, although Roberto will be up for parole soon.

The FBI lab ran Bliss's DNA through missing persons and found out she'd been missing since she was eight years old. Her poor family. I'm sure they'd thought she was dead, never to be discovered. What emotions they must have felt when they got that call. I can hear Florence booming those words, "Miss Daviess, are you sitting down? I've got some big news for you. Your daughter Briane is alive and well."

Briane Daviess. Bliss was so deep in the life, she'd buried and completely forgotten her own name. I can't imagine the mind-numbing horror of an eight-year-old girl being sold into that life. What a crock of manure to call it "the life." They should call it the slow death.

It's been a long haul. The twists and turns haven't been easy. But building a new life has been worth every step.

I will always carry scars—emotional and physical. But my scars and my past will never define me.

* * *

God has been good to me.

Please don't get freaked out because I brought God into it. Believe whatever you want, but don't judge me for what I believe. He was with me in my deepest darkness like an unseen hand holding onto mine. He walked through hellfire with me, and he brought me out.

You don't have to agree. You can say it's my way of dealing with trauma.

But he's real to me.

My recovery took some time. I had to get completely free from that world. You might think I'd want to cling to Bliss and Tawnya, some of the other girls who'd suffered as I had and survived. Eventually I hope to reconnect with them, but deep wounds take a while.

I needed to bury that life and forget it ever happened, but I couldn't escape the nagging feeling that other girls were suffering as I had as I went on with my life.

A few years later, I ran into Natalie at a women's conference.

No, it wasn't some pastor's wife's comfy churchy message that got me. I sat in a group of women, church ladies I would've called them when I was young. They seemed so together, disgustingly perfect or disgustingly fake. I chose to think the latter—until they started to talk.

Their hair and their outfits were like beautiful bandages hiding hideous wounds. They each had a story. And as the we rounded the circle and neared me, closer and closer, that nagging feeling surfaced. Not like a bird peeking out of a nest. Like a blue whale launching from the deep into a backflip. I had to tell my story.

Natalie asked if I was okay. Wide eyes around the circle showed that the other women wondered the same. My heartbeat set a new record. My throat tight. My mouth dry. But that nagging feeling erupted into cleansing tears. Natalie pulled me closer, her steady arms holding my shaking body.

"Do we need to go?" she whispered.

I shook my head like a kid shakes a pop bottle. "No." I must've sounded emphatic. I startled myself. I looked around the circle, lifted my chin, and said, "I can't sit and do nothing. I have to share my story."

None of these women knew me except Natalie. None of them knew my history. I was tea-sipping, mall-shopping Mrs. Williams, dressed in the same beautiful bandages and designer hairstyles as they were, but in that moment, I felt as naked at Selene on a stage.

I laid it all out there. Beginning to end in a whirlwind. I expected narrowed eyes and pursed lips, but I was met with tears and hugs. They hadn't been where I'd been, but they each had their own pain, their own story, and we all shared one heart.

That was the real turning point for me.

"Natalie, it's not enough to be a good person. I want to do for others what you did for me."

Now, I work alongside Natalie. A lot of broken halos out there. A lot of fallen angels.

My dream is to give them wings.

Sex-trafficking takes someone who's beautiful and ruins them.

Now, I take those who think they've been ruined and show them they're still beautiful.

ACKNOWLEDGEMENT

Thank you to my friends at The Skipping Stone, Grit into Grace, and Stripped Free.
You inspire me with your selfless love.

Thank you, survivors.
You give hope and courage to those still trapped.

A special thanks to my wife. You demonstrate inexhaustible patience.

Deepest gratitude to the author of life who smiles on our dreams and erases our shame.

ABOUT THE AUTHOR

John Matthew Walker is a physician with a heart for victims of sex-trafficking.

His dream is to awaken hope and inspire compassionate action.

Follow the author at
johnmatthewwalker.com

Made in United States
North Haven, CT
24 April 2023

35840561R00125